D0820347

The Touch

Liu Hong was born and grew up in China. She came to England as a student and now lives in Wessex with her husband and children.

Also by Liu Hong

Startling Moon
The Magpie Bridge

The Touch

Liu Hong

review

Copyright © 2005 Liu Hong

The right of Liu Hong to be identified as the Author of
the Work has been asserted by her in accordance with the
Copyright, Designs and Patents Act 1988.

First published in Great Britain in 2005
by Review

An imprint of Headline Book Publishing

1

Cataloguing in Publication Data is available from the British Library

ISBN 0 7553 2460 9 (hardback)
ISBN 0 7553 0602 3 (trade paperback)

Typeset in Meridien by Avon DataSet Ltd,
Bidford-on-Avon, Warwickshire

Printed and bound in Great Britain by
Clays Ltd, St Ives plc

Headline's policy is to use papers that are natural, renewable and
recyclable products and made from wood grown in sustainable forests.
The logging and manufacturing processes are expected to conform to the
environmental regulations of the country of origin.

HEADLINE BOOK PUBLISHING
A division of Hodder Headline
338 Euston Road
London NW1 3BH

www.reviewbooks.co.uk
www.hodderheadline.com

To my family

With thanks to:

Dr Xu Zhongmin

Susie Jolly

Hazel Orme

Jessica Woollard

Mary-Anne Harrington

for love, support and inspired editing

1

Hold the needle as you would a tiger. Once it's in, wait for the *chi* to connect, with the same patience as you would attend the most respected guest.

These had been my mottos for as long as I had practised. They came to me naturally, like breathing. But today they did not help – I was not listening to the message. I was held by the voice that had first said those words to me so many years ago.

I fought the memory, and turned to examine my patient.

It should have been no surprise that my first patient on my first day back at work as an acupuncturist was an asthma sufferer. And at first I didn't see anything unusual about her. Polite, if quietly stubborn, Lucy seemed no different from other young Englishwomen I had encountered since I had arrived in the country. She said she had suffered from asthma on and off for about twenty years.

I found the points easily enough – it helped that I had practised on myself the previous day: *tian tu* (heavenly prominence), *ding chuan* (stabilising breathlessness), *feng men* (wind gate) and . . . *ying xiang* (welcoming fragrance). When the needle pierced her skin she shivered slightly and murmured something. Even to my foreigner's ears it did not sound like English. 'I beg your pardon?' I leaned forward.

'*Deti le*?' She blushed. Then: 'Perhaps I said it wrong, but I thought that was how you described the sensation. . .'

'Oh, you mean *deqi le*.' It meant 'reaching the *chi*' – the sensation of the needle hitting the right point.

She nodded and, perhaps not trusting herself, said no more as I positioned the next needle.

So, she had been to an acupuncturist's before, and had bothered to learn the Chinese phrase. This small effort and her shyness disarmed me, and I smiled at her despite myself. I reached out to pick up her hand and take her pulse, and all trace of nervousness vanished. Her hand was soft and baby smooth, dimples set deep between each knuckle. It had been some time since I had touched another person deliberately, not since my husband and daughter left me, over a month ago.

Breathing deeply, my eyes closed, I put my fingers to Lucy's pulse. Suddenly I was no longer conscious of the treatment room, so bare, with its smell of new paint. I was a doctor again, doing something I had done for years before I set out with my husband to this new country. I listened and waited patiently for the pulse to come through, deep inside her. There it was, thin, fast and distant. As I pressed harder I felt her flesh yield, and the pulse faded. How trusting she was, as I had been once. When I looked up, her eyes were fixed on mine, full of questions that she was either too shy or too well mannered to ask. I recognised this type of patient.

I let go of her hand.

Soon Lucy settled into sleep. I tiptoed through to the other room – the reception and dispensary where Xiao Jin, my student secretary, worked. The window was the most decorated part of the room, with a startling picture of a man before and after treatment for eczema. It had been the first thing that had caught my eye when I saw the clinic, and I found it repugnant. Why choose such an ugly picture to advertise the clinic? I had wondered.

Xiao Jin stood in front of the row of glass jars lined up against the wall behind the counter. Brown sacks of dried herbs, delivered this morning, lay at her feet. She was stocktaking, murmuring their names in her Beijing accent: *'jin yin hua* (honeysuckle), *ye ju hua* (wild chrysanthemum), *dang gui* (Chinese angelica) . . . *shao yao* (peony root).

The Touch

I closed my eyes again and the picture of the man with diseased skin faded as the herbs' pungent scents filled my nostrils. 'Yellow flower,' I had said, holding it up to show my grandfather. How proud I had been and how tall he had seemed to me then, with the basket on his back. The twigs and grasses he had been picking looked dull – a colourful flower had caught my eye. 'Wild chrysanthemum.' He had smiled. 'Pretty, isn't it? And useful, too. That is why you are named after it, Juju, chrysanthemum, good for bright eyes.'

'*dang gui* . . .' Xiao Jin's voice carried on.

'*dang gui*, due-to-return, tonic for women.' My grandfather's gentle voice echoed, in the restaurant where I had had the most delicious egg fried rice. I had reached forward with my chopsticks, put a little tentatively into my mouth: it was smooth and tasted like my favourite pine mushroom.

I stood quietly so that Xiao Jin wasn't aware of my presence, but each time she said a name, and untied a sack, I found myself saying it with her. The voice from my past was clear now: he was pronouncing the names in his strong north-eastern accent, the way I'd learned to say them. As more jars were opened, the fragrances became as insistent as voices: 'We have met before. When? Where?'

'Don't they smell awful? This batch is especially strong.' Xiao Jin turned, waving a piece of paper in front of her face, and gave an exaggerated cough. I stepped back, and she stared at me curiously.

I escaped to the treatment room. What was happening today? Everything was conspiring to draw me to the past, which I was determined to avoid.

Lucy was still lying down, her eyes open now. 'How do you feel?' I asked.

'Wonderful.'

Her answer unsettled me: I might have expected, 'fine', but 'wonderful' seemed too much.

I strode back through the reception area to open the front door, letting a gush of cold, damp air into the clinic. then I wrote down the herbs I wanted Lucy to take. But I knew as I inscribed each name on the paper that for me it was already too late. The assault on my senses had opened a floodgate. When the door of the clinic was locked and Xiao Jin had gone home, when I had nowhere to escape to but the small upstairs bedroom where more herbs were piled in their sacks, I would be unable to resist. The past would rush in. That I had travelled so far would make no difference.

'Do you think she'll take it?' Xiao Jin asked, reading the prescription. It contained some of the most bitter-tasting herbs, the best medicines.

'Yes, she will,' I said, remembering Lucy's look of pleasure and 'wonderful'. I had confidence in her, so bright, so open, so strangely at home with my treatment. Something about Lucy touched me. I wanted to protect her, to cure her, and I was sure I could, but it frightened me that she could give herself so freely.

2

The autumn I was due to start school, I had a particularly bad cold. I was as hot as a furnace – the cool towel my mother placed on my forehead steamed with the heat – and soon my coughs and sneezes turned to wheezing. Finally, after I had refused the water she'd offered me for the fourth time, she declared that enough was enough: she would take me to hospital. She dressed me – asking my older sister, Ling, to look after the house – which took quite a while as I could hardly stand. Mother was trembling, and shaking her head as she did up my buttons. I became more and more frightened as I fought for breath, and she was muttering about my late father, whom I had hardly known as he died when I was very small. She seemed to be saying I had something called asthma – and this had happened to him.

She sat me on the back seat of the bicycle and we set off. I sneezed as soon as the cold air hit me – I hadn't been outside for days. There was a strange taste in the air and my chest tightened, as I coughed and gasped. 'Mummy, is it New Year again?' I asked, but she didn't answer, just pedalled. I was puzzled: the air smelt as it did after the fireworks had been lit on New Year's Eve. There was a tightness and smoky aroma that always excited me as I anticipated the loud bangs to come. Other girls might be scared and cover their ears, but not I.

On the other side of the bridge the road was unmetalled and bumpy. I gripped the seat while my mother twisted and turned the bicycle, trying to avoid the potholes. I watched the chemical-factory chimney puffing. Almost a landmark, it was a familiar sight, but today I couldn't take my eyes off its plume of black smoke. Perhaps I'd been sitting on the bicycle for too long; my hands and feet were tingling and the tightness in my chest was worse. My head felt heavy and dizzy, and I coughed, gasping for air. I felt as if someone was trying to strangle me and I opened my mouth to shout for my mother but fell off the bicycle.

We were still a long way from the hospital, and instead of continuing on her way, my mother rushed me home. Luckily, Laoye, her father, had taken a break from his travels and had just arrived at our house. He took one look at me and reached straight for his medicine box. Before I knew it, he had stuck some needles into the front and back of my neck and on the inside of my elbows. I did not protest, and was relieved when, soon after he had positioned the needles, I could breathe more easily. Laoye stepped back and watched me, wiping sweat off his face.

As my breathing returned to normal, I noticed that the needles were still in my flesh. They did not hurt, but I found them uncomfortable and tried to brush them away. But Laoye held me down gently and laid his hand on the inside of my wrist, as I had seen him do with his patients. He closed his eyes as if he were in a trance, and I had an opportunity to observe him closely – it had been a long time since he had stayed with us. I liked Laoye's face: it was long, with smiling eyes, and his skin was brown from all the time he spent outdoors on his rounds. I liked his big hand on mine and the assurance of its firm yet gentle touch. I'd always known that when I was with him everything would be all right. After a minute or two he let go of my hand, rose and took out the needles.

'I'm thirsty,' I said. My throat was dry now that the alarming breathlessness had gone.

'Let her have as much liquid as she likes. Hot water will do,' Laoye said.

'How about some rice congee?' Mother asked, sounding

relieved. I could see she felt more confident with Laoye there.

'What happened to me?' I asked. 'Is the New Year really coming?'

'You've been poisoned by the air from the chemical factory, like so many people in this part of the city. And what's all this about New Year? Bit too soon, isn't it?'

'I smelt fireworks.'

'Fireworks? Next you'll say the Americans are dropping bombs on us!' Mother's voice was loud but I sensed that she was not angry with me. She disappeared into the kitchen and came back almost immediately with a steaming bowl of rice congee, which I swallowed quickly.

'I don't understand.' She sat down next to Laoye. 'Why would the smoke suddenly affect her like that when she's been brought up with it?'

'We all cope in different ways. Her body must have decided now that it has had enough. I can understand that.'

Mother looked at me, then at my sister sitting beside me. I peered at Ling, too, my big sister, taller, prettier than me. I suspected that Mother loved her more than she loved me. I was sure she always looked at Ling more affectionately. Ling was 'easy' she said, and I was 'trouble'.

There was a knock at the door and Mother rose to answer it. She came back to Laoye. 'It's next door asking for you. They know you're here. How quickly news travels. Still, they're so kind to us that you'd better go. Grandma Li has been so poorly lately.' Laoye picked up the white wooden box with the leather strap that he took with him wherever he went. Mother went too.

Soon she returned to cook our dinner. After we had eaten, she hurried us to wash for bed. As she brushed Ling's hair she told her she'd been a good girl to keep the house clean and tidy, and said that I should learn from her. Ling smiled.

Neither of us wanted to go to bed until Laoye had returned for his dinner, but late in the evening he still had not come back. Ling had tired of waiting and gone to bed, and I had yawned and yawned when at last he pushed open the door. He smiled at me but went straight through to the kitchen. I knew I must wait because he would want to wash himself thoroughly – Mother had already prepared the water. But Laoye spent a long time in there and soon a pungent smell wafted through the kitchen door. Curious, I peeped in.

I saw him putting leaves and twigs into a blackened pot on the cooker. He heard me and turned round. I understood: although Laoye had often made brews like this before, this one was for me. The smell was sharp and strong, but I didn't mind. At least it drove away the stink from the chemical factory, which still seeped into our house.

Now he held the pot down to me. 'Will you drink it?' he asked.

'I will if you think it will make me well,' I said, and his face lit up. I loved my *laoye* so much that, no matter how bitter the medicine, I would do as he asked.

'Good child. I knew you would.'

But it was more bitter than I could have imagined. I spat out the first spoonful, then tried another, then another, but I could not swallow the medicine. Mother came into the kitchen and saw what was happening. 'Father,' she said hesitantly, 'are you sure she can take this? Perhaps I should get some sugar?'

'No.' Laoye stopped her and poured some more of the brew into the bowl. 'Sugar will reduce the effect of the herbs. Juju,' he turned to me, 'I want you to think of this as a soup, not a bitter medicine, that will help you breathe properly, like Ling, like me. We want you to get better. Drink it up quickly, please.'

I held my nose with one hand, picked up the bowl with the other and started to gulp it down. But it came straight again up. My weak stomach had betrayed me, when I had so wanted to prove to Laoye that I was brave enough to drink the medicine.

Laoye sighed and took the bowl from me. 'That's enough, Juju, you've tried your best. Laoye isn't cross. We'll try something else.'

At night all of us huddled in the one big bed. Ling hugged me and soon I heard her breathing evenly beside me and knew she had fallen asleep. But Mother and Laoye were still whispering to each other, on the other side of the bed, thinking we had both dropped off.

'Poor child . . . Did you see how hard she tried? But I'm worried about her. She will have another attack once she's exposed to that foul air again,' Laoye warned.

'But what are we to do? There's no escaping it – it's the air we all breathe,' Mother replied.

'You could do as I have done and move to the country.'

'Father, I have a family. We can't take to the road like homeless wanderers.'

I listened avidly.

Once Laoye and Mother stopped talking the room was quiet. Ling turned in her sleep and her leg rested on my thigh, heavy and reassuring. I thought of pushing it away, but clasped her arms instead. There were thoughts I could share only with her. Although Ling never confided in me – she seemed to have no secrets – I could trust her implicitly. On the other side of the bed, I heard Mother's breathing, heavy and sometimes irregular, like her temper when she was awake. I liked listening to Laoye best: his soft snoring was the most reassuring sound of all.

For several days Laoye stayed with us, devising more palatable brews for me, treating friends and acquaintances. But each night he argued with Mother. They didn't disagree in front of me, but I heard them when they thought we were asleep. It was all about me: should I stay or should I go? But go where? I was desperate to ask.

Then one day he left again. I had been playing in the street and knew immediately when I came back and found his medicine box gone. The house felt emptier. I missed the bitter scent of the herbs that hung about him. Perhaps if I had been braver, if I had managed to hold down his remedies, he might have stayed, I thought sadly. At night I struggled to summon their smell and imagined Laoye in some far-off land.

The next few days I had to stay indoors as Mother was terrified I would fall ill when Laoye was not there, but I had been fine so gradually Mother accustomed me to going out again when the wind was high, the cloud not too low and the chemical factory shut for lunch. She watched the chimney as if it was a weather mast. Ling was instructed to keep an eye on me for any sign of breathing difficulties.

I made few friends. I had always liked to play alone and what few friends I had I lost because I had to stay so much in our house. I knew I was due to start school soon, and I dreaded it: it would mean going outside and mixing with new people.

I prayed for my first day of school to be foggy but it was raining, which meant I could go out. When I walked towards the bridge I smelt the air: there was a dense trail of fireworks in it.

I shared a desk with a big boy called Determined. No sooner had I settled in than he knocked my pencil to the floor. 'I don't want a girl next to me,' he said loudly. The boys behind us laughed, and some girls joined in. I turned away my face. 'What are you looking at?' he asked.

'I wasn't looking at you,' I said.

'Yes, you were. How dare you?'

'You're so ugly that I wouldn't want to.' I became angry.

'If you say that again. . .' He raised his fist.

'Quiet!' the teacher shouted. 'You, and you,' she pointed at the boy and me, 'stop disturbing the class.'

Determined grinned, and turned to the teacher as if nothing had happened. My face burned at the injustice – I hadn't disturbed the class: he had started it.

At break the rain stopped and everyone went out to play, but nobody came to play with me. I stood near the classroom, pretending not to care. It was not as if I was used to having friends, but being ignored made me feel more alone than ever.

At the second break I still stood alone. Determined had forgotten about me and was chasing another boy. Bored and lonely, I was sure that the smell in the air had grown stronger and began to fear that something bad would happen.

At afternoon break a few girls asked me to join in with them. I thought they'd invited me out of pity and I hated being patronised, but they needed one more girl for their game. I relented. It was my favourite game: a catch played with a rice-filled cloth ball. I became so carried away with it that I didn't notice the smell growing more intense until my head began to feel odd. I was breathless anyway from running. My hands and feet were tingling, my chest and throat tightened. When the ball hit me I collapsed on to the ground.

I was rushed to hospital, where the doctors made me feel better. But this time when I got home, Mother watched me like a hawk and I was not allowed to go out even for a stroll. When she couldn't take any more days off work she locked me into the house and arranged for one of our neighbours to send me food for lunch. I felt I was going mad. I begged Mother to send for Laoye – I was convinced he would make me feel well again. Finally, on the third day, to my delight, he arrived. 'Laoye! Laoye!' I shouted. 'I can drink the herbs – let me drink the herbs.'

He laughed and Mother laughed behind him. 'Silly child, don't boast,' she said.

'I'm not,' I said. 'Give them to me and I'll show you.'

I drank the whole bowl.

Mother shook her head. 'Ling could never do that. She's so fussy about her food.'

Laoye didn't say anything at first, just looked closely at my face, then leaned forward and put a hand on my head. He gazed at me as he addressed my mother: 'All children are fussy, but this one has courage. Eating bitterness,' he murmured, as if to himself. 'She'll need to get used to it, this one.'

In bed that night, as the lorries sped past our house, Laoye and Mother argued about me again.

'She's suffering from asthma,' I heard him say to Mother, 'and she has allergies too. She should leave now, before it's too late. Do you want her to suffer like your husband?'

'You don't need to remind me of that, Father.'

'Remember how his health was destroyed.'

My mother sounded distraught now: 'Father, I said you don't have to remind me. But what can I do? I can't have her in hospital – it's too expensive.'

'Let me take her. She can travel with me. I can treat her, and teach her too.'

'You're mad – she can't live like a vagabond. Beside, you know what being outdoors does to her.'

'Not everywhere is so polluted. Why should she stay where the air is poisonous? Even she knows it is not good for her. Yet you make your home in this foul-smelling place.'

Silence. I heard my mother turn away angrily – the conversation was over. I thought of what Laoye had said about me eating bitterness. Was there something unusual about me? Had he singled me out for some grand plan?

'Listen, I'll take her to the countryside, to my home town where your cousin still lives. The mountain air will do her the world of good, and there will be nothing to upset her,' Laoye begged.

Mother did not speak for a long time.

I smiled in the darkness. I wouldn't be sad to leave home, just happy to have more precious time with Laoye.

3

After three weeks' treatment with acupuncture and herbal medicine, Lucy had improved dramatically. She seldom wheezed now although her cough still troubled her. I learned, as she began to be more talkative, that she had indeed seen an acupuncturist before, when she was working in London. What alarmed me, however, was how evangelical she was about it. To her, it was more than a treatment, it was a way of life. While I could understand the joy and trust she had found in Chinese medicine, when Western treatment had failed her, I was taken aback by what I saw as childish naïvety. It seemed that her happiness hung on my treatment and I was not prepared to bear such a responsibility. The unease I felt grew heavier each time she visited me.

On a sunny day in the fourth week, she came in like a fresh breeze. She'd taken all the herbs I'd given her – she had boiled them carefully in a specially purchased earthenware pot, she said, as if she had done her homework well and expected to be praised.

I imagined her drinking my medicine in the front room of her house. I had never been inside an English home and imagined hers to be a suburban semi with the pot-pourri, the matching curtains and sofas I had glimpsed through other people's windows. It would have a round table set for tea. In fact, in my fantasy she was not drinking a herbal brew at all, but milky tea. Despite her enthusiasm, I could not imagine this foreign woman drinking the bitter infusions I had prescribed for her.

She sat down, noticed the small purple hand rest I'd bought and placed her hand on it. The velvety smoothness offset the paleness of her skin. She looked up to smile while her hand stroked the cushion. 'Lovely,' she said.

I was glad she had noticed it and as I met her smile I pointed at the wall behind me. 'The acupuncture chart,' I said. It was another recent addition to the room.

She nodded. 'I have one – not exactly the same, but similar. I love all the characters.'

I pointed out the ones relevant to asthma and she studied them carefully. When I told her their meanings she gasped and marvelled at the aptness of their names. 'Stabilising breathlessness? Welcoming fragrance? How clever.

'You haven't been here long, have you?' she asked.

'We've been open for about four weeks. In fact you're one of our first patients.'

'Lucky me. Finding you was the best thing that's happened to me for a long time. Of course,' she continued, 'I've done my bit. Eliminated dairy products from my diet, which was hard as I'm a big fan of cheese. I really want to do it right this time. Dr Lin, I feel sure you're the one person who can cure me.'

Her words embarrassed and alarmed me so I began to examine her. I took her pulse and kept my eyes closed long after I had finished. I wanted there to be silence between us, to curb her enthusiasm. Her pulse was encouraging: she had improved, I was pleased to note, but was still not completely well. Illnesses like asthma don't go away in a fortnight, however effective the treatment.

I let go of her hand and waited for her to stand up and leave. She got up but, mistaking my intention, walked over to the treatment couch and lay down. 'Welcoming fragrance,' she murmured to herself in Chinese, evidently thinking of the chart I'd just shown her. 'Well,' she smiled again, 'is it welcoming fragrance first?'

'We're not doing any points today.'

'Oh, why not?' She looked as if I'd denied her a treat.

'Let's just say that acupuncture has done its best for the moment.'

She rolled down her sleeve. 'What a shame,' she murmured, and got up.

I explained that it was important to follow the needles' good work with herbal treatment. This was the time to consolidate our achievements. I wrote down the names of the herbs quickly. I knew too well what she needed now. 'Take these herbs for four weeks,' I said.

'Surely I don't need more herbs.'

'Yes, you do. You might not feel ill, but you are still not cured.'

'Is it possible to have more acupuncture in that case?'

'Herbs work better at this stage.'

For a few seconds the room was quiet. Lucy studied the chart behind me. I knew she was buying time, trying to think of a response. She said slowly, 'If it's all right with you, I prefer to be treated with needles.'

I tried to keep smiling. 'I'm afraid the course of treatment I've designed for you means you need to stop the needles for a time and concentrate on the herbs. If you want to get better, you must keep to it. But of course, it's up to you.'

She left quietly after paying for the herbs. But I wasn't sure she would use them. For a moment my professionalism deserted me and I knew how sad I would feel if she stopped her treatment. I felt like grabbing her hands and making her promise to come back. It was not just a matter of pride: I was starting to care about her.

I sat down before the desk, my fingers on the hand rest – I could still feel her warmth there. This was not China, where my patients were obedient, docile and familiar with my vocabulary: heat, damp, *yin, yang*, balance, a hot or cold food, knowledge that was part of their everyday lives, handed down by word of mouth from generation to generation. They came to me when they felt they were going to fall ill rather than waiting until it had happened.

The insistent murmur of my next patient roused me from my

thoughts. I glimpsed through the door the tall, thin figure of Mr Lincoln, clutching a plastic shopping-bag, in which he would hide his prescriptions – I gathered it was a double shame that he should see a Chinese acupuncturist about his low sperm count. He worked in the building trade, he explained, and builders were not renowned for open-mindedness.

Normally I found his subterfuges touching and had always gone out of my way to help him relax. But today, after Lucy, I wasn't ready for him. Although the two had such a different attitude to my skill neither treated it or me with the respect it deserved.

Xiao Jin chatted with him, as she did with all of my patients, and showed him into the treatment room. I saw the blush spreading up his neck as he murmured in response. Xiao Jin was not the most diplomatic person in the world and I waved her out.

Mr Lincoln fiddled with his plastic bag as he told me the good news: his sperm count had gone up and he wanted to continue the treatment. But as I sat down to write a prescription he leaned forward suddenly: 'Would it be possible to have the herbs prepared here?'

'Why?'

'It's . . . The smell upsets my partner.'

His face couldn't have been redder. I put down the pen. I'm not a man and would not presume to know how he felt, but it seemed that he was too sensitive to what other people might think of him. Still, I was not his psychiatrist. I sighed. 'You can take the herbs in capsules, but they are less effective and you will need to swallow around twenty at a time.'

His eyes bulged. 'So many? Are you sure?'

Suddenly I was angry. My sympathy for him vanished, replaced with an increasing impatience at the way these English patients insulted me with their lack of trust. 'It's up to you,' I said. 'I was trying to save you the trouble of boiling the herbs. If you aren't sure, why don't you go away and think about it?' I bade him a cool farewell.

Xiao Jin's commiserations at the end of the day did not help. They seemed superficial: she wasn't so involved in the patients' lives as I felt. These setbacks were hard for me to take. I sent Xiao Jin home early, with assurances that she would be paid for the hours she hadn't worked. After she'd gone I sat in my quiet treatment room, plagued by remorse. How had I failed to see that my patients needed more information? They came to me in desperation, with such hope in their eyes, and I awaited them with equal anticipation – I had forsaken my family for them. What a cruel irony that they did not understand the medicine on which they pinned their hopes.

A persistent sound grew stronger – raindrops on the small window set high, as in a prison cell on the wall opposite the door. Xiao Jin had opened it that morning, when it was sunny and warm. I stood on a chair to close it, hearing footsteps and traffic outside.

We were so cut off from the rest of the town here. For the average passer-by, we must seem a curiosity, so much more alien than the local takeaway outlets. There, they could sample familiar things, a soup or a stir-fry, the combination of sweet and sour – but mine was a closed world of incense, needles and mysterious herbs. No wonder Mr Lincoln was afraid of ridicule. How much of their treatment did my patients understand? What did they think of me?

When I replaced the chair I found on the floor a photo of a little boy and a woman – Lucy, her face squeezed so tightly to the child's that it took me a minute to recognise her. It must have fallen out of her bag.

I sat down again slowly, and felt in my pocket. I took out the worn-looking photo from my wallet and placed it next to Lucy's on the table. They were both passport-sized photos and even the blue background was the same. But I had a feeling that Lucy's, unlike mine, had not been taken at the airport before a departure. My daughter's arms were round me and her face pressed close to mine, as Lucy's was pressed to the little boy's. You could not see the tears on my daughter's face, though – I had wiped them away.

I stood up – I had to get out. From my experience of the last few days I knew how, slowly, the darkness would descend.

I stuffed an umbrella into my bag and locked the clinic behind me. It was nearly five weeks since I'd arrived on a late-night coach from London. A few weeks before that I had answered an advertisement in a Chinese newspaper, recruiting a qualified acupuncturist. The pay wasn't much but it was far more than a waitress would earn. There would be one day off each week but I didn't need spare time because I had no family to attend to – at least, not in this country.

It was only on the bus, as I left London behind me, that I allow myself to feel excited. The only other time I had felt so alive was when I had graduated from medical college. I was barely twenty. For a precious five years, I had studied and lived as far away from my home town as possible, as far away as I could from the wound that had eaten away a large chunk of my childhood. Those five years had restored my faith in my fellow human beings. I had come away full of the importance of my job, the knowledge that I could take away pain and make a contribution to the world.

Now I was no longer so optimistic, but I relished the idea of a new beginning. At forty I would finally be an independent woman, earning my living, and, perhaps, I would help a few people along the way. In treating Lucy I had begun to find a purpose here. Her transformation from breathless patient into a contented woman was something to be proud of. It helped me make sense of what I had done – my sacrifice in leaving China and my family. I must bring Lucy back to the clinic. I hoped again that she hadn't gone away for good. I remembered the look on her face as she left – she had lost faith in me, I was sure.

I turned down a path leading to a canal and hurried past fishermen huddled along the bank. The rain had stopped and a bright sunset emerged from the cloud. A group of small boys with helmets on bicycles raced past, shouting, 'Excuse me,' aiming for the deepest puddles. They left a gust of refreshing air in their wake and I breathed deeply slowing my steps. The sudden movement seemed to intensify the stillness of the bank. I felt an overwhelming desire to immerse myself in its green-ness, and sat on a stone slab and hugged my bag to me.

Something hard jabbed my thigh and I felt in my pocket to check that my purse was still there. I took it out, and looked again at the extra photo I'd tucked into it next to mine. I must return it to Lucy.

Now, in near darkness, I walked slowly back up the path. One of the anglers nodded to me, but largely I was ignored. What did he make of a Chinese woman in a white gown wandering through the dusk? Did he spare me a thought at all?

I lingered at the door to the house that was not my home and an image flashed into my mind: a widow threw a bag of beans on the floor, then picked each one up. The beans were numerous, but so would be the empty minutes in the rest of her life alone. 'One, two, three. . .'

Had I read it in a book? Was it a scene from a Peking opera? No matter. But it seemed to mirror my life, my feelings now. 'One, two, three,' I counted, staring into the dark to trace the minutes I was missing in the life of a little girl, my daughter.

4

On the night before I'd finally left home, the air was so dense that I couldn't believe I was the only one who noticed it. There was a new heaviness in the smoke from the chemical factory. Perhaps someone from another part of town had set off their fireworks early. When I heard a shrill sound outside I called to Laoye: 'I knew it! It's New Year!' Mother ignored me and busied herself with packing my bag, but Laoye came to the door. As we poked our heads out, we heard the sudden screech. 'There! Fireworks!' I shouted again, and looked up to the dark sky to search for a colourful display. After a short while, there was a loud bang, followed by a sound like someone screaming from the direction of the factory. Laoye grabbed my hand, pushed me indoors and shouted for Mother.

It was the first gunshot in the fighting between the different factions of radicals devoted to Chairman Mao. In our town it started with a clash between the chemical-factory group and its rival the steel factory, who were the more hot-blooded of the two sides. But I learned this later on, when I could no longer smell the fireworks. My disappointment was immense, but Laoye and Mother showed me little sympathy.

They debated whether we should leave that night or the next day. From time to time they would go out to listen to the gunshots. Laoye would have taken me sooner, but our neighbour told Mother we should not go out or we might be caught in crossfire.

We set off the next morning, when we were sure that the shooting had ceased.

21

Laoye didn't lead me: he strode ahead, not looking back, trusting me to follow. He only held my hand when we walked past the bridge near the chemical factory, which was quiet, the chimney sad and empty. After the bridge he let go of my hand and we joined the morning bicycle traffic. This was the same route I would have taken to school, but today, instead of joining the children with their schoolbags, I went the other way to cleaner air and a new life, with a worn red nylon travel bag over my shoulder. My mother wouldn't let me carry anything when she and I walked together, but Laoye insisted that I had my own pack, which I loved. I didn't mind missing school and my asthma had turned out to be a blessing in disguise: it meant I could spend all the time in the world with my *laoye*.

I knew that in many people's eyes my grandfather was a strange man. He wore the same blue top and grey trousers as every other man but his walk and his bearing made him different. I looked at him now, carrying his medicine box as if it were a weapon. To me he was like those heroes in the films Mother had taken us to see, handsome but plainly dressed, who performed extraordinary acts of courage, rescuing those in distress. They were often Communist agents in disguise under Nationalist rule. This again was like Laoye: an air of mystery hung about him. I straightened my back and raised my head high, imitating him.

As we reached the station he turned to me. 'Now, listen,' he put a hand on my left shoulder, 'I know you're a big girl now, but this is a place where lots of people gather. There might be bad people who want to take children away from their families so. . .' He produced a piece of thick yellow string from his bag, tied one end round my wrist and kept hold of the other. At first I wasn't sure that I liked it, but I was soon too distracted by the crowds at the station to care.

The noise made me dizzy – dialects I didn't understand, people cursing, ducks quacking and cars sounding their horns. Occasionally I saw children of my own age, snotty, wary-looking but alert, with no strings attached to them. I pointed them out to Laoye, who shut his eyes as if the sight of them pained him. 'Juju, they are homeless. Nobody cares for them.' He steered me away from them whenever they came close.

I envied their freedom, the way they wove so freely through the crowd, but if I had to be bound, I was glad it should be to Laoye. It was a kind of honour. People wearing rags lay sleeping on mountains of luggage on the dirty ground. Where had they all come from? Where were they going? Were they all escaping from the dirty air in this city?

We stood at the ticket queue until I got pins and needles. The sun had long risen and was overhead now, burning us. The warm clothes we had worn against the morning chill now clung to us uncomfortably. There wasn't any shade to shelter in.

Even the calling of the snack-sellers failed to arouse my interest: all I wanted was to find a cool place to sit. I felt distant from everything and, eyes closed, leaned on Laoye to doze. When I heard a shout I didn't move, but I felt Laoye stiffen. I opened my eyes and blinked: the sun was still blindingly bright. 'A boy has collapsed,' I heard, and saw a crowd gathering. Laoye ran towards it, and I followed, still bound to him.

At first the crowd wouldn't let us through but then Laoye said loudly, 'Let me pass. I'm an acupuncturist.' As if by magic the crowds parted. I saw one of the homeless boys lying on the ground. Laoye knelt down, felt his pulse, then reached for his bag. Swiftly he stuck a needle between the boy's upper lip and his nose, another into his elbow and yet another on the outside of his thumb. Then he gazed at the boy with the same tenderness he sometimes showed me. But when he became aware of the crowd that surrounded him, he seemed afraid. Quickly he gathered his things and started to walk away. I followed reluctantly, eager to watch the boy wake up. When we reached the edge of the crowd, we heard, 'He's come round.'

Laoye turned, saw me and seemed surprised. I tugged at the string, wanting to go back. He smiled. 'It's only sunstroke,' he said. 'He'll be all right.'

We had lost our place in the queue. I couldn't remember where we had been but even if I had, the people behind us would have refused to let us back in. Laoye glanced up at the scorching sun and cursed for the first time. Now that we were out of the queue, we could sit in the shade and enjoy a brief moment of comfort. I was thirsty and hungry, and remembered the egg fried rice Mother had prepared for my lunch. But . . . where was my bag?

Laoye looked at me and realised what had happened. Without a word he took out a Thermos and handed it to me. I drank, quenched my thirst, but when I remembered what I had lost, I began to sob.

A tall dark man stepped into the shade. 'You are going to Tu Fei Wo, aren't you?' he said, in a heavily accented voice. Laoye nodded. He squatted and pressed something into Laoye's hand: 'There – have my ticket.' Laoye looked surprised. 'I saw you help that beggar boy. You deserve to be helped in turn.'

'Thank you, young man.' Laoye reached for his purse.

The dark man shook his head. 'No, no.' Then he leaned closer. 'My mother has been bedridden after a stroke for years, and I wonder. . .'

Laoye stopped smiling. 'I'm only an old man who knows a few tricks, like how to revive people with sunstroke. I'm sorry, I can't help your mother.' They stood up and I saw that another crowd had gathered round us. Their closeness made me feel anxious. Laoye gathered up his bag and took my hand. Then he pressed some notes into the tall man's hand. 'Let's go,' he said, and pulled me forward.

By the time we were settled on our hard seats I was exhausted. Suddenly I was homesick. If I had been at home I'd have been playing with my sister, who would just have come in from school. Now I knew why Mother had made such a fuss about my departure: this was how it had felt to her. I sobbed, and only stopped when the ticket inspector arrived – I was frightened of him. Then I was distracted by the adults around me, who were singing along with the loudspeaker in the carriage and waving their arms in the devotion dance. It gave them an excuse to stretch and I saw a number yawn, which made me laugh. But the noise went on so long and they danced so wearily that I grew sad again. We were poor, but had never been in want, and I had never lost anything before. Should I tell the police? Laoye shook his head, and said we didn't know who'd taken my bag.

'Listen, Juju, I'll tell you a story.' I turned to him, eyes wet. 'Once upon a time,' he began, 'there was a little boy . . . of about your age, I think.'

As the train jolted along I glimpsed a side of the city I'd never seen before: a child squatting to pee, some clothes hung out to dry, a tired-looking woman pouring water from a bowl, everywhere paper being tossed about by the wind . . . It was satisfying to fly past it all, to escape something that could never catch up with me. It was getting dark; I leaned closer to Laoye, whose soft voice soothed me, along with the humming of the train.

Once upon a time, he said, there was a little boy who had read all the classics and wanted, like their heroes, to rob the rich and save the poor. For that reason, he escaped from his parents one day to follow a *kung-fu* master. He admired his master very much and worshipped him as if he were a god. He was a good pupil and became the best of all the apprentices, and his master was proud of him.

He took the boy to many competitions to meet other fighters, and to test his strength. Soon he thought he was invincible: there wasn't a kick he hadn't learned or a strike he hadn't mastered. Eventually he grew proud and looked down on other people. A beggarwoman lived near where the pupil and his master lived. Although they often gave her food, they laughed at her bent back and ragged clothes. Then one day, the master fell ill after a violent fight, so ill that no doctor and no medicine could save him. Those strong men felt helpless, until a woman came to the master's bed. 'Drink this,' she said. It was an infusion of dried herbs. The young man, as he now was, recognised her as the ragged beggarwoman he'd often scorned, but the master drank the medicine and was cured.

'What do you think the story tells you, Juju?'

I thought for a minute. 'Always drink your medicine?' I could not help feeling proud that I could drink up Laoye's bitter brew.

He laughed. 'Yes, that's a good point. But what else? Who do you think is the strongest in this story? Who is the hero?'

I thought harder. 'The master?'

'But the master was dying. . .'

'The beggarwoman?' I said uncertainly.

'Yes. I think so. She saves lives, which means more than winning a fight, doesn't it?' Then he leaned forward to hold me. 'I want you to grow up to be truly strong. I want you to be a real hero, like the beggarwoman.'

'Like the beggarwoman,' I murmured. I thought of Determined sitting next to me at school and how he had insulted me because I was a girl and no one had stood up for me. 'Can girls be heroes?'

'Of course, I happen to know more girl heroes than boy ones. Anyone, girl or boy, can be anything they want to be. Don't let anyone tell you otherwise.'

That was not how Mother spoke: girls are girls – they don't play with mud, and they don't fight. When I told her that my ambition was to be a driver when I grew up, because I wanted to travel the country, she said, 'Girls don't become drivers. You can be a nurse, or a teacher like Ling.'

'Real strength is in your mind, your head. It's how much you learn, and . . . how quickly,' said my grandfather.

My head was drooping low on Laoye's chest, and although I heard his words, they went in one ear and out of the other. I was too sleepy to absorb them. The last thing I heard him say was about gaining when you lose, or was it losing when you gain?

'And the situation all over the country is bright, with Chairman Mao's Red Guards in control of propaganda stations. They took up arms and fought. . .' The Tannoy on the train had woken everyone. I rubbed my eyes and looked up into Laoye's tired face. 'Are we there yet?' I asked.

He laughed. 'You'll have another sleep before we get there.'

For a while I amused myself by watching the trees, houses and telegraph poles flying past. They were like curious but impatient children, peering in at the window, then disappearing. Soon, houses and trees were scarce. There were just telegraph poles now, and fields, where people worked with stooped backs. I wondered how many days it would have taken us to walk this distance.

'Maybe a month for me as I am used to walking.'

'And what about me?'

He laughed and shook his head.

The sun was rising, lighter as it tried to tear away from the horizon, but the clouds we were heading towards grew thicker. Gradually they took shapes and I discovered, with excitement, that they were not clouds after all, but hills and mountains.

I'd only ever seen mountains in pictures. Real ones were on a scale I hadn't expected. After the dull drab houses we had left behind, the mountains were intriguing like a scene from a story book that made me fidget with anticipation.

The train hurried towards them, like a dog to its master. Suddenly the windows were full of exposed rock, and tree roots hanging overhead. We burrowed into a dark tunnel in the hills and emerged to a view of waterfalls, like giant white birds. My heart beat fast. 'Where are we? Are we still in China? It's so clean!' I shouted.

Laoye leaned on the window and watched with me, pointing at this tree and that flower, telling me their names. 'The mountain is one big treasure house,' he said, rubbing his hands, 'like the mountain in the story when the little boy goes hunting for riches.'

He told me of many herbs, grasses and blossoms to be found there, and of an elusive herb called the *lingzhi*, which grew on the cliffs and was reputed to restore the dead to life, and to bring a person's beloved to them in their dreams. Everyone had searched for it so it was hard to find now.

'Even for you?' I asked.

'Even for me.' He lay back to smoke his pipe. I knew that this was a sign that he did not wish to be interrupted. When he was smoking like this, he always wore a far-away look. It was at times like this that it struck me he had troubles of his own, and had had a life before I was born.

I was sure he had secrets he kept from us all. His actions often puzzled me, even on that trip. After he had warned me about strangers, he had rushed to help a homeless boy. But when that kind man who'd bought us tickets asked for help, he had refused it. Now that I came to think about it, I realised it had happened before. Although Laoye never hesitated to help our neighbours or friends when they were ill, he hated it if they made too much of it. Once, Auntie Xu from across the road had had a red silk banner made in Laoye's honour after he had cured her father of arthritis: 'To Dr Lin – such a superior doctor – Huatuo the ancient saint reborn' was embroidered across it in golden thread. Auntie Xu delivered it herself, followed by a crowd, and Laoye was furious. When Laoye threatened never to treat her father again if she did not stop this performance, poor Auntie Xu broke down in a flood of tears. 'I said I expected nothing. Is that clear?' Laoye had said.

We spent another night on the train and arrived at dawn the following morning. The station was quiet, the waiting room candlelit. 'This is the nearest town to my village,' Laoye said, and led me out of the station. How different the air was from what I had been used to: it was like a delicious drink. My lungs were filled with freshness.

But the town was unfriendly: all the doors and windows were shut, frozen by the cold weather. We hurried to get on to a bus, which was full of people talking loudly. Nobody smiled. They were tall – especially the women, who carried large cloth packs, their faces reddish-brown like baked sweet potatoes. We sat at the back, stamping our feet, squeezed between a smelly man with an oily fur coat and a woman holding a clutch of chickens bound together with a string. She had hard eyes.

I clasped Laoye's hand. 'Why is nobody smiling?' I whispered.

'Don't worry, Juju. Their hearts are warmer than their faces,' he said, and leaned closer to me. 'Do you know what Tu Fei Wo, the name of this place, means?'

I shook my head.

'It means "the nest of the bandits". In the old days, this area was notorious for bandits, who camped up there on the hills.

But have no fear,' he winked, 'all that was in the past. There is no danger, now that we are liberated.'

I sat back as the bus charged up the mountain path. As we drove through the rugged scenery, the sharp features of my fellow passengers began to seem a part of it. It no longer mattered that they didn't smile because, like the mountain and river here, I found them beautiful.

I craned my neck as the bus wound round the mountain, like a creeper on a tree. 'Are we there yet?' I kept asking.

'Not for a long time,' Laoye said.

The rising sun warmed us, melting the stiffness, and I leaned on Laoye so that I could stretch my hand inside his shirt to scratch his back – his favourite treat.

'We are going back to Tao Yuan,' Laoye said, yawning.

5

It took me a while to recognise the man who stood outside the clinic, examining our window display, as Mr Cheng, even after Xiao Jin's annoyed exclamation: 'What do you think he wants?' Eventually his posture gave him away – he was nodding, with both hands behind his back. I knew he had been a provincial health official before he came to England, which was when he must have adopted that stance. It was the way he had stood to address my husband, when he had worked in his London clinics.

Mr Cheng owned a chain of acupuncture clinics dotted around England and Scotland, all called Harmony. It was said he had come to England some twelve years ago. He had started by setting up a *tai chi* school in London, which became popular and prosperous, then gone on to establish the clinics. He was a successful businessman.

'It's Mr Cheng,' I whispered to Xiao Jin, who was working on the stock list for once, instead of talking on the phone to her friends.

'Who?' She frowned.

'Mr Cheng, our boss.'

Xiao Jin had never met him before and I could see how Mr Cheng's unpromising appearance didn't fit her image of our employer. The way he studied the grotesque before-and-after posters made him look like just another curious passer-by. But I saw something else in his face: where others were fascinated,

31

disgusted, appalled, even, his expressed ownership and pride.

Xiao Jin rushed to open the door, all smiles. He straightened at her approach, seeming almost annoyed that he had been discovered. 'Everything all right?' He nodded to Xiao Jin, barely acknowledging her extended hand, and stepped quickly inside. I remained behind the counter. 'Dr Lin,' he said. 'May I see you in your treatment room?'

I knew why he'd come: we weren't making enough money. I hadn't worked in my ex-husband's London clinic, which was one of Mr Cheng's, but I knew from my visits there that they had much more custom than ours.

He sat down in my chair and motioned me to sit opposite him, on the patient's chair. It was more comfortable, with two cushions, but still lower than his. I felt odd sitting there and ill-at-ease in his presence, as I had felt at my interview. I was relieved that the job I had applied for was in a small provincial clinic: the thought of being under his nose in that big London clinic had not appealed to me.

He asked to see my notes, and flipped through them quickly. I soon saw that he was not interested in the range of ailments I was treating, but in the frequency with which the patients returned. I gave monosyllabic answers, watching his nicotine-stained fingers moving through the papers and felt the slow burn of irritation.

When he turned to Xiao Jin's sales notes, he shook his head and raised his voice: 'No single prescription should exceed ten grams. I thought I'd made that clear in the rules.'

'Yes, but. . .' I hadn't thought he meant it. I didn't often prescribe more than that amount, but I objected to being restricted.

'Rules are rules. I'm not running a charity.'

I tried hard to restrain my anger. 'Many of our patients are new and I want them to have instant results, which will keep them coming back for more.'

His eyes rested on the small cushioned hand rest. My heart thudded as he rested a hand on it, palm up, limp but arrogant. His eyes moved over me and he leaned back in the chair. 'I see you make your patients comfortable here. I wouldn't mind a treatment myself, Dr Lin.'

I straightened my back, gritted my teeth and pretended not to have understood what he meant. I smiled at the wall and tried to divert his attention away from me. 'I'm glad you like what I've done – but, of course, it's you the patients should be grateful to, Mr Cheng. It's your clinic.'

He smiled, pleased with the flattery. His eyes drifted to the medicine box on my table. 'Where did you get that?' he sneered. 'It's ancient.'

'It's a family heirloom.' I tried to sound casual but tensed inside. I wished I hadn't put it somewhere so obvious.

He leaned close to examine it. 'It looks out of place here – not very hygienic,' he said hesitantly.

'If you don't like it, Mr Cheng, I will remove it.'

'Ah, there's no need.' He yawned and stood up. I stood up, too, showing respect to a senior, but secretly I wanted to hurry his departure. In all of this he was simply exercising his power so that I knew who was the boss.

'But, remember, we need to economise.' He paused at the door, as if the thought had suddenly come into his head.

Talking about business and money put him at ease. He was in his element. Ours was one of his lowest-performing clinics: he understood that this was partly because it was new, but he expected us to catch up quickly. How did we advertise our work? he asked. I told him that we put up notices in libraries, shops and community centres, but most patients came to us through word of mouth.

'How about contacting the press, the local *Gazette*? Get a journalist to write an article about you. Tell them stories about China – the English love them. Does Xiao Jin work hard? Do you really need her for so many hours?'

'Sometimes more, sometimes less. It's hard to say,' I replied truthfully. I really needed a medical assistant, rather than a secretary, but I knew it was out of the question that he would agree to pay for another qualified person. And I was sure Xiao Jin was eavesdropping – another reason to keep quiet.

'I'll give you three months,' he said, eyes cold and distant, hands behind his back once more. 'Remember, talk to the press, advertise, get the word out. You will see more patients.'

We said goodbye frostily at the door and he got into a blue Ford, the back windscreen obscured by mud, and drove off.

'I bet his wife doesn't want to be seen dead in that car,' muttered Xiao Jin, after he had sped away. 'Reduce my hours? I should have asked him for a pay rise. All those heavy sacks have done my back in. Does he think I'm a common labourer?'

Although she had made it obvious that she'd overheard our conversation, it was unclear to me whether she thought I was doing her a favour or a disservice in answering him as I had. I didn't care. I knew deep down that we saw the clinic differently: for her it was just a job but for me it was meant to be a new life.

Back in my treatment room I opened the small window to let in the air. I wanted to rid it of every trace of Mr Cheng, his smoky smell, even the dent his hand had made in the hand rest. At around the time of my separation from my husband, Mr Cheng had paid me a great deal of attention. I hadn't liked him then and I liked him less now. I recalled his high-pitched voice and felt uneasy: something about him was vaguely familiar and made me think of things I'd rather forget. I turned to the medicine box, gleaming on my table. I stroked the worn leather strap, and felt, for a fleeting moment, as if I had touched the hand of its original owner. A shudder went through me. Mr Cheng had said it was unhygienic, but I had seen in his eyes that he was unsettled by it. If only he knew what stories the box contained. I decided to remove it upstairs to my bedroom. Despite what he had said, I was sure he would prefer me to keep it out of sight. Also I didn't want him to become too curious about it.

And he wanted me to tell stories from a past that I had wanted to bury for ever. I laughed bitterly. I had a feeling that my story was not quite what potential patients would want to hear. But he had been serious I knew.

In the end, Mr Cheng's words had their desired effect on us. Xiao Jin spent a day at the market giving away leaflets – to escape the boredom of the clinic, she told me – and a couple of days later a fair-haired woman from the *Gazette* came with a small notebook to talk to me about 'life in China as a barefoot doctor'. She persuaded me to be photographed in front of my Li Shizhen poster.

Xiao Jin giggled as she read the article aloud: '"During the Cultural Revolution I became a barefoot doctor, treating local peasants and their ailments. . ."' But she also seemed shocked. 'Really? You were a barefoot doctor once? You don't look . . . I mean, you seem so young. I didn't think you would remember the Cultural Revolution.' She looked at me expectantly, her young cheeks flushed. The heavy words sounded light in her mouth.

I smiled, trying to match the bland expression I had worn for the newspaper photograph. I was amazed at how easy it had been to tell that story. The place was real enough and much of what I had told the journalist had been true, but no one would ever know what I had kept to myself – not in this part of the world, anyway. Telling it, I had experienced a strange sense of relief, as if that was how things had actually happened. Now, seeing it on paper, I could almost believe this new version of events. The journalist was certainly taken in, hooked like a fish. I had given her just what she wanted.

'Dr Lin?' Xiao Jin asked.

'Yes?'

'Is it true, then, what happened?'

I nodded, and she stared at me as foolishly as the journalist had.

I fiddled with the latch of the medicine box. I had an urge to open it, but I held back. My story is safe, I told myself. See how easily these people are taken in.

6

My aunt, a tall, stern-looking woman, with the high cheekbones typical of the women round there, handed me two big baskets lined at the bottom with newspaper. 'You like cherries, don't you?' she asked.

'Of course.'

'If you can fill these baskets with them – put white in this basket, and red in that – by the end of the day . . . you can eat as many as you like.' She scrunched up her face to the rising sun. I needed no more encouragement.

For the first time, I experienced how fresh cherries should taste and I couldn't get enough of them. Plucked from the tree, in which I startled opportunistic birds, they tasted warm and almost alive. In no time I was off the ladder, climbing into the branches. I was the monkey king sent to guard the imperial orchard and feasting on celestial peaches to his heart's content. Up here, I could see the neighbours' houses and the grown-ups working in the field, my cousin, not much older than me, among them. Then I looked further, to the rocky mountain called Black Hill, which I had travelled up the other day on the dusty, noisy bus. Clouds trailed across it like a silk scarf, and I imagined I could see Laoye, who had left early that morning to gather his 'treasures' – the herbs.

The days between Arrival of Autumn and Frost Descent were the best time for the ones he wanted, he had told me, and there was not a day to lose. I thought of the look of concentration on his face as he knelt down to pray in front of the small clay statue of an old man with a long white beard and a walking stick, standing on a bed of herbs. He was the 'herb god', he had told me, who protected him. After his prayer he bathed himself. The water was cold and his teeth chattered as he splashed it on himself. I asked why he was bothering to wash so early in the morning. He had grinned and said it was to show respect. Respect to whom?

'To the Being who yields all the fruits and leaves for me to pick.'

'What is this Being?'

'It is the soul of the mountains,' he said, after a little thought.

I pondered his words now, high in the tree, and tried to imagine what the soul of the mountain might look like. It was hard to conjure up a picture of a soul, so I thought instead of the rocks, fruits and rivers I had seen on the walk we had taken shortly after my arrival. We hadn't gathered herbs then – we were just paying a visit, Laoye had told me.

I wondered whether he would be picking herbs like the *lingzhi*. In the old days, he had told me, people had to rise early in the morning and meditate, so that all unclean thoughts were banished, dress in white and make offerings. Even then it was not guaranteed that you would find the *lingzhi*. Only the brave and true would glimpse it.

I strained to look for him, and thought briefly that I could see him just under the cliff. There was a cave, he had said, which he had discovered a long time ago while looking for the *lingzhi*. Only he knew about it and he had made me promise not to tell anyone else. He was probably there now, resting, for it afforded a good view of the valley below, our village included. Could he see our house from there? I waved.

The sun had climbed high now: it must be hot for those people in the field, but here, in the shade of the tree, it did not trouble me. Dreamily, I carried on with my work, occasionally dropping a cherry or two into the baskets beneath. Once or twice my hand would post a warm wriggling caterpillar into my mouth – I was so used to the feel of the soft, ripe fruits. When

38

it first happened, I screamed and flung it away. After that, I didn't mind so much: I just put them back on the tree – there were enough cherries for us to share, I thought generously.

I was in Tao Yuan, the earthly paradise described by Tao Yuanming. Our village was commonly known as brigade number one of Red Star Commune, Laoye had explained, but his special name for it was Tao Yuan. Tao Yuan was not just this bit of the countryside but the place where one was happiest, where the air was clean, food abundant and the land beautiful. Laoye had discovered his Tao Yuan and had brought me here, but one day, he said, I would discover my own.

I thought briefly of my mother and sister. Although I had missed them on the train, now they just seemed far away.

When the sun became too hot, even in the shade, I climbed down, but not before I had spotted Auntie with a big basket setting off for the field – lunch for the families. She walked with a limp which was why she wasn't in the field with her husband and my cousin. When she came back, her basket was empty. There was no lunch left for me, she said apologetically, flashing a tight-faced smile in compensation, and I saw bits of vegetable stuck between her front teeth. I told her I wasn't hungry anyway, I had stuffed myself with cherries. In the afternoon, I carried on eating and playing on the trees.

When Laoye came back, just before dark, I was feeling ill and vomited most of the cherries I'd eaten. Laoye stormed off. Soon I heard raised voices in the other room, from across the yard, as he told off Auntie for letting me eat so many.

As the darkness closed in, I felt guilty. Auntie was not a generous woman, but she had given us a room to live in, and cooked our food, although I hesitated to light the oil lamp. There was no electricity and she was strict about when we could use it. Sitting in the dark through the long evenings had been hard to get used to. It was all right when Laoye was there, telling me stories, but sitting on my own, I saw only dark shadows that frightened me. I tried to be brave – Laoye would think less of me if I showed my fear.

When I heard him coming to find me I called to him, 'Laoye, I'm here,' and lit the lamp so he could see me. His face was tired, but in his hands he had a bun and a warm bowl of rice congee. Then I felt hungry and it didn't take me long to empty the bowl. Afterwards I blew out the light.

I sat for a while till my eyes got used to the darkness. Then, against the moonlight outside, I saw Auntie coming out of her room briefly, perhaps to check that the lamp was out. I'd been just in time. I could hear Laoye next door in the kitchen. I knew what he was doing: he knelt in front of the herb god statue, thanking it for protecting him from snake bites and falling off the cliffs.

He spent longer than usual, kneeling and praying. When he finally came into the bedroom in the dark, he stroked my face.

'Laoye, you were a long time with your statue.'

'I was thanking him for looking after you as well as me. You could have fallen off that tree and hurt yourself. Why did you eat so many cherries?' he chided.

'It was fun in the trees and I liked the cherries. I thought I could see you beside your cave.'

He nodded. 'I thought I could see you, too.'

He was silent for a minute. Then he patted my head. 'You must have recovered well from your asthma to do so much for your auntie. I was right to bring you to the countryside with me.'

Panic rose inside me. 'But, Laoye, you're not going to send me back, are you now I'm well?' I gripped his hand tightly.

'Not if I can help it. Besides, I'm not sure you're completely cured yet,' he said, to my relief. 'You're here to stay. What I was thinking of just now was . . . Wait.' He shuffled down from the *kang* on which we were sitting to look for the matches.

He came back with my schoolbag and relit the lamp. 'But Auntie. . .' I whispered.

'Sssh. Don't worry about her. We owe her nothing.' He spoke in the casual tone he used sometimes when there were just the two of us. It made me giggle.

He spread out a piece of paper on the table and laid beside it a pencil and a rubber. 'What's this?' He drew a thin circle.

'A ball?'

He shook his head, then drew little lines round the circle. 'Now what's this? A round thing that you see every day, without which there would be no light.'

I thought of my day in the tree. 'The sun.'

'Good.' He nodded. 'Now, if I take away the lines here, representing the rays, you have only the circle, and if I stretch the circle, you have this.' He drew an oblong. 'And if I put a dot in it to represent the bit in the middle, which you can't see for the brightness – there. That's your first word to learn. Sun.' He dropped the pencil on the table and leaned back, his hands behind his shoulders to massage his neck.

I stared at the paper, transfixed.

'You see, our ancestors, who invented the characters, took their ideas from the real thing,' he murmured. 'If you understand how they thought, you will be able to unlock their wisdom.'

'Is that really how you write the sun? Just draw an oblong with a dot in it?'

'More or less. Nowadays it's been simplified with a line in the middle, like this. This is how we write it now.' With one hand still massaging his neck, he used the other to straighten the dot into a line. I crawled up behind his back, put my hand where his had been and tried to rub his shoulders. They were so knotted that I knew there was little I could do. Still, he smiled and nodded his thanks.

When my wrist was sore, I rested my hand on his neck. 'Teach me another,' I said, liking the warmth and the familiar feel of him.

He grinned. 'Look out of the window at the moon,' he said gently, so I did. 'How would you express that?' he asked. 'Imagine you were the ancestor who was going to invent a character. Imagine you are the first person ever to look at it.'

It was still and quiet, so quiet that we might have been the only people in the world. I often felt like this in Laoye's presence, bigger, stronger, cleverer than my usual self.

'How would you draw it for someone who'd never seen it?'

I gazed at the moon again. It was all curves, so curvy, full and watery that it seemed about to float down from the sky and fall on us. He waited, while I fiddled on the paper. Finally I drew a shape like a quarter watermelon. 'Like this?'

He put two wiggly lines in the middle. 'Now what?'

'I'd stretch it like you did with the sun.'

'Try it.'

I stretched the quarter melon into an oblong and straightened the two lines in the middle.

He rubbed off the vertical line at the furthest right-hand side and added a little foot at the end of the top line. Then he turned the notebook so that I was looking at the oblong standing up, with the feet dangling at the right-hand corner. 'That's the moon. Unlike the sun, which is round all the time, the moon changes shape, doesn't it? That's why it has to have an opening. It is more flexible, softer, like water.'

I heard an owl. I thought of the ancestor who had invented the word 'moon' – had he done it on a quiet night like this, when there was only the owl and him? I felt close to him, and to Laoye. We had a pact, I thought, him and me. Like the ancient masters, he would teach me all the knowledge he had.

Laoye rose to go into the kitchen, but I couldn't tear myself away from the words on the piece of paper. I had been surrounded by words for as long as I could remember; characters in red or black on slogans and posters pasted along walls and hanging in corridors, complete with many exclamation marks. But there was something magical about the characters Laoye was teaching me.

I stared at the sun: straight lines, square shape, complete; then at the moon, curved and open. I wrote them again, 'sun' and 'moon'. I liked writing them, straight, curved. Straight, curved. Closed sun and open moon. 'This is fun. Can we do more? Can I invent another character?' I begged.

And during our time in Tao Yuan, Laoye and I invented many more characters.

7

In the early days of our brief romance, Zhiying often encouraged me to look at the moon. He had seemed offended that I did not regard it as especially romantic. I explained to him that I had to pay attention to the moon as part of my work, that I had been taught to look to it for guidance: its appearance would dictate whether or not it was appropriate to use needles; its shape would determine the method I used. He had laughed and said, 'What a funny school of medicine,' and I would remember, chillingly, that what Laoye had taught me was a different system from my husband's, whose textbook quoted Chairman Mao on its front page. Laoye's medicine had been used since the beginning of our civilisation, from the first herbalist, Shennong, who had died testing herbs so that practitioners who came after him would not be poisoned. I kept silent, though. I never talked of Laoye to Zhiying. I had locked that story away in my heart: I needed to keep those two parts of my life separate.

Tonight I looked for the moon – I looked at it often these days, not always professionally. Open-ended moon. Foreign moon. But it was the same moon wherever you were. Did Tiantian look at it sometimes? Was anyone teaching her to write its name?

I had woken from a dream of her that had felt almost real, but it had vanished, leaving no memory. How tempting new life was, yet how hard to live day by day. In the curious time between sleep and waking I could almost smell her clean scent. I missed her as if she were an amputated limb.

Eyes closed but awake, I became more aware of where I was, here, now. I could smell the herbs next door. At night their scent was stronger, as if they had forgotten they had lost their roots and were flourishing again, living and breathing in my room. In my mind I travelled down to the treatment room and remembered how Mr Cheng had sat there earlier, looking as if he owned not only the space but me. How wrong he was. This was my space, my shell, waiting to be filled.

I seemed to see the medicine box, now lying under my bed. After Mr Cheng had gone, I had taken it upstairs. It had felt heavy, as though it was full of my grandfather's accumulated wisdom, and also of my guilt. I recalled its weight, now anchored in my room, intimate, like a tumour that had grown inside me. I had learned to live with it, and now it was a part of me. But I needed to keep it closed, private, sealed off.

The problem was Mr Cheng,

Our publicity drive had created a stir, a rush of interest in the only Chinese clinic in town. An old man with a crackling voice rang to say he'd stayed in Nanjing during the thirties, would that be near where I had come from? A teacher asked if I knew which animal year came next for their school project. A man came in to buy diet tea for his wife and ended up being treated for arthritis. Quite a few Chinese turned up, Cantonese from the restaurants and takeaways, some with good Mandarin, others who struggled to speak English. The mainlanders were mostly students, like Xiao Jin, and we gave them a ten per cent discount. I defied Mr Cheng over the volume of herbs I prescribed, which was crucial for the Chinese patients who had been treated with herbs before so needed a larger dose, and told Xiao Jin to omit it from the records.

Our takings shot up. Mr Cheng phoned to congratulate us, but there was something else he wanted to discuss, he said. Many people had called him about asthma cures: could we advertise ourselves as a specialist asthma clinic?

'I'm no asthma expert, and you know as well as I do that the essence of Chinese medicine is that it treats individuals as

44

individuals. There isn't a cure-all for asthma. We can't give people false hope,' I said.

'But there's no harm in saying we specialise in it, surely, Dr Lin?'

'Mr Cheng, I am no specialist, as I told you.'

'Don't be modest. If you're as good a doctor as you are a story-teller, you'll go far.' He laughed. 'And, yes, I'd like you to keep feeding them stories. It's what they like to hear.' He had contacted the editor of a bigger newspaper, who had been interested in me doing a series of barefoot-doctor anecdotes.

I said I had no more stories to tell. He laughed and said I was too modest.

When the sun streamed in through the thin curtain I woke again and gasped at how late it was, then realised it was Sunday, my day off. I headed for the Old Town Park – I'd heard a number of my patients talk about it. Spring was more evident here, with rows and rows of bright yellow daffodils. I walked purposefully, self-conscious to be alone among families with children and young couples arm in arm.

A brass band played near a fountain and a crowd gathered. I listened for a while. I recognised the tunes but could not name them. Its members were mostly old men, with one or two teenagers, and the crowd cheered each time they finished a piece. I heard a couple next to me say that the old men were retired workers from the former Great Southern Steelworks, and remembered an article I had read in the *Gazette* on the town's history: the steelworks had been the main employer. I thought of the chemical factory that had dominated my childhood city. I had once belonged somewhere, and I envied those men, growing old in the place they had lived all their lives. I remembered the poisonous fumes, but also the communal baths, our friendly neighbours and the local sweet shops. There had been bands too, playing sentimental songs.

Suddenly I could not bear the memories the music had evoked and I walked slowly to the other side of the fountain where some children were paddling in the shallow water. Brightly coloured wellies gleamed in the sunshine. A boy was pleading with a girl to let him play with her paper boat, but she ignored him. The boy's face stirred something in my memory and I heard a woman say, 'Let him have a go, Sarah?' Her voice was faint and fast, wheezy. I'd heard it before somewhere.

Sarah ignored her.

I felt in my pocket and found a folded leaflet of Xiao Jin's. I made a paper boat and handed it to the little boy, but the girl saw it first and snatched it. Now the little boy grabbed the first boat, which was rather wet.

The woman turned. 'Connor, what do you say to the—' She didn't finish her sentence. It was Lucy.

'Hi.' She shook water off her hands. 'Somehow I knew I'd bump into you.' I smiled awkwardly, mumbled a greeting, and we studied the two children bent over the paper boats. 'That's my son, Connor.' Lucy pointed to him.

'I know,' I said, remembering now why his face was so familiar. I brought out the photograph and handed it to her. 'You left this at the clinic.'

'Oh, thank you.' She wiped her hands on her jacket and took it. 'I saw the article about you in the *Gazette*. I really enjoyed it – it helped me understand Chinese medicine better.' She blushed. 'I was a bit silly about the herbs, wasn't I?'

My mind went blank. I could barely remember what I had said to the journalist, and I wanted to tell Lucy it was not her fault – after all how could a Westerner expect to understand ancient Chinese treatments? But after a short silence I asked, 'How are you, Lucy?'

The band started up again and, dancing to the rhythm of a marching tune, Connor came to give Lucy a damp hug. She held him and kissed his cheek, then he ran back to the fountain. 'I'm back on my pills and inhaler,' she said. 'I'll get used to them again. What brought you here?'

'I wanted to see the spring – and the children. I was thinking of my daughter.' It was the first time I had mentioned her to anyone here.

Now Lucy was full of questions. 'You have a daughter? How old is she?'

'Four.'

'Same age as Connor. Where is she?'

'At home.' She raised an eyebrow, and I added reluctantly, 'In China, with her father.'

She stared at me, but said nothing: I saw the accusation without her having to utter it.

I turned my eyes to the children. Connor had the paper boat I had made for him and suddenly I wanted to take his chubby little hands, and get wet with him. I restrained myself – Tiantian hated being distracted when she was playing. I turned back to Lucy, with her pale, drawn face. Overwhelmed by loneliness, I wanted to hold her, too. I gathered my courage: 'Will you come back to the clinic?' I said, trying to sound casual. 'I want you to let me treat you properly.'

8

Market day. I was determined to get up first, but Laoye beat me to it. In the other room, Uncle and Auntie were loading their donkey cart noisily. In the faint light I saw the baskets of cherries I had picked. Laoye made me drink some hot water while he finished his packing. Then Auntie came to tell him that there was no room for us on the cart. Laoye said we would walk, perhaps find a lift along the way.

He hoisted a big basket full of herbs on to his back and beckoned me. Dogs serenaded us with barking on our way through the village which was quiet, as it was still very early. Buoyed by the prospect of the market, I skipped ahead. Once out of the village, we headed away from the mountain and into the plains. The fields around us were nearly empty now that the harvest was in, and we startled birds pecking at the leavings. I ran ahead, shouting, 'Watch me!' to Laoye and sang a song my sister had taught me. '"Our motherland is a garden, and the flowers there are colourful. If you . . . if you. . .' I always got stuck there, but it didn't bother me – I loved being with Laoye.

I heard what I thought was singing behind me, and looked back to see Laoye striding along. As he came nearer I realised he was reciting a poem. His head swayed gently from side to side. I heard words like 'sweet' and 'warm,' and ominous ones like 'poison' and 'cold'.

He looked down at me, smiling. 'Would you like to learn it so that you can say it too?'

I nodded.

'You remember how I cured you and the boy who had sunstroke? The secrets are in the poem. My teacher taught me when I was young.'

His smile disappeared and he looked away into the distant hills. Then he bent down to me. 'I'm not allowed to teach girls, but it is a rule I disagree with. Besides, you are a special girl, aren't you?'

I smiled up at him as the warm light of the sun, rising over the horizon, touched my face. Thousands of insects were caught in its beams, dancing like little lost fish. I felt a warm glow in my heart, and I was so happy I wanted to cry. My hand gripped Laoye's sleeve.

He still looked serious. 'You must promise not to share the secrets with anyone, not your auntie, not even Mother.'

'I promise.' It would be an easy promise to keep.

'*Mahuang xinwen, juhua weihan. . .*' he began.

The rest of the journey flew as I learned the poem. I jumped and ran, matching my pace to the rhythm of the words. Even the hills appeared less high and intimidating – I was so grown-up I even had a secret from my mother.

When I felt tired we hopped on to a passing tractor and overtook my aunt and uncle, even though they had set off before us.

We arrived at the same town to which we had come on that cold morning to catch the bus for the village, but now it was alive. Shop and restaurant doors were wide open, sucking people in and ejecting them like eager mouths. People hurried to and fro, followed by horses, donkeys and dogs. Scents lingered in the air, surprising me.

We found a place to the eastern end near the cattle market. Laoye settled me on the ground with some thick straw he found nearby, then went off in search of breakfast. He came back with two steaming bowls of soy milk and some warm buns, which we ate slowly.

The sun was rising steadily now and people flowed in, smelling of food. At first no one came to us, even though the cattle market near us was in full swing. The animals bellowed and bleated while their owners engaged in mystifying transactions. They all wore thick hats and coats with long sleeves, and the pair nearest to us were involved in a tight handshake, eyes locked on each other, although their lips barely moved. I had the impression that the hands were doing the negotiating but nobody apart from the two men could see what was going on.

Finally they slapped each other's shoulders and one took the other's horse. The owner put both his hands back together in a lock, the posture he had adopted before the negotiation, and several men congratulated him on his successful deal. But I thought he was sad: I'd seen him pat his horse when he arrived. Now his hands were idle, with nothing to occupy them.

I put down the milk bowl, stretched and yawned. I was weary, but couldn't bear to sleep in case I missed some fun. 'Go and look round.' Laoye nudged me. 'See how Auntie's doing.' He put some money into my hand.

You couldn't have missed the fruit and vegetable part of the market if you'd tried. From a distance it sounded as if hundreds of people were quarrelling. I approached apprehensively. The stall-holders, mostly women, pointed at their produce with flushed cheeks and lively gestures. At first I had to concentrate hard to understand their accent: for 'I' they said '*An*' rather than '*Wo*' and their sentences almost always ended on a rising note. Soon enough I grasped that they were boasting about their wares, but the way they called to you made you think you'd come to a big party, a family reunion: 'Little Sister, Auntie, Big Brother – hey, pretty girl with the pink bag. . .'

I went from stall to stall, not wanting to miss anything but cautious about what I would buy. I let the sellers see my money to show that I was a serious customer and they let me touch the green spinach, bright yellow apricots and delicious-smelling tomatoes still on the vines. My eyes feasted on colour. It was not until I registered that the baskets containing cherries were familiar that I realised they were the ones I had picked. My aunt might have noticed me but she continued to call in her loud, sweet voice, 'Freshly picked cherries, just off the tree. . . . Look at this, Big Brother!' She reached out to a man walking by with a pipe while her other hand dug into the cherries. 'How fresh, Big Brother! Buy some, buy some for my big sister.'

'I'm not married,' the man retorted.

'Take some for your mother, then – there's nothing the elderly like better than fresh fruit, so soft and sweet.'

'Why can't I just buy some for myself?'

'Well, of course! You deserve it! Go on – treat yourself.'

The man laughed and walked on. Auntie's face froze and she let the cherries fall from her hand. The basket was still full: she hadn't sold any. 'Laoye sent me to come and help you,' I said.

'Did he?' she said, uninterested. I squatted and nodded to my cousin, who sat beside Uncle with a sack of sweetcorn kernels. They came from the cobs that the brigade gave each family to rub. We were paid to do it, but had to return the rubbed-off corn, although most families kept some for themselves and the brigade usually turned a blind eye to it. But my uncle and aunt, who were greedy, kept more than most. Beside the sack was a basket of eggs. They had chickens of their own, but those eggs had been given to them in return for Laoye's treatment – I recognised the basket: it belonged to Grandpa Ying, one of Laoye's regular patients. I wondered if I should tell Laoye what Auntie and Uncle were doing because he never accepted gifts from his patients.

I leaned over the cherries and stroked their delicate skin. They still smelt lovely but were nowhere near as fragrant as they had been when I had just picked them. Two white ones were buried among the red. I removed them. Together, the white looked whiter and the red redder. They were like day and night. Red in nature was delicious – so different from the red of posters or armbands.

A tall figure was standing next to me. 'Those cherries do look good, Little Sister. Let me have some.' The man who had walked past us a few minutes ago had returned.

Before I could answer him Auntie's excited voice shouted, 'Red or white?'

The man hesitated.

'White is sweet and red is . . . delicious,' I said.

He laughed. 'Well said, Little Sister. I'll have half a kilo of each.'

'Half a kilo white, half a kilo red. There you are,' Auntie said proudly, and swept the cherries into two bags made of old newspaper. It was her first sale of the day. After that, it was as if a spell had been broken: the cherries sold quickly. Auntie's voice rose with each sale and she smiled broadly at me. The baskets were half full now, and there were bruised ones in each scoop. Their colour was dull but the scent was more powerful. Auntie picked out the bruised ones and offered them to me, but I wasn't hungry. I just wanted to smell and look at them.

I went to find Laoye, the money he gave me still warm in my hand – I hadn't bought anything. There was a crowd but Laoye stood out as always. He was not surrounded by people but those who wanted to see him engaged him in long conversations. Laoye talked, and they nodded. He didn't shout.

'You found Auntie?' he asked, when he saw me. I nodded and sat down, tired and hungry now, but I didn't say so. His silent dignity had transferred itself to me. I wanted those who came to listen to him to think that I was part of that enlightened circle. A tall, well-dressed man squatted next to us. He looked like an official but was friendly with Laoye. I could tell they'd known each other for a long time. He didn't buy anything, and for a while Laoye and he barely spoke, just watched the market and exchanged glances.

The midday sun was scorching hot. In my mind I saw those cherries again and wished I'd had some while I was with Auntie. I leaned against Laoye and closed my eyes. Then I felt a tap on my shoulder. It was the official-looking man. 'Are you hungry, Juju? Shall I take you to lunch with your grandfather?' How did he know my name? I looked at Laoye, who smiled and smoothed his chin. 'Come along,' the man said. 'Let's give her a treat. I'll take care of the rest of this – I can always take more *ma huang* for my dispensary and I know I can trust yours.'

Uncle Ma's chemist's had two big wooden doors and they

were wide open. As I went in from the heat and bustle outside I was calmed by the dim cool and the hush. The scents seemed almost to jostle for our attention. I gripped Laoye's hand. Uncle Ma did not light a lamp. As my eyes became accustomed to the darkness, I saw two girls standing at the glass counter in front of a wall covered with little wooden drawers. Uncle Ma made a gesture and they took Laoye's sack inside. Uncle Ma went with them.

When we were alone, Laoye held my hand and took me to the drawers. He stood on tiptoe to open one and scooped something out. 'Wild chrysanthemum,' he said, and placed a single stem of a dried yellow flower in my open palm. At the gentle pressure of my fingers it crumbled and the petals fell like rain to the floor. I swooped to pick them up, smelling their sweet, spicy scent. 'They are for bright eyes,' Laoye whispered. As I stood up he held a white blossom to my nose and I detected a light fragrance that reminded me of face cream my mother had worn when I was younger. 'Honeysuckle, for cooling internal heat.'

Now I realised why Laoye had said the mountain was a treasure house: it was full of flowers and blossoms that were not only beautiful to behold but useful to treat all sorts of illnesses. On our brief trip to the Black Hill, he had shown me pretty flowers like these. But then, bewildered by the array of colours and scents around me, distracted by birds and rabbits, I hadn't taken them in. Now, seeing them arranged neatly in a chemist's and smelling their scents, which had intensified somehow with the drying process, I began to understand the poem I had been reciting all morning: it abbreviated the names of herbs and flowers, but now Laoye told me their full names and showed them to me. The medicines were not necessarily made from the blossoms: sometimes it was the roots or the stems. '*Jin yin hua*, honeysuckle, internal heat. Chrysanthemum, *ye suhua*, bright eyes,' I repeated to myself, and pulled out a drawer. In it, instead of flowers, I saw a pile of stones. I pulled out another and was surprised to find pungent twigs. Laoye explained that the heavy things were arranged in the lower drawers while the lighter herbs were at the top. 'Can stones be medicine?' I asked.

'Yes, we use minerals – animal bones too.'

'I like the herbs better,' I said, and asked Laoye to lift me up so I could smell the blossoms on the top shelves again.

That was how Uncle Ma found us when he came back to the shop. 'Starting her early?' He smiled at Laoye and counted out some money for him.

Laoye put me down, took the money without checking it and breathed out heavily. 'We'll see.'

As Laoye turned from the shelves I remembered something: 'Where is the *lingzhi*?'

'The *lingzhi*?' Laoye seemed puzzled.

'Yes, the herb that makes you dream of the person you miss?'

Uncle Ma shook his head. 'We're out of stock, I'm afraid. It's not every day that you find something as precious as that. Your *laoye* is the best herb-picker around here, and if you want to see *lingzhi*, he's the man to show you.'

'Will you, Laoye?' I turned back to him.

He nodded. 'I'll try.'

Before we left the shop, Uncle Ma took me to the backyard where many more fresh herbs were stocked. The smell was overwhelming and I wondered how the people working there could endure it. Using big straw choppers and other equipment, they cut, ground and sliced grasses and twigs, sweating and grunting with the effort.

We stopped in front of a two-storey building in the quieter part of the town. A delicious smell floated out to us. It was a restaurant and I had never been inside one before. Two other people were eating bowls of noodles, and we sat down at a table by the wall with a vase of yellow chrysanthemums. I was opposite Laoye, who stretched and spread his limbs, blinking at the sun shining through the window. Uncle Ma picked up a stiff piece of paper from the table, looked at it briefly, then put it down again. For some reason, the two men reminded me of wandering cats who had found their home. It looked as if we would stay there for a long time.

I got up and stole behind Laoye. As he was leaned back in his chair I put my arms round him and hugged him tightly. He chuckled and struggled a little but I wouldn't let go. I buried my face in his shirt and smelt herbs. 'I want, I want, I want. . .' I said. I heard Uncle Ma make noises of mock-disapproval, and felt shy. I snuggled into the warmth of Laoye's neck. He reached behind him to tickle me and finally I collapsed into laughter and let him go.

'Where is Lingzhi?' Uncle Ma said, and my ears pricked up.

'Lingzhi?' I looked round, confused.

'Oh,' Uncle Ma laughed, 'Lingzhi is the name of the woman who runs this restaurant.'

'Can Lingzhi be a name?

'Of course,' Laoye said, and took me into his arms, 'and it's a beautiful name.' His eyes narrowed dreamily. 'Let me tell you about the first Lingzhi. She was the youngest daughter of the emperor Yan. She died young, just before she was to be married. Her soul floated to the Wu mountain and was the morning cloud that clung to the mountain half-way up and the soft evening rain that wet the grass. Later, she grew on the mountain as a herb. It is said that whoever eats it will dream of the person he or she misses most. . .'

'Ah, here she comes now.'

At Uncle Ma's words Laoye turned sharply, and his face lit up.

I followed his eyes and saw a woman in a worn dark red silk coat walking slowly down the stairs. Her face was partly obscured by steam coming from the kitchen. When she arrived at the foot she paused to smooth her hair, and I saw her red lips and white teeth. She walked towards us, elegantly, as though she were floating. Like most women in the town, she was tall and had high cheekbones but, unlike them, her skin was delicate and her manner gentle. She was about Auntie's age, maybe older, but different from Auntie in ways I couldn't describe. I knew, though, that if Auntie had worn that red coat, it would have looked wrong on her. On this woman it was just right.

Uncle Ma stood up. 'Sister Lingzhi, how is Younger Brother today?'

She nodded at him. 'He's just drunk his medicine. A magpie

told me there'd be guests today, but who'd have thought. . .' She turned to Laoye, who stood up slowly, taking off his yellow hat. His face was red and I noticed now that he was wearing his new white shirt.

'Shall I go up and see him?' he asked in a low voice, his eyes avoiding her face. Why, when she was so lovely?

'No, of course not. You will have lunch first. Now, who is this?' Her eyes, which had been steady on Laoye, had settled on me.

'It's little Juju. She's staying with me. She needs a change from the city air.'

He didn't say that I was his granddaughter, but she seemed to know who I was. Her eyes scrutinised me, which made me nervous, but then they softened to a half-moon. 'So, you are the special girl I've heard about.'

'Juju, this is . . . Auntie Hu,' Laoye murmured.

'Auntie Hu,' I repeated and bowed. For a moment she regarded me silently, as though I had said something interesting. Then she bent down to the piece of paper Uncle Ma had picked up earlier, with four-letter words on each line. Laoye leaned forward and their eyes met. His lips moved, but no sound came from them. Auntie Hu looked at him as if she had heard the words he hadn't uttered. Then her finger moved along the paper and she pronounced them slowly, as if she were a student learning from a teacher. Laoye nodded, a gentle smile on his lips, a fond expression I had thought he kept for me alone. Suddenly I was jealous. 'I'm hungry,' I said loudly, and put my hand on the piece of paper so that Auntie Hu could not read on.

She looked at me and I thought she might scold me, but she giggled and laid a hand on my head. 'Little monkey,' she said, softly, so that only I could hear.

She disappeared into the steaming kitchen and we heard a sudden rush of sounds – her high-pitched voice and murmurs in response.

The men sat down. For a moment I thought they had forgotten me – I poked Laoye, then tapped my chopsticks on the table to attract Uncle Ma's attention. Suddenly they were laughing and talking all at once.

Now food smells escaped from the kitchen and more customers came in. I recognised the cattle traders. Auntie Hu greeted them and led them to a table near the noodle-eaters. I had a feeling that our side of the room was a special place – the chrysanthemums were fresher – although the cattle traders seemed content where they were. There was something unusual about Auntie Hu's place: it seemed busy yet at the same time it was peaceful.

'Did you hear they're going to close the market soon?' Uncle Ma, who had also seen the cattle men, turned back to Laoye. He spoke in a whisper as if he was worried someone else might hear him.

'Why?'

'You know how things are, these days.'

Laoye was silent for a while. Then he said, 'It can't be true.'

'I've seen the document. No one below my level is meant to know yet, but I'm afraid it will happen.'

I thought of the feast of scents. I thought of the lively women. I thought even more of the things I'd been curious about and only half understood. These impressions had seemed to me the real goods at the market, there for me to pick and choose. I had taken note of the ones I'd like to return to – like sweets I'd saved to enjoy later. But now that I might never experience them again I knew how special they had been. Why was the market to close? Where would all the people and animals go? I wanted to ask Uncle Ma and Laoye but their serious faces frightened me so I kept quiet.

The cattle traders were eating now, but I knew that our food, when it came, would taste more delicious than anyone else's. Auntie Hu was cooking it herself, I was sure. So I waited patiently. But Laoye and Uncle Ma were distracted, impatient – perhaps they were upset by the news of the market. I'd never seen Laoye so restless before. He kept peering into the kitchen and straightening his back as if he wanted to be prepared for Auntie Hu's return.

Soon the room was empty, except for us. I was becoming desperate with hunger when I saw Auntie Hu coming out of the kitchen carrying a pretty yellow bowl with little birds round the edge, filled with egg fried rice. 'Let Juju eat first. She needs feeding up,' she said, and put the bowl in front of me. Laoye and Uncle Ma nodded but said nothing. I peered curiously into my bowl: small vegetable cutlets were buried among the rice; it looked very pretty.

Auntie Hu went back into the kitchen and came back in a little while with a thin slim-necked white bottle and two matching cups. She placed the bottle in a bowl of hot water, and I smelt alcohol. She leaned forward to pour it, first for Uncle Ma, then Laoye, and wiped up a drop from the table with her sky blue apron.

All this time we sat and watched her, no one saying a word. I'd seen Mother serve wine to Laoye sometimes, but not as Auntie Hu did, as if it was a sort of ritual and she might sing while she was doing it. 'Eat,' she said to me, when she noticed me watching her. Laoye raised the glass, nodded to her, then brought it to his lips. He did it slowly, and with deference, as he did everything else in that restaurant.

When their food finally arrived, Uncle Ma and Laoye were already half-way through the bottle. Laoye undid the top button of his shirt. His flushed face made him look young. Each time he swallowed a mouthful of wine his hand went up to smooth his hair.

Auntie Hu joined us from time to time: she stayed just long enough for me to feel as though she'd sat with us throughout the meal. She made me feel drowsy, a warm sensation I wanted to hold on to.

When they had finished the wine she brought more, but Laoye put up his hand: 'No. I don't want to be drunk today. Take me upstairs and let me have a look at Younger Brother Hu.'

She studied him briefly, wiped her hands on her apron, then took it off slowly. Her hands went up to smooth her hair, which was tied in a knot at the back of her head. Then she turned and started to walk upstairs. Laoye picked up his white medicine box and stood up so abruptly that he nearly knocked over the table. I was about to follow him when Uncle Ma stopped me: 'Stay here. Laoye is going to see a patient who's bedridden. He needs to see him alone.'

'Who's the man?'

'Auntie Hu's husband. He's an old friend of ours.'

'Do they live alone? Don't they have children?' I looked round the large room, which seemed even larger now without any customers except us.

Uncle Ma hesitated, then said, 'No.'

'Why not?'

'Uncle Hu, her husband, was too ill to have children.'

'Oh,' I said. We waited in the silence. 'Don't you want to go and see him, too?' I asked Uncle Ma.

'No. I live in this town, I see him often enough. But your *laoye*, he hasn't seen him, them, for a long time.'

I sat down again. The room was too quiet and I grew restless. Outside I saw a dog wagging its tail in the sun and wanted to go out and make friends with it. But Uncle Ma seemed to want to chat.

'Do you like Auntie Hu's food?' he asked.

'Yes.' Its taste was still in my mouth.

'People like it here because she tells them which food to have, which to avoid.'

'Is she a doctor?' I wondered aloud.

'Auntie Hu? No – but she's an excellent cook. She knows about medicine as she is the daughter of a famous herbalist. Your *laoye* helped her learn which herbs to use for which illness.'

So that was why she had been so pleased to see him. She had been waiting for him to tell her what to put into her cooking! I thought of the mouthwatering food we had eaten. Normally I kept to things I knew in other people's houses, but everything had smelt so delicious I had tasted it all, even the dish Auntie Hu had enjoyed. I had asked her what gave it its particular flavour and she had answered, smiling at Laoye: '*Dang gui*, due-to-return.' Then she urged me to have some more.

'It's particularly good for women,' Laoye cut in, glancing at her.

She had seemed proud then, and I realised that Laoye had taught her this.

Now a question occurred to me: 'But didn't you say Auntie Hu's father was a famous herbalist?'

'She came from a medical family and her grandfather was a well-known acupuncturist.'

'Why didn't Auntie Hu learn about medicine from her family?'

'You're a sharp girl, aren't you?' laughed Uncle Ma, gazing at me as if he'd only just met me. 'I can see why your *laoye* has chosen to pass on his knowledge to you. Well, they didn't teach her because she was a girl.'

'So?'

'So your *laoye* taught her instead.'

'Was that how they came to know each other?'

'More or less.'

I felt annoyed. Why was he so vague?

'She was a clever girl.' He smiled and added, 'Like you.'

Instead of pleasing me this revelation upset me. I had thought *I* was Laoye's special girl, the only one. Well, he had never said so, but somehow I had had the impression that that was the case. This was disappointing news.

'But how do you know all this, Uncle Ma?'

'Well, let's say I'm well connected. And I used to work in Auntie Hu's family clinic. I knew them all well.'

I was getting cross with Laoye for taking so long. When he finally came down, he seemed a little distracted, and the drink must have affected him for he slipped once on the stairs. Auntie Hu came down soon afterwards, but her mind must have been elsewhere too because she nodded at me as if she barely recognised me.

Laoye and Uncle Ma argued about payment while Auntie Hu and I watched. When they both offered her money, she took it from Uncle Ma's hand. Laoye picked up his empty basket, and I noticed a new blue bag on his shoulder. Was it hers? What was in it? 'We'd better set off before it's too late.' He nodded to Uncle Ma and Auntie Hu, and took my hand.

On the edge of the town, beyond the open market, there was an earth-god temple. Laoye took me there and knelt for a long time in front of the giant earth-god statue. I hung about on the threshold to watch him crouching low but he stayed there so long that I became bored. This seemed so different to his private ritual of praying to the herb god at home, and the giant statue had such vacant eyes. Yet there had to be a good reason for him to honour the earth god – he was never foolish.

A man in a blue robe peered at me from a corner of the temple. I stared at him. There was something about the air in the temple that I didn't understand or like. It smelt mouldy and it was gloomy. Finally Laoye rose and I saw him putting the money Uncle Ma had given him into the plate in front of the statue.

He was silent on the way home and I dared not speak to him, even though I wanted to ask him about the temple, the kneeling and the money. Although we had less to carry, his back was bent, like an old man's. I recited the poem he'd taught me earlier, hoping it would make him smile and talk as he had on our way to the market, but he seemed absent. 'Did the poem help you when you were treating Auntie Hu's husband?' I asked finally, sensing a connection between his sadness now and our visit to the restaurant.

He jumped, as though I'd woken him from a dream. 'Auntie Hu's husband? He's much improved.'

Something in his voice confused me: it sounded flat, as if the news was less positive than it sounded. Was Laoye not overjoyed that his treatment was succeeding? I could imagine how happy it would make Auntie Hu. When I imagined her joy I was filled with warmth – the pangs of jealousy had disappeared as soon as we left her house. Laoye was my grandfather: how could anyone compete with me for his love? Besides, I remembered something else: 'Laoye, Uncle Ma said that Auntie Hu does not have children. Is that true?'

Laoye turned sharply. 'He told you that?'

I nodded. 'I asked him if Auntie Hu had any children and Uncle Ma said she didn't because Uncle Hu was too ill.'

He was silent.

'Shall we see Auntie Hu again?' I asked, after a little while.

'I hope so, Juju.'

After that his spirits rose a little, and he told me more of the herb poem.

Then I remembered something else. 'Laoye, is it true that people come to Auntie Hu's to get better?'

'Who told you that?'

'Uncle Ma.'

'Well,' Laoye chuckled, 'I certainly feel better each time I go to her restaurant. She's such a good cook and she knows a little about the hot and cold nature of food.' He paused. Then he said, 'Uncle Ma exaggerates. He's very fond of Auntie Hu.'

'What is the hot and cold nature of food?'

'Hot and cold?' He was thoughtful. 'Well, I suppose if you want to learn about medicine, you should know about it. Haven't you come across this idea before?'

I vaguely remembered Mother saying sometimes that I shouldn't eat too much chilli because it would make me too hot, and I told Laoye this.

'The important thing is not whether something is hot or cold but whether the person is of a hot or cold temperament.'

'Well, I am hot,' I said firmly.

He laughed. 'So am I sometimes. But no one remains hot or cold constantly, we change all the time, and as a doctor you need to determine what condition your patient is in so that you can treat him or her properly. That is why pulse-reading is so important. You touch your patient's wrist and it is as if you are touching their lungs, their kidneys, their heart.'

That night, Laoye taught me two new words. He took last night's piece of paper and added a vertical line with two loops to the left-hand side of each character and pointed to the moon saying, '*Yin*,' and the sun, '*Yang*.'

I copied them down, noticing again how straight the lines of the sun and how curved the lines of the moon were, and added the loops.

Laoye spoke close to my ear: '*Yin* is north of the water and east of a mountain. *Yin* is the underside of a leaf. *Yin* is water. *Yin* is a girl. *Yang* is south of the water and west of a mountain. *Yang* is the bright side of a leaf. *Yang* is fire and *Yang* is a man.'

Yin was Auntie Hu's face in the shadow, enveloped by the steam from the kitchen as she came downstairs; *yang* was Laoye's smiling eyes as they reflected the sunshine and chrysanthemums in the vase.

9

The sun was warm and the wind soft, almost too soft. But I was surprised to see Mark, Lucy's husband, wearing shorts, although they suited him. Lucy and Connor were also lightly dressed, in T-shirts and jeans. When we started to climb the hill Mark, broad-shouldered, carried the picnic in his rucksack, while Lucy lagged behind with Connor.

Unlike Chinese hosts, they did not constantly engage me in conversation and I couldn't decide what to make of it. To feel offended was too mean-spirited, but to act completely at home was beyond me. I made a show of examining the hills: Mark told me they were called 'downs' when I mentioned them. 'Downs,' I repeated. Their curves somehow suited the word, so I repeated it, and saw Mark smile. Was he laughing at my accent? With strangers I always suspected the worst. But as his smile deepened, I decided he was being friendly. I looked back at the house, not the suburban semi I had imagined but a thatched cottage at the foot of a green slope. We had had some tea there before we set off and I had felt enveloped in comfort and warmth, after the solitude of my room at the clinic.

Mark was a tall, well-built man, yet his manner was boyish – Lucy even addressed him in the tone she used with Connor. As we stood waiting for her and Connor to catch up, Mark's legs twitched as if he were impatient for the next move. 'Aren't you hot?' he asked, as I stood next to him, a little breathless.

'*Chunwu qiudong.*' The words slipped out of my mouth, taking me unawares. Until then I hadn't realised that that was why I'd dressed as I had in a woollen top that stretched below my waist.

'What did you say?'

'It was something my grandfather used to tell me, meaning "Wrap up warm in spring but freeze in autumn."'

As I spoke I thought of Tiantian. I had always had to remind her to put on warmer clothes. She never seemed to feel the cold, whatever the weather. I imagined her little body and felt a pang of sadness as I remembered that Zhiying, my ex-husband, would dress her now.

We walked on a little way, then Mark said, 'Why should you wrap up warmly in spring?'

Why indeed? I wanted to take off my woolly top. What did a soft spring day in England have to do with the rough windy days of north China? 'I suppose it is about having your body in tune with the season, with nature. In spring the weather is unpredictable – in my part of the world anyway. You don't want to be caught when there's a sudden chill,' I said cautiously, choosing language and concepts that I thought he'd understand rather than those that played out in my mind: spring, element of wood, growth, the liver – part of the *chunwu-quidong* complex I had absorbed in childhood. Spring was a time to be cautious; spring was a bad time for asthma patients or, indeed, anyone with chronic illness, which flourished at this time, as if to remind the sufferer of its existence. I looked down at Lucy and Connor, slowly coming towards us.

'Fascinating.' Mark nodded and looked at me thoughtfully, as if he'd heard not only what I'd said but also what I'd omitted. We moved on, chatting, to the top of the hill, and as the fresh, cold wind blew, I felt a twinge of cold and pleasure – and something I hadn't experienced for a long time: excitement. My patients, like Lucy, hung on my every word, but that was because of my profession and the white coat I wore. To them I was a doctor but this man had suggested I was interesting as a person.

In front of us a round ridge encircled the top of the hill like a necklace. I grew bold enough to point it out to Mark. He said it was a prehistoric construction called Wanbury Castle. We moved out of the wind, and Mark lay on the grass and closed his eyes. I hesitated, then sat down beside him. The downs overlooked a valley, interrupted occasionally by lonely farmhouses and churches. I stared at the expanse of green, a playground for the eye that somehow could not get used to its vastness. Soon I felt the awkwardness in me disappear, rendered insignificant by the embracing generosity of the land. It melted something hard that had built up in me over the years.

The grass stirred in the soft wind, like a wave in the sea, and for a moment I wished I could lie down in it as Mark had done. But I had to be alone to do that; I couldn't relax in the company of others. I watched Lucy and Connor approach, tried to fix the image of the downs into my mind, then closed my eyes.

When I opened them I realised how close Mark was lying to me. He seemed to have fallen asleep. An ant was crawling up his leg and I suppressed the urge to flick it off. When he stirred I took my eyes off him. On impulse, I pulled off my thick top to feel the warmth of the sun on my skin.

Then I felt Mark's eyes on me, smiling, as if he approved, but he didn't say anything. He pressed his hands on the ground, got up swiftly and set to work spreading out the picnic: rug, jars of pickles, dips, sandwiches. Plastic plates, knives and forks. His hands were big but deft. I wanted to help, but I was intimidated by the range of cutlery and Mark's self-sufficiency. Despite his friendly smile, I was suddenly shy and wanted Lucy to catch us up.

She appeared, red-faced, laughing, with Connor on her shoulders. They collapsed on to the rug, upsetting Mark's arrangement. He frowned but I was relieved to see them. Lucy coughed, took out her inhaler, then looked at me and laughed. 'Aren't you hot?'

'Oh that's *chunwudong* – is that right, Juju?' Mark said.

I nodded, despite his awkward pronunciation, which I liked somehow. Encouraged, he continued, rearranging the knives and forks: 'It means you should wrap up warmly in spring.' He grinned at me, as if we shared a secret.

'*Chunwudonc,*' Connor repeated, large eyes staring at me unblinking, reminding me of his father. Then he said, 'Your face is flat.'

'Connor!' Lucy exclaimed.

But I laughed. Normally I would have been embarrassed, but today I felt light-hearted and confident, so much so that I put my face close to his. 'I am wearing a mask. This is not my real face.'

He put out a hand tentatively to touch me and I pressed it to my cheek. He screamed and I let go. Then we laughed.

'Me, too, I'm wearing a mask!' Mark laughed.

'No.' Connor giggled and reached out to grab his father, who ran away, with the child in pursuit.

'*Chunwudonc, chunwudonc.*' Mark carried Connor on his back and was pretending to be a train now. For a while the hill was noisy with their rendition of the Chinese word. I sat listening to the echo, feeling carefree like them, wanting to join in. This was unlike me – it must be the spring air, I thought.

Seemingly out of nowhere, Lucy sat down next to me. 'So *chunwudong* – is that why you don't want to give me acupuncture just now? I've been wondering.'

As I watched her eager face I was reminded that, besides being my new friend, she was also my patient. I'd almost forgotten. Fleetingly I felt regret. I had so enjoyed that light-hearted moment.

'Is that right?' She moved closer to me.

'What? Oh – sorry – yes. In a way. We are still at the tail end of winter. I didn't want to introduce an evil wind into your body with the needles,' I said, although my heart was not in it.

She listened carefully – too reverently, I thought. I remembered the sensation of her flesh yielding beneath the pressure of my fingers and felt uneasy. She had come back to the clinic the day after our chance meeting in the park and had since been as eager and co-operative a patient as she had been before our brief rift, still I wished she would question me more and not acquiesce so easily. If only, I thought, she would treat me as Mark did, as if I was just an interesting person, relaxing with friends.

'I wish you had explained that to me,' she said softly, trying to disguise the implied criticism.

I smiled, feeling shy again. She had been my first patient at the clinic and I had been more nervous than she was. Communication with her had not been at the forefront of my mind. I was too busy concentrating on my diagnosis.

It was only when we had started to eat the sandwiches, cut into triangles, the crusts removed, that I remembered my own contribution to the picnic. I brought out the noodles and the egg fried rice. Mark offered me some Coca-cola.

Lucy pointed to it. 'I wouldn't have imagined you drinking that!'

'No.' I shook my head. 'It's too sweet.'

'So, you prefer bitter things. Like those horrible herbs you gave Lucy to drink. They give me nightmares.' Mark laughed with such an engaging twinkle in his eyes that, although I didn't like what he had said, I could joke too.

'Chinese torture,' I said.

It was only after I said it that I remembered it was a remark Mark had made to Lucy which she had recounted to me at our last appointment, when we had chatted long after the session. Blushing, I glanced at her, but she looked away.

Mark rose to tidy away our picnic, with the same efficiency and ease that he'd set it out. Watching him, I thought briefly of Zhiying, who loved to take charge when we were cooking and entertaining. He was so sociable – he must have another partner by now. He would make a good husband for someone else. I mulled over this thought and felt a little sad.

We drank tea and Lucy asked, 'Tell us about your family.'

'My daughter's called Tiantian, which means "ease".' It had been Zhiying's idea, a reflection of our earlier days when I had found what I had thought was true happiness in his company – peace and contentment, which I'd mistaken for love. After what I had experienced in childhood I had craved an ordinary, uneventful life.

Lucy asked what she must have wanted to ask since we had met last time in the park: 'How could you leave her behind?'

'I'm selfish. I want a life of my own,' I said flatly. Sometimes it was easiest to put myself down. I couldn't sink lower than this.

There was a silence, and I saw that I'd embarrassed them. Mark, who had been bouncing Connor on his knees, now held him tight and rocked him to and fro. Suddenly I was terrified that my only friends here would think me as heartless and selfish as I had declared myself to be. I tried feebly to explain: 'In China, it's not uncommon for children to grow up with their grandparents.' I paused: it was true that many did, but in our case, it was more complicated. I would dearly have loved to keep Tiantian with me, but my husband had convinced me that it was best for him to raise her with his parents in China. In a moment of weakness I had agreed, and now I regretted it every day.

'I have a colleague from Taiwan who sent her children home to their grandmother. . .' Mark began. He looked for help to Lucy.

She spoke quickly: 'And in Britain many parents send their children to boarding school.'

Aware as I was of their kindness in this condemnation of their own people, I still wanted to change the subject. I resented having to defend myself. Why were the English so obsessed with my childcare arrangement? The Chinese accepted it as the only logical way – in fact, some of the those I had met in England had done as I had. That it was common to send a child away did not make it right, though, or my longing for Tiantian any easier to deal with, but talking to the English made me feel even guiltier about it. I always sounded as if I was trying to find an excuse for my actions.

'What did – no – what does your husband do?' Lucy had changed the subject for me, although the conversation didn't get easier for me.

'We were both doctors when we met, but now . . . he's an entrepreneur.'

'What kind of business?' Mark asked.

'Import and export. He went back to China because it is better for his business.'

'Will he return?' Lucy asked cautiously.

'I don't think so. We separated. Things weren't working between us any more.' We were not divorced – neither of us had felt the need for that. He hadn't had an affair, so far as I knew, and I hadn't fallen in love with anyone else. We had just gone in different ways.

There was more, of course, but I didn't know them well enough to go on. Lucy and Mark exchanged a glance and Mark coughed. Connor spotted a rabbit at the other side of the ridge and leaped up to chase it. Mark followed him – he ran a little too fast, I suspect out of relief to be away from me.

'You could . . . I don't mean to be rude, but if you decided to bring Tiantian back, the government would help with childcare costs and I'm sure you could get help with babysitting,' Lucy said.

That had never been an option for me and my husband. Tiantian had devoted grandparents in China, and families should look after their own. Why would we depend on outsiders?

Mark and Connor waved at us from down the slope. Next to me, Lucy waved back. It seemed for a moment that we were in a sort of paradise, an English Tao Yuan. Its spring was brief but warm, its people cool and reasonable. I had stepped into a perfect world where there was no want, no will to conquer, where perhaps I might be allowed just to be. I thought briefly of that other Tao Yuan, the one I'd found and lost, and felt a sharp pain. I should beware of such sentimental notions – there could be no such place for me now.

I began to worry that my unhappiness was impinging on my hosts. I told Lucy I wanted to go home 'There's work to be done at the clinic.'

She didn't press me to stay, for which I was grateful, merely asked, 'Are you sure?' in a voice that implied she knew I was. Then she called Mark.

He walked me down the hill, without small-talk. In the car, he concentrated on the road and spoke little, beyond asking for directions.

A mixed feeling of emptiness and relief washed over me as I opened the door at the clinic. The familiar scent of the herbs embraced me, making me suddenly aware of what the day had meant to me. It had been a step into a new world, an English world of closeness and familiarity. Now I was back in my cell. Mark stepped in and peered around. I held the door, wondering if I should invite him in for a drink.

Then he leaned forward and kissed my cheek. 'Goodbye,' he said, and left.

10

Something expensive, yet familiar landed in my hand. 'White Rabbit!' I exclaimed, and looked up to see Ling smiling at me. It hadn't occurred to me until then that she might be shy with us, but it was so long since we had seen each other. It must have been a new experience for her to be on a bumpy tractor. From the way her hands held tightly to the metal sides, I could tell she was nervous. Her eyes darted between the hill in the distance, the endless fields and my cousin, who wore his father's old winter coat and a big hat that made him look like a woolly dog. He peered at my sister while he fiddled with the arrow made of twigs that he was holding. I was not the only one who was intimidated by her grown-up sophistication – I could see its effect on him, too.

It was a few weeks after the Spring Festival. Laoye had stopped going up to the hills and stayed indoors to teach me. Neighbours dropped in for long chats with him, talking deep into the night, with only the flicker of their pipes to indicate where they sat. Patients came with presents, which Auntie gleefully accepted behind his back. Sometimes I thought he knew but turned a blind eye to make our stay easier in her house. He'd already started to talk about moving out – the brigade leader, the man in charge of production and our pay, a friendly man who had benefited from Laoye's treatment, had promised him a hut at the edge of the village – just what we wanted.

For some reason Mother and Ling had not come to see us

until now. Laoye did not tell me of their visit until the day before they were due to arrive and I had been both nervous and excited. Excited because I was about to see Ling, nervous because I was worried that Mother might want to take me away now that she knew I had recovered from my asthma. I stole a glance at her now, talking quietly to Laoye at the front of the tractor. They did not mention me, and there was no sign that they were plotting anything. Laoye had promised to argue on my behalf should Mother threaten to take me home and, trusting him, I tried not to worry.

There were a lot of things I wanted to ask Ling and tell her, but just at the moment, on the way to Laoye's and my temporary home with Auntie, I had run out of conversation. How long had we been apart? It seemed a long time yet no time at all. I shared my White Rabbit sweets with her and my cousin, and our jaws moved slowly as we savoured the creamy taste.

The tractor roared through the centre of the town. Soon a familiar house came into view. 'Auntie Hu!' I shouted, and saw that Laoye was craning his neck. But the door and the window upstairs were closed.

'Who lives there?' Mother asked.

'Someone I know who runs a very good restaurant,' he replied simply, and I was puzzled: surely Auntie Hu was more than an acquaintance. I wanted Mother to sample her delicious meals – Auntie Hu might tell her of food that would cure her headaches, I thought, peering at her now. Her face was always so tightly knotted with a deep wrinkle between her eyebrows. Only Laoye could bring her relief with his needles.

I felt in my pocket for the treat I had saved for Ling: pine nuts that Laoye had bought me at the market. I brought out a handful and explained she must bite hard to crack the shells. She tried but frowned.

My cousin grabbed a few from me. One by one he put them into his mouth and made frighteningly loud noises with his teeth, then spat the cracked nuts into his palms. He showed Ling how to take the kernels out of the shells, but didn't bother with me. Ling handed one back to him and said, 'For you.'

He blushed and murmured something.

'What did you say?'

'I don't want them. You have them,' he repeated.

'What's your name?'

'Guizi – "precious".' He answered quickly and eagerly, and didn't ask hers.

I waited, then told him, 'She is called Ling.'

He was silent.

'How old are you?' my sister asked.

'Twelve.'

'I'm fifteen so I'm older,' Ling said. 'You must call me Elder Sister.'

'Elder Sister Ling,' my cousin whispered, and I could tell he would have called her 'Younger Sister Ling' with the same relish. From then there was a lot of 'Elder Sister Ling' on the tractor – it seemed he took every opportunity to use her name.

My aunt and uncle were equally besotted with Ling, and went out of their way to be generous. Auntie let her use the light whenever she wanted to and made such a fuss about her cleanliness, her prettiness and her polite way of addressing everyone that Ling blushed. I overheard Auntie saying to a neighbour, 'The city folks are indeed different from us. Look at how white her skin is, and her manners!'

'But I came from the city,' I felt like saying to her, then realised that I didn't count. Ling fitted in with her image of a city girl while I did not.

Mother and Ling filled our *kang*, which had always felt empty when only Laoye and I were in it. Hugging Ling, I told her of my trip to the market, the adventure with the village dogs and my climb up the hill with Laoye, all of which sounded flat and dull, so much less exciting than it had been. Soon I lost interest in my stories and overheard Mother whispering ominously to Laoye, of grave matters that made him sigh: the chemical factory, shooting, food rationing and school. School came up more and more frequently and I was alarmed to hear my name repeatedly, though Mother lowered her voice when she uttered it. But I tried to comfort myself. Laoye would argue on my behalf. Laoye was her father – surely she would listen to him. As I listened to her, I remembered how I had buried my face in her chest at the station when I had first seen her and realised only then how much I'd missed her. Her hand had stroked my hair – which was smooth for once as Laoye had made me brush it that morning; usually, here, I did not bother.

When I opened my eyes again it was to wince at a brightness that seemed too stark for morning. I searched for Ling and saw her squatting by the window, pointing at something. I squeezed beside her. The glass was frosted with white flower patterns, and she was blowing on them to melt a clear patch. We looked through it to see a background of pure white and my cousin grinning from ear to ear, throwing something at us.

'Snow!' I shouted, and jumped up. Mother chased after us to give us gloves, scarves, extra layers. I hugged Ling so tightly that she screamed.

Outside my cousin threw a snowball, which missed me and landed on Ling. 'Black dog becomes white dog, white dog becomes fat dog,' I heard Laoye shout from where he was watching at the door with Mother.

'Black dog, white dog, white dog, fat dog,' I repeated breathlessly, stamping my feet with cold and joy.

It was not just the dogs that looked fatter: everything else, the hills, the houses in the village, all wore a fluffy white coat. We went through the streets calling the children out to play, showing Ling off. I felt a sudden affection for the village, which I had sometimes looked down on. I thought now not of the annoyance I felt with all the children who dropped in on us at mealtimes so that we had to feed them, but of how their parents left eggs and meat in gratitude to Laoye. The villagers' hard faces, which had made me suspect they had been bandits in their youth, looked softer now. As the snow fell on them, I even saw a smile or two.

The snow kept falling and Ling had gone indoors. Soon even my cousin went inside, obeying his mother's call. But I stayed out, dizzy and happy with the changed world around me. I defied Mother, who asked me to come in, because Laoye laughed and said, 'Let her be.'

'Big raindrops fell harder and harder, and then there came a call from Beijing, asking me to go and join the army but alas, I am still too young,' I sang, twirling around with my arms wide-stretched, my head tilted up to meet the snowflakes, some melting in my mouth. Even though it wasn't rain, even though there hadn't been a call for me, I still sang, relishing the feeling of being wanted and warm. For the moment I was safe where I was and I wanted things to remain as they were.

I sang on hysterically. Part of me must have known even then that it could not last.

That night, in Auntie's big room, we had warm potato soup and hot steamed rice – refined rice that Mother had brought as a present. She had a city resident's rations. 'Ling is such a well-behaved girl,' Auntie said, and we all looked at Ling, whose clothes had remained immaculate, even after our play outside.

'But you all had a good time, didn't you?' Laoye said. 'Juju, did you beat the boys in the snow fight?'

'Oh, you shouldn't try to beat the boys! You're only a girl,' Auntie said.

Laoye looked disapproving. 'What do you mean, "only a girl"?' he said, voice rising.

'Oh, come on, it's just a game.' Auntie turned to Mother again. 'I'm sure Ling'll find a good match when she grows up. She's such a gentle creature.'

It was Laoye who broke the news to me after I had gone to bed: 'Your mother wants you back,' he said flatly.

'But you said I could go to school here and I will, if I have to,' I pleaded.

'It's not just about school. That would have been all right with your mother, I think.'

'Why, then, do I have to go back?'

'Because your mother is getting married again.'

'What?' I asked stupidly, shocked. I didn't know what that had to do with me.

'It means you will have a new father, and he wants his family around him.'

A new father? I sat up, but Laoye held me down. 'Sssh.' He stroked my hair. 'Your mother will move from your old home with this new . . . your father. You are going to a brand new school and will live in a lovely big house.'

'I don't want a new father. I want to stay here with you.' The thought of a new 'father' filled me with horror. Laoye's hands felt for mine in the darkness, but he said nothing. 'You promised,' I said bitterly.

He gripped my hands. 'I can pick out the stars in the sky for you if you want me to, but, Juju, you are your mother's child.'

I stared at the pretty window, still frozen with the white flower pattern, and felt the hurt in my heart. Moonlight filtered in, leaving broken shadows on the *kang*. It seemed only yesterday that I had been so happy learning magic words with him and now . . . If even Laoye could not keep a promise, who could I trust? Was it part of growing up to realise that good things could not last? I felt my eyes warm and I snuffled. I had known it all along: I would have to leave Tao Yuan. It could never be mine.

I turned my head away and, for the first time, hardened my heart against Laoye.

11

‘How can you sleep with that smell?’ Lucy hovered at the door of my bedroom. She was early for her appointment and as I was free I had invited her up. The treatment room downstairs had begun to feel more welcoming, but it was not my private space. It was not somewhere I wanted to relax with a friend.

‘Smell?’ I sniffed. Then I knew what she meant. It was the herbs in the storeroom next door. A few sacks even lay in a corner of my room. Used to it, I took it for granted.

How could I sleep with the smell? Perhaps it helped me to sleep, I thought. As I stood there with Lucy, I tried to imagine what it was like for her. For someone who hadn't been brought up smelling the herbs, drinking the medicines, she knew a great deal. It made me want to introduce them to her as Laoye had introduced them to me at Uncle Ma's chemists all those years ago. I wanted her not only to like their smell but to appreciate their qualities. However, her eagerness held me back. I remembered that she might need words of caution and a healthy dose of cynicism more.

‘I'm used to it,’ I said, ‘but I'm sure you must find it repulsive.’

‘I wasn't sure at first, it's an acquired taste, but I'm beginning to like it.’

She sat on my bed, and blew at her fringe as she spoke, then gave a pearly laugh. It was hard not to laugh with her. I sat down next to her, and she picked up Tiantian's photo from the dressing-table, the only decoration on it apart from an alarm clock. 'Ease, you told me her name meant. Now I see,' she murmured. 'She looks like a happy child.'

The photo had been taken when she was three, with her thick dark hair in two plaits. Each time I looked at her, I remembered how she had squirmed on my lap and protested as I had struggled to get her looking so neat. I felt a stab of pain deep inside me as I thought of how much I had already missed of her growing up. Who was plaiting her hair now? I wondered.

'Connor's got eczema.' Lucy sighed and put down the photo.

'So has Tiantian,' I said, 'I used to bind her hands to stop her scratching.' Lucy looked horrified. 'When she was small,' I added, but Lucy's expression said that even that was unacceptable.

I switched back into professional mode. 'I can give you some cream for him, but I would start by changing his diet,' I said.

'No dairy products?'

I nodded. 'More vegetables.'

'It's hard.' She sighed.

I knew. Tiantian was stubborn and made each meal a battle of wills. Was that why I'd given her up, admitting defeat when he, my husband, would not even try? He'd let her eat anything even though he knew it was bad for her.

As if echoing my thought Lucy continued, 'It was all right when I was feeding him – I just dug my heels in – but Mark. . .' She shook her head. I was surprised that she had criticised her husband in front of me. I nodded and said nothing.

She sauntered across the room to open the window and lean out. 'It's nice to be in the town,' she said. 'I've always wanted a room like this where you can watch people come and go. It's so quiet where we live.'

Once again she had surprised me. It had not occurred to me that she might feel anything but happiness and contentment with her family in her perfect little cottage. I had yearned to feel as comfortable here as she did there. But perhaps she had a point and I, too, should appreciate what I had and open the window to watch the bustle outside.

I sat on the bed, but part of me wanted to stand beside her at the window, pointing at things, laughing. Suddenly I wished I did not have to work that afternoon.

'Dr Lin.' Xiao Jin's voice rang up from downstairs. 'When you come down, could you bring some more *ma huang?* We are running out.'

'All right,' I said.

'Also,' she had remained at the bottom of the stairs, 'your next patient is due in five minutes, at two o'clock.'

'Oh, that's me,' Lucy said, and we laughed.

'We're on our way,' I called back.

'*Ma huang?*' Lucy frowned.

'It's one of the herbs you had,' I said, going over to one of the sacks to untie it.

'I remember now,' Lucy said, following me. 'I checked it out. *Ephedra sinica,*' she touched the dry yellow twigs and murmured, 'whose main component, ephedrine, relieves the narrowing of the airways that occurs during an asthma attack. My book tells me to use it cautiously as it can be toxic to the liver.'

Like many of my patients, Lucy was hinting at doubt. They rarely questioned me directly, as if they might offend me – it was as though, by quoting a book or an opinion, they might sound less mistrustful. I was getting used to it, difficult though it had been at the beginning, coming as I did from a background in which there was no need to prove that Chinese medicine worked.

I watched her bring the twig close to her nose and sniff it. 'They're magical, aren't they? They look like ordinary twigs, but. . .'

'They have to be picked between Descent of Frost and Arrival of Winter.'

'Really? What are they – Descent of Frost and Arrival of Winter?' She was fascinated.

'The time of year just before winter sets in. If they are not picked then their potency is weakened.'

'You sound as if you've picked them yourself.'

'Not me. I've seen them straight after they'd been picked though.'

Laoye had picked *ma huang* in those first few months that I'd spent in the countryside with him. He had piled it on the floor to dry. When I had put a twig to my mouth he had stopped me. Treat all herbs with caution, he had said. Respect them and they will cure you. Trifle with them and you will suffer.

'Juju, are you all right?'

Lucy's voice woke me from my reverie. She was looking intently at me, expecting me to say more. I shook my head. Even though my early memories of Laoye were happy, they were now coloured with pain. They hurt more because I had trusted him so innocently. I was suddenly relieved now that I hadn't told Lucy more.

I took a handful of the twigs, retied the sack and knotted the string, then headed for the door. Lucy followed, still holding a twig. 'Anyway,' she said eagerly, 'I much prefer to see what I'm taking – boiling the herbs – than just popping white pills. God knows what they put in them.'

While I was treating Lucy Mr Cheng turned up. He sat in a corner, watching, unusually patient, which unnerved me. When Lucy rose to leave he leaned forward. I introduced her, and hoped he would go. Instead he smiled and chatted to her, wanting to know what treatment she had received and asking how well she had responded to it. He gave her a long lecture on the superiority of Chinese medicine, the ignorance and superficiality of which I found nauseating. But, to my alarm, she listened attentively. The smile on her face as she left made me want to hit him.

He turned to me triumphantly when the door closed. 'See? A satisfied patient. We need more like her. She is the sort of patient I had in mind for our specialist clinic – the sort who keeps coming back.'

'Mr Cheng,' I tried to remain calm, 'I've told you before, I am no expert on asthma. . .'

'That doesn't matter and, anyway, you'll seem like one to these foreigners.'

'I will not do it,' I said simply.

His expression changed. 'Don't think you're my only doctor.'

I didn't say anything. It would be hard to find another job, but I had already considered looking for one.

He stared at me. 'You are more stubborn than I thought. What's your problem with running a successful clinic?'

'I don't want to lie to my patients.'

'Don't you see? You'll be doing them a favour, making them happy. Look at how keen she was. The herbs won't do them any harm.'

For someone who owned so many clinics, he did not understand the discipline of herbal medicine at all.

'I might have to go ahead without you,' he went on. 'You must consider your position carefully.'

12

I stood alone in the playground. It was comforting to remember that Ling was in the same school. She walked me to my classroom every day then went to her own. The new school was affiliated to the transistor-radio factory, where Uncle Guo, our new father, worked. The chemical factory, near where we used to live, had been my real father's workplace. It had paid his pension and provided free housing for us. But now that our mother had remarried – for our benefit, she had hinted – we had to move from there.

In this house everything was new and contrasted with our old home, which was dark and cluttered but warm. Ling and I even had a room to ourselves, thanks to our new father's status – he was the propaganda director of the factory. We had a spanking new radio, which was my greatest delight. It looked so grand that I wondered whether Mother married Uncle Guo just so that we could share it. It occupied pride of place in our house on the top shelf of the sideboard. When it was not in use, it was covered with a piece of red velvet, and Mother, Ling and I often wiped invisible dust from its surface. It had a gold-embroidered front and intriguing numbers and charts on the bottom half. Two knobs stuck out proudly, like guards at a palace entrance. It was so much more than a mere appliance. Unlike the rest of my life, it was predictable and fun, full of ancient stories, contemporary songs and comedy, of which I never tired. The only problem was that Uncle Guo – whom we had to call

'Father' – was in ultimate control of it, and he was only interested in the news and the weather forecast, which were dull. Now it was not enough to ask Mother's permission: her view only counted when my stepfather wasn't around.

It was hot in the sun, but I didn't want to go to the shade where all my classmates huddled together in the lee of the low brick bungalow that was our classroom. I tried to imagine what Laoye might be doing at that moment – visiting patients? Preparing herbs? Or was he sitting in his secret cave, thinking of me?

He had promised to come and fetch me if I needed him. 'But how would you know if I did?' I had asked.

'How did I know when you were first struck down by asthma?' he asked. 'Remember, you are very special to me, Juju,' he added. 'Whenever you need me, I will come.'

I nodded, only half convinced. I enjoyed being reminded of how unique the bond was between us, but I couldn't help remembering that he had said I was my mother's child.

Absently, I drew on the ground with a stick the characters I had learned from endless copying. None of the teachers explained to us, like Laoye did, how each character had been formed. Our Chinese teacher came into the room, asked us to take out the textbook, and said, 'Read after me. Lesson one, long live Chairman Mao.' We would read the sentence, and repeat it several times. Then he would write the characters on the blackboard and we would copy them into notebooks lined with squares. Our homework was to copy until we had them by heart.

Maybe I just hadn't wanted to hear the bell ring. When I looked up again I was the only child left outside. Suddenly I felt sick: the doors of the bungalows stood upright, like soldiers lining up to accuse me. Then I heard a chorus of students reciting the familiar quotation from Chairman Mao, 'Study well and progress every day', as we did before each class. A uniform clattering of chairs indicated they were standing up to greet the teacher and another meant they had sat down and the class had begun.

I didn't want to be alone in the yard any longer, and tried several wrong doors before I finally located my classroom. As I knocked on the door I felt a burning sensation down below and was about to turn away when the door opened. It was our maths teacher. I waited until she spoke to me.

'Why are you late?' she asked.

'I've been to the toilet.' Confessing that I had not wanted to join the class seemed a bad idea.

'Find your seat quickly.'

I sat down and relief swept through me. But I couldn't settle because the burning sensation had intensified. I tapped my feet and squeezed my thighs together. When I couldn't bear it any longer, I raised my hand.

'What is it?'

'I . . . need to go to the toilet,' I whispered.

Her response seemed calculated to humiliate me: 'You were late for class because you were in the toilet and now you want to go again. If you disrupt the class now, I'll report to your father. Aren't you ashamed of yourself?'

When the warm trickle burst out of me I felt a brief satisfaction – the tension had gone. But a puddle accumulated despite my best effort to will it away.

My neighbour screamed: 'Teacher, Lin Ju wet herself.'

I opened my mouth but couldn't speak.

I was escorted to the back of the classroom in disgrace. There I stood and listened to the rest of the lesson, the last class of the morning.

Ling came and took me home. She washed me and helped me change into clean trousers. She cooked lunch as usual but I didn't feel like eating. In the afternoon, I spent every break in the girls' toilet. I had been afraid to drink anything, too terrified of embarrassing myself again. Listening to the giggles and jibes of the other girls, my shame turned to anger. Since I had been branded an outcast, I felt as though I had nothing to lose. During break when the teacher wasn't looking, I picked a fight with the girl who had exposed me and was given a detention at the end of the day. Later I was marched home by the maths teacher.

My stepfather listened to her silently, nodding from time to time. When she had finished he offered her tea, which she declined. When she left, the room fell silent and I remained standing in the middle of the room while my stepfather circled me.

He switched on the radio, and listened to the news, then the weather forecast. I stayed where I was, not daring to move. Once the forecast was over, instead of turning the radio off, as he usually did, he turned it up. I was puzzled until, without a word, he struck me – so unexpectedly that I screamed. But the sound was drowned by the revolutionary opera playing on the radio.

'See if you dare to lie again,' he said, raising his fist.

'I didn't lie!' I shouted, at the top of my voice.

'How dare you answer back? When your seniors speak, you remain silent.'

'Talk! talk!' a voice shrieked on the radio, a Nationalist torturing a Communist agent.

'I wasn't lying,' I repeated.

The slap landed before I had finished my sentence, a heavy blow to my head that sent me flying into Ling's arms. 'Father, please,' she begged, voice trembling.

He pulled me away from her and pushed me on to a chair. 'Now, admit you lied to your teacher.'

'No, I didn't.' He hit my face, as the female voice was singing: 'For the sake of the Party I will surrender my body and soul.'

'Mother!' Ling screamed and I saw her coming.

Then tears welled in my eyes. I ran to her. 'Lao Guo, what's happening?' Mother said, ignoring me.

'Ask her, the little liar.'

'I didn't lie. I just needed to go to the toilet and was too shy to say so,' I sobbed. Mother would understand.

'Don't argue,' he said, coming close to me again.

'Lao Guo.' Mother held his hand. Then she said something that surprised me: 'Not her head. If you must beat her, then hit her bottom.'

Wildly, he searched for and found the broom. 'Admit that you lied!' he hissed.

I sobbed, and found my whimpers filled the suddenly quiet room – Ling had tiptoed over to turn off the radio. She came back, knelt in front of him and held his hands. 'Please, Father, it is all my fault. Please beat me instead.'

My stepfather looked as if he was about to strike her, too, when there was a knock at the door. Our neighbour must have realised now that the radio had been switched off that this was a real beating, not a torture scene in the opera. At first my stepfather ignored it, but the knocking went on. Eventually he went to open the door. It was our neighbour who stopped the beating, not my mother.

I sobbed myself to sleep. In the middle of the night, I woke gasping for air. My wheezing brought Ling, Mother and eventually my stepfather out of their beds. The asthma had returned. But I smiled between each gasp. Now that I was in trouble, Laoye would have to come back.

13

The phone woke me. Its echo carried along the bare walls and up the wooden stairs. It stopped and I reached out a hand, half-awake, expecting to touch a small, soft, warm body. When I felt nothing, I curled up and burrowed towards the wall. I hugged the pillow and tried hard to ignore the itch that radiated out from my core. I wondered if Mr Cheng had been on the phone. Since the day when he had threatened me with dismissal I had been expecting a call to say that my services were no longer required.

The bareness of my room woke me fully. Roused from such a deep sleep, I had expected to see the clutter of the home my husband and I had shared briefly in London. Tiantian's toys, my books, suitcases that acted as wardrobes, packed with little knick-knacks from China – silk fans, tea, bamboo artifacts, items we could give as presents, and daily necessities, toilet rolls and toothpaste, things his parents had insisted we brought to England as they were so much cheaper in China.

I sat up. A light breeze made the thin curtain twitch. Since Lucy's visit I had slept with the window open. The weather was warmer anyway. At this time of day, before the traffic started, I sometimes heard a rider trotting down the street. The first time I heard it I had wanted to wake up Tiantian so that she could see the horse. I still hadn't got used to not having her beside me.

I thought of Zhiying only on mornings like this, when I remembered what it was to feel desire. He had been the first and only man I had slept with. Although he was a considerate, patient lover, I found lovemaking messy and bewildering. Having Tiantian became a good excuse to avoid it, and soon I was sleeping next to her, not him.

When I got up I nearly knocked over the tulips on the table. Lucy had brought them with their vase when she had come to visit – christening your room, she had said. It had felt such a personal thing. My husband had never given me flowers, and I was not even sure that Lucy saw me as a friend. They had been buds when she had given them to me, and now they had bloomed. She had sat on my bed and touched my things, and after that, somehow, my room had felt like a different place. For a while I gazed at the vase, noticing how its whiteness highlighted the tulips' yellow. On impulse I leaned forward and ran my fingers down its smooth narrow neck. 'It's mine,' I murmured.

I washed carefully. My limbs felt stretched and heavy. The problem now was keeping them and myself occupied. It was an odd feeling. As I scrubbed them the flesh reddened. I pinched my thighs until tears came into my eyes. A sound came from deep inside me – a groan? Laughter? Whatever it was, I let it out and felt better.

I stepped out of the shower and hesitated. There was no mirror upstairs, but there was one in the treatment room. Xiao Jin wouldn't be here so early, I decided, and went downstairs barefoot, carrying my clothes in one hand, the other on the cool wooden bannister. I was fresh after my shower, and suddenly light-hearted: this had begun to feel like my own home, not Mr Cheng's property. I was overwhelmed by an uplifting sense of independence.

The mirror was above the sink. I saw a thin woman, hair still black, breasts still firm. I smiled at my reflection then remembered the moment I had told Zhiying I was leaving him. He had taken it badly. When I saw the hurt in his eyes I felt it inside myself. He had whispered, 'Why? What have I done wrong?'

'Why?' I stood in front of the mirror and asked myself again.

Even now I did not have an answer. I had had an urge to be free. Beyond that I could say no more. He had not believed me: he had thought I was in love with someone else – one of my male colleagues, a waiter in a restaurant, even a customer. His jealousy was almost amusing. If only there had been another man. I wished I had met someone to fall in love with.

It had been a hard decision, preceded by many long nights. In the small hours I sat watching him, fast asleep: he slept like one who had no secrets and I believed he had none. I envied him his easy conscience. And perhaps that was why I had had to leave: I could not live so close to another soul yet be unable to unburden myself. A couple of times I nearly woke him to talk, my heart so full of pain and guilt that I feared it might burst. I was sure that he would not condemn me, and I longed for him to hold me and tell me to forget it all, it had happened such a long time ago, when I was only a child. But as I watched him he would turn, muttering in his sleep, and I would hesitate. How could I tell him my secret and be sure that he would not use it against me in the days, months, years of our life to come? How could I tell my secret to anyone freer, more innocent than I?

He suspected nothing. I had hidden this part of my past life from him so well that I had nearly fooled myself, but finally it had come to claim a price. It had eaten a chunk of my soul and now had parted me from my family. More and more, these days, when I thought of Zhiying, I remembered with nostalgia the days of our courtship: there had been panic and fear on my side, but youth had given me confidence to conquer the guilt. He was a decent man and we were in love. It was only after our move to England that I had begun to relive the nightmare of my childhood.

What to do now? I shuddered and looked away from the mirror. What would any of my soul-searching achieve? We could not change the past – the things we'd done, the decisions we'd made. Had we known where we would end up, would Zhiying and I have lived our life together differently?

Back upstairs I dressed slowly, gazing at the photo of Tiantian as I always did. Where she was concerned, I was all generosity – so generous that I had let Zhiying take her away from me. She'd fare better with him, I had thought, with grandparents, uncles and aunts, than she would with me, all alone in this foreign country, penniless and friendless. However desperately I missed her, I had been at ease with that decision, though hard it was to justify to others. Her absence was the bitter price of my separation from Zhiying.

I leaned forward to touch the photo frame for reassurance, but felt again the stab of pain. Despair hit me; emptiness and silence gathered, like the distance between me and her. If only I could hold her again. If only I could feed her, bathe her, watch her play and sulk.

A sound at the front door brought me back to the present, a voice I'd heard before. I lifted the curtain and peered down. A huge, silvery car was parked just outside the clinic and a broad-shouldered man stood at the door. The impatient shifting of his feet was familiar. 'Mark.' His name slipped out.

At the sound of my voice he looked up.

I saw immediately that there was something odd about the way he held his shoulders and neck.

'Oh, hi,' he said. 'Could you. . .?' He motioned to the door.

'Wait.' I dressed quickly, carrying with me the image of Tiantian smiling as I hurried down the stairs. I held on to it every day as I went down to the clinic: her smile had come to represent all the love and approval I needed. Wrapped up in thoughts of my daughter, I was at the foot of the staircase before I realised it was only a quarter past eight.

I opened the door. 'Hello.'

'I've . . . hurt my neck in a car accident,' he said. His awkward posture made him look almost comical, but pain showed on his face. 'Lucy said I should come to you.' The car was parked on a double yellow line. 'I mustn't stay long.'

Relieved, I went to fetch Xiao Jin's appointment book. He hovered at the door. 'I'm sorry I came so early. I was on my way to work and thought I'd pop in instead of ringing. Lucy gave me your number but I lost it.'

'How about this afternoon? I'm free between three and four,' I said.

'Perfect.' He nodded slowly and walked away. I followed, feeling that some further exchange of pleasantries was required. He was the first soul I had seen that day, and I wanted to talk about Tiantian, tell Mark something about her, to relieve the pain of her absence. But he didn't look back. I watched him drive away to join the rush-hour traffic.

My first patient was Mr Robinson, an old man who liked to talk to me about the stories he had read of China, and of the Cultural Revolution. He was chatty and cheerful and I wondered whether it was partly for the companionship that he came. He reminded me of my elderly patients in the big city hospital where I worked just after graduation. Some days they came just for a chat, but they were entertaining and I didn't mind. Those had been happy days, when I had colleagues to share jokes with, other light-hearted young graduates from all over China. We were new to the city and nobody there knew who I was. It was there that I had met Zhiying.

The clinic was quiet and the day passed slowly. I found myself looking forward impatiently to Mark's appointment. All day his pain-filled face hovered at the back of my mind, merging somehow with my cherished photo of Tiantian and making me anxious. Although I suspected he was suffering from nothing more serious than whiplash, I hated the thought of him being in pain.

But at three o'clock Xiao Jin led in someone else. 'What happened to Mark?' I asked.

'Who?'

'Mark, Lucy's husband. He's hurt his neck.'

Just then Mark came in and Xiao Jin looked up from the appointments book. 'I see,' she said, looking at Mark. 'Did you put this in?'

I nodded.

'But it's for next Wednesday,' she said triumphantly, pointing to the date at the top of the page.

Mark turned to go but I could not let him leave in such pain.

Lucy would not like it, I told myself. She had sent him here: I mustn't disappoint her. 'Mark, I've double-booked myself. Would you mind coming back around six? I can treat you then.' I didn't usually work overtime but I had made a mistake and this seemed the easiest way to deal with it.

It was nearly six thirty when he turned up, rushed and bothered. He leaned on the door, with his car key in his hand, as if he was not going to stay. The traffic had been bad, he said. He never understood why there was so much in such a small town, although it was nothing compared to London where he used to work. We chatted about London for a bit. He was going to be sent on a trip to China soon, he said, to Shanghai. Had I been there? No? He looked surprised.

The conversation was reassuring. Earlier I had disliked his businesslike tone and the brisk way he'd walked off. Now, though, I thought we were talking quickly to avoid silence. The topic he'd chosen, traffic, seemed forced, but we had little in common. The room was too quiet and echoey whenever either of us finished a sentence. At last the traffic outside had quietened and I had exhausted what small-talk I had. I pointed at the chair and heard the change in my tone, the doctor's voice, and found the formality oddly comforting. Although his curiosity about me had made me warm to him when we'd first met, it was my skill as a doctor that had persuaded him to seek me out, and I wanted to impress him. He sat down and I asked him to start at the beginning. 'Tell me what happened.'

'I had an accident a week ago,' he said. 'The car behind didn't stop in time at traffic-lights. I'm taking painkillers but they're useless. I've also been to a chiropractor. It felt better for a few hours, but then the pain came back.'

'How do you feel now?'

'My neck hurts like hell, just here.'

I reached for his hand and realised, when he lowered his head for me to examine his neck, that, unlike Lucy, he had not seen an acupuncturist before. I was pleased that he was new to it. 'I need to feel your pulse,' I said. 'Rest your hand here.' I patted the hand rest. He peered at it and laid out his hand, palm up, then palm down. He laughed. 'Which way?'

I smiled, reached out to take his hand and turned it. It felt big in mine. The pulse was fast and heavy. I lowered my eyes when his caught mine and rose to straighten the newly changed sheet on the treatment couch. I needed to examine him but for some reason I couldn't ask him to take his shirt off. I dared not risk turning back in case he was still looking at me.

After what felt like hours, I heard him say softly: 'Dr Lin, would you like to examine me now?'

I turned and saw that he'd undone the top two buttons of his shirt. Relief engulfed me: he had solved the problem for me.

I stood near him, holding the needles. 'So, where on your neck does it hurt most? Here? Or here?'

'No . . . yes – yes . . . Ouch, that's right. There.'

I stuck a needle in, twisted it clockwise, then anti-clockwise. He sighed and closed his eyes, in the way that Tiantian had flinched at pain. A little amused, I pondered the way he had addressed me: 'Dr Lin,' I had asked him to call me Juju when we were on the downs, but 'Dr Lin' sounded more deliberate and somehow knowing. Was he mocking me? I did not know him well enough to judge.

I gazed at him for a minute, then realised I needed more needles. 'Wait here,' I said, and hurried to the other room to fetch them.

When I came back he smiled as soon as he saw me. 'Oh, there you are, Juju, I was worried you might have just left me here.'

This time Juju sounded right. Surely it was not surprising that he was confused about what to call me. The relief and joy on his face made me smile back at him.

'So this is what acupuncture is about! You stick needles in where it hurts most? It seems to be doing the trick, though.'

'That one was called the *ah-shi* point, meaning, "Yes, that's it".'

'It was spot on. The pain's gone. Oh, it feels wonderful.'

'Are you ready for more?'

He nodded, and I asked him to lie down on the couch. Then I tried some other points: *yin tang*, the impression hall, *feng chi*, wind pool, and *jian jing*, shoulder well. When I reached down to his knees for *zu sanli*, the foot-three-miles point, he chuckled. 'What have my knees got to do with it?'

'All these points are along the same meridian. Whiplash blocks your energy and blood channels temporarily. What I'm doing is unblocking them,' I said, and watched him close his eyes, almost as if he was enjoying it. I sat down in the silence, a silence which was mutual and welcome. Neither of us hurried to fill it with conversation. I felt it was safe to observe him now that his eyes were closed, and studied the still figure in front of me, his knees bent and arms folded. I thought of our picnic on the hill, of how confident he had seemed. Today he was vulnerable and I felt at ease.

After twenty minutes or so I took off the needles, sat him up and massaged his neck. I did it automatically, as I so often did for my patients after an acupuncture treatment. But as I worked I thought of my husband. After a hard day at the clinic, he had often asked for a neck rub. I wondered if Lucy did the same for Mark.

I wrote down some herbs – the real test of whether Mark had been convinced by my treatment. 'More Chinese tortures,' I said, and knew that I had wanted to conjure Lucy's presence. Seeing Mark without her felt wrong.

He seemed eager to do the same: 'Lucy will be so pleased I came,' he said, standing up and rubbing his eyes, 'though I wouldn't have called this torture.'

It was getting dark as he left, yet I resisted turning on the light. I watched the traffic that Mark's car had joined, the rush of people going home to their nests. Before today I'd mentally followed my patients as they left the clinic and formed vague impressions of their destinations, but today I had a definite picture. I had been to their home, which exuded warmth and other things I craved.

'Mark,' I murmured, then, 'Mark and Lucy . . . Lucy and

Mark.' I pronounced their names as if it was a mantra, and the more it felt like a mantra the more I said it.

'Lucy and Mark . . . Mark and Lucy,' I repeated, until it was dark, as I massaged my own sore neck.

14

━━◆━━

How quiet it was up here, though I was so absorbed in my play that I wouldn't have heard a thing. As I turned the brown tuning button I made my own sound, pretending it was the noise of the radio. There were several to choose from. I was sitting on a mountain of disused radio parts. The one I was playing with looked complete, with its golden embroidered cover, the square wooden frame and the knobs that controlled volume and the channels. It resembled the one we had at home. There were three channels: the local one, another for the province and Central China Radio. I loved the provincial one: it broadcast stories from the Three Kingdoms and other heroic tales. I turned the tuner to it now and pretended I could hear the stories. They were serialised in daily half-hour slots, and although they coincided with our lunchbreak at home, it was hit and miss as to whether or not we got to hear them. It depended on my stepfather's mood. This radio was smaller but more stylish than the grand one we had at home. I examined the fancy calligraphy across the front but couldn't decipher what it said.

Two other children sat next to me. Some days there were six or even seven of us, all murmuring to ourselves, imagining our own favourite channel. I wondered if they also got beaten at home by their father, or perhaps their mother, and if they were forbidden, as I had been, to listen to what they liked. Perhaps they had similar thoughts – it would explain the sense of solidarity I felt with them. We looked out for each other. When the tractor came to dump new parts, we warned each other to get out of the way and avoid a scolding.

Playing like this I could forget everything. It was only towards evening when I was tired and hungry that I would consider going home. I was careful not to skip school too often, and so far no one had noticed that sometimes I wasn't there. The school was going through a strange time anyway. The teachers were often called away to attend political meetings. They encouraged us to treat them as equals, and to tell them when we thought they had done wrong. It was not just our school: the radio told us every day that we were 'little revolutionary generals who would lead the way'. The maths teacher had been criticised and one of the senior classes had even persuaded the headmaster to criticise himself in front of us all. I had not felt vengeful when the maths teacher had stood before us with her head low. Discipline was part of a teacher's job, I understood that, and it was not her I hated but my stepfather.

When the loud Tannoy system sounded inside the factory we all looked up. It played a song I could barely understand, something about how strong the workers' muscles were. A poem followed, written by someone from the propaganda department. I listened half-heartedly, resenting its intrusion on my own secret broadcast. I wondered if it might be the work of my stepfather. Once in a while I heard him giving a speech over the Tannoy, a high-pitched voice that sounded different from the way he usually spoke. I wouldn't have recognised him if I hadn't heard him practising at home.

He had left me alone since the day I had had the asthma attack. I wouldn't say he feared me, but he certainly avoided me. I noticed him getting closer to Ling though; she called him Father now, but I had not since he beat me.

When the bell rang the workers thronged out of the buildings. They chatted among themselves, as if they had been waiting all day for this moment, and competed to see who could shout loudest. Those coming out of the nearest block were responsible for the gold-embroidered covers on the radios. I had once peeped into their workshop, which was full of colourful threads. There were lots of women and the real radio was always on. They were coming out now, each with a plastic basin filled with soapsuds, and towels in their hands. They sang on their way to the public bathhouse, drowning the blare of the Tannoy.

I wished I could make the moment last. I was desperate not to have to go home. I imagined that everyone I saw had a happier home than I did. I wished Mother hadn't remarried. I missed the days when there had been just the three of us.

When the other children and the security guards had left, I rose slowly. I knew this part of town well now. Last week I had wandered as far as the railway station, which was even more crowded than it had been when I had gone there with Laoye. Lots of Red Guards were clustered about, shouting slogans and slapping their red books. I stood at a distance. The crowds excited me, but they were intimidating, too. I thought I might have been able to take advantage of the chaos, but I didn't know which train would take me to Laoye's and I didn't have any money, although I saw many Red Guards getting on to the trains without tickets and nobody stopped them. Once I had gathered my courage and gone to the platform entrance, only to be told that they didn't believe I was a Red Guard: I was too small. I fled when they asked where I lived.

Perhaps I should steal Ling's red armband next time, I thought, as I stepped into the stream of workers coming out of the factory on their bicycles. I knew some, and some knew me through my stepfather. Occasionally they gave me lifts. I could smell soap on the wet hair of the female workers coming out of the baths and wished I could grow up quickly to be as free as them, or as free as they appeared to be, with their hair flowing as they rode swiftly past.

'Hi,' someone called from a bicycle. I looked back and recognised him. He'd ridden past me a few times but I'd never seen him inside the factory so he was not one of the workers. He reminded me of my stepfather – he was about the same age. 'Climb on, I'll give you a lift,' he said. 'It's all right, I know where you live.' He stood with one foot on the ground, and waited.

I hesitated. I felt suddenly shy, I didn't know why. 'Hop on. I have a nice surprise for you at home.' He smiled.

I looked at the darkening sky, then hopped on to the back of his bike.

'Juju, what are you doing? Get off now.' Ling's voice came from nowhere and I looked up to see her flushed red face.

'I was only giving her a lift,' the man said in a low voice, stuttering a little.

'She doesn't need one. She's coming with me – we live just round the corner,' Ling said.

'No, we don't—'

Before I could finish she was glaring hard at me and grabbed my hand. 'Come, Mother was getting worried about you.'

The man put his feet back on the pedals and rode off quickly. Ling whispered, 'He's a pervert, I can tell. Where have you been all day?'

'Just . . . wandering around.'

'You've been to the station, haven't you?'

'No, not today.'

'You're mad! You could be taken and sold like a slave to the peasants in the countryside.'

'What's wrong with the countryside? Anywhere is better than here.'

She glared at me again, was about to say something, then took my hand again instead and we started to walk towards home. After a while she turned to me and said: 'You were looking for Laoye, weren't you?'

'No, I wasn't.'

'Well, don't try to be difficult. Guess what?'

'What?'

'He's here. Laoye's here – he's been waiting for you all day.'

After that she didn't need to lead me by the hand. I wished we could fly home. Just as we were about to cross to our street we were stopped by a fleet of lorries, the liberation yellow-green ones, painted with red slogans. 'What do they say?'

'To warmly . . . send educated youth . . . to the countryside,' Ling read slowly, as we stood by to let them pass. We watched the young people on them, looking proud and chanting. I thought of the teenagers I had seen at the station and felt superior and grown-up – although Ling was older than I, she hadn't been to the countryside: that flying visit to collect me didn't count. But I held my tongue. It was not right to show off, especially when she was annoyed with me.

Our home smelt of delicious egg and tomato soup, Laoye's favourite. Hearing my stepfather's laughter I slowed down.

'Don't worry,' Ling whispered. 'He's in a good mood. Laoye is treating him.'

The first thing I saw was Laoye's white medicine box on the sitting-room floor. My heart jumped. He was really back, as he had promised. But how had he known I had had another attack? Had Mother told him? In my heart I knew the answer: it was because there was something special between us. He had known because I was his favourite granddaughter.

When my stepfather's face turned to me it wore a rare benign look. We normally only saw it when he was drunk, and it usually meant we were in for a political lecture on the Current Situation. I had learned never to trust it. It could change suddenly. I approached him slowly. He seemed a little calmer than usual today.

'Juju,' Laoye called, from the *kang*, and I ran to him. 'Have you come to take me away?' I wanted to ask, but I was too scared to say it in front of my mother and stepfather. I hugged him tightly. 'Where have you been all day?' he whispered.

'I've been trying to find you,' I wanted to say, which was nearly the truth. But I couldn't say anything. I simply clung to him.

'You missed school,' Mother said, and I peered at my stepfather nervously, even though I knew that, with Laoye there, he wouldn't dare hurt me.

'Spirit of rebellion,' my stepfather said, raising his glass. I could smell alcohol on his breath. 'I'm sure the Red Guards would approve. They have been smashing up the old system. It's a trend we should encourage. Well done, Juju.'

I couldn't disguise my surprise. Was this the same man who had beaten me because I'd disobeyed my teacher? What had changed? Were these jokes and smiles a response to Laoye's treatment?

Mother, however, remained reassuringly constant: 'Well, next time you miss school you must let us know, otherwise. . .' Ling whispered something in her ear and Mother looked horrified. 'What? You were nearly abducted?'

'It was only a man I knew wanting to give me a lift,' I said finally, upset that she was making a fuss about something so trivial – she had not lifted a finger to help me when my stepfather had hit me.

Mother sighed and said to Laoye, 'You see what she's turned into? My words fall on deaf ears.' She turned to my stepfather: 'Lao Guo, you should take your daughter in hand.'

I shuddered, but he smiled and raised his glass. 'Well, I trust her to know what is right and what is wrong. She seems to be on the side of the revolutionaries and that's fine with me.'

I looked around the room, relaxing a little. I knew that Laoye would not have arrived empty-handed and, sure enough, a few sacks lay on the floor. Pine nuts, hawthorns and chestnuts. I eyed them greedily as I gobbled the dinner Mother had saved for me. The radio was on, not the news but a traditional story on the provincial channel. Normally I would have had my ears glued to it, but there were better distractions today. I wanted to eavesdrop on the adults' conversation. Mother and Laoye's voices were prominent, but occasionally I heard my stepfather's, high-pitched with excitement, reminding me of his speech on the factory loudspeaker but somehow less threatening now. Surely this was too good to be true: Laoye's return, my stepfather beaming at me and my favourite radio programme. All this before I had started on the mouthwatering treats.

Ling cracked open a few pine nuts, expertly now, and beckoned me. But I had lost my appetite. They were from my Tao Yuan. I wanted to know when I could return. I wished I could run to Laoye and ask him how long he was staying and if he planned to take me away again. But I knew I had to be patient.

15

'Look what we've got for you,' Lucy said, pushing Connor forward.

He waved something in his hand and shouted, 'A present! A present!' He reminded me of Tiantian when I gave her a new toy. I tried to match my excitement to his and bent down.

'Open it!' Connor urged, and I took it from him and started to unwrap the pink paper.

'I hope you don't mind, but I thought your wall looked a bit bare so. . .' Lucy said, as I unrolled the paper. It was a picture of an ancient man dressed in robes, with a long white beard. He carried a basket filled with flowers and grasses on his back, and in the background was a cloud-clad hill. The inscription in Chinese at the top of the picture said, 'Shizhen picking herbs'.

'Do you like it?' they asked eagerly.

I leaned it against the wall, next to the acupuncture chart. The chart was in black and white with small neat print, mapping out the meridian points on a naked male body, which looked almost too precise to be real. The picture of the man was too brightly coloured and the crudely painted figure had a disproportionally large head. I thought it was horrible. The two pictures couldn't have been more different.

'Who's the man?' Connor asked.

'He's a famous herbalist, from ancient China, called Li Shizhen,' Lucy said, then turned to me: 'Is that right? I ordered it after reading about it in a magazine. It reminded me of your

stories about your grandfather. What did you call him – Laoye?'
I turned sharply. How did she know?

'Your article in the *Gazette*, remember?'

I bit my lip. I shouldn't have mentioned him. It had been a slip of the tongue. Afterwards I had thought long and hard about it. But nobody here knew about my past.

I met Lucy's eyes and tried to sound casual. 'Yes, Laoye.'

'Laoye.' Lucy turned to Connor: 'Can you say it? It's Chinese for "grandfather".'

'Laoye,' Connor said slowly, as he stared at the picture of the ancient herbalist. Then he gazed at me: 'Have you got a grandfather as well?'

Lucy and I laughed. 'Connor, everyone has a grandfather,' she said.

I looked at him for a minute, and said quietly, 'Mine died a long time ago.'

Luckily Connor did not dwell on it. He dropped his eyes from the picture and ran to the reception area murmuring his version of 'Laoye'. For a moment his voice echoed. Lucy and I stood in front of the picture and I thought how unlike Laoye the figure in the picture was. Laoye was self-deprecating and quiet, the opposite of the exuberant, dramatic man it depicted. It seemed odd to be confronted by Lucy's image of Laoye, but she had not known him. Even I had only known him as a child. I had heard stories of his youth, but I had had no idea of what his personality had been like. We cannot imagine our grandparents as young people because they are old when we first know them.

Perhaps that had been my first mistake: to believe that that old man had no other role in life but to be there for me.

'You must have loved him very much.' Lucy said, and I nodded.

'We have an expression for it,' I said. '*Ge beir qin*. It describes the special bond between grandparents and their grandchildren.'

Lucy repeated slowly: '*Ge beir qin*. Well.' She turned to me brightly. 'And what's that other word – Laoye? It all sounds so poetic. You should give me Mandarin Chinese lessons. I'd love to learn.'

I went to the door, concerned that Connor was alone in the reception area. 'Mark came to see me about his whiplash,' I said. This was the first time I'd seen Lucy since his visit, and I had expected her to mention it. She hadn't and I wanted it to be out in the open.

'I know,' she said, as she followed me. 'I'm glad he came, he hadn't seemed very keen.'

'He was late.'

'That's just like him. I hope you didn't mind.'

'No,' I said, relieved. Now there was no secret – and how absurd it had been to feel so awkward about seeing him.

'How did you treat him?'

'Acupuncture and . . . herbs, of course. He said he didn't mind taking them.'

'I haven't seen him boiling them. I'm sure I would have noticed the smell too.' We were in the reception area and Connor was tiptoeing across to open one of the lower drawers. Hearing our conversation he rushed up to Lucy. 'Daddy threw his herbs away.'

'What did you say?' Lucy asked, holding out her arms to him.

'Daddy threw his herbs away. I saw him.'

I remained at the door. I had wondered whether he would take them and it didn't surprise me that he hadn't.

Lucy blushed. 'Well, I don't know why he did that, but he was enthusiastic about the acupuncture. He told me about the *ah-shi* point. He made such a fuss about it. Why didn't you use it on me?'

I laughed to ease her discomfort. '*Ah-shi?*' I said. 'It's a point we use to kill pain – I often use it on new patients, who might be sceptical because the effect is usually instant. I didn't use it on you because you were not in pain and did not need convincing that acupuncture could help you. It is one of the basic points – like kissing a child when he has hurt himself.'

'Kiss it better, Mummy,' Connor murmured, took a stone out of the bottom drawer and put it into his mouth. Lucy rushed to take it from him and gave it to me. I told him its name and what it treated, and he listened. I lifted him up to show him the twigs and grasses I kept higher in the cabinet, but he was more interested in the stones and insisted on opening more drawers at the bottom.

'I'm sorry,' Lucy said, and once again took the stones from him.

'There's no harm done and it's good that he's curious. We'll watch him,' I insisted, and laid some on the floor so that he could play with them.

Lucy knelt next to me, watching Connor making patterns with the stones. She was at ease and I was prompted to ask the question that had been on my mind since I'd met her. I tried to sound casual. 'So, where and how did you meet? You and Mark, I mean.'

'Mark?' Lucy paused. Then a smile lit her face. 'We met in London, at a party, at a friend of a friend's house. We just got talking, you know. And. . .' I waited, expecting the long story of a romance, but she seemed to lose interest. 'It's all such a long time ago. We were much younger.' She rose to follow Connor, who had abandoned the stones and was climbing the stairs.

We ended up in my bedroom, where Connor spotted the photo of Tiantian: 'Who's that?'

'My daughter.'

'I want to play with her.'

'I'd love you to meet her, but she's in China.'

'You must bring her here, you know,' Lucy said. She was talking to me as if she knew me well. I liked it.

'She will start school this autumn,' I said, remembering Tiantian's voice when I had spoken to her on the phone last weekend. As usual I had rung at the wrong time when she was anxious not to be late for a birthday party. I could not imagine her missing me. 'She's quite happy now—'

'Sssh – what's that?' Lucy said.

I listened. The downstairs door handle was being twisted. Someone was trying to get in. Xiao Jin? But it was the weekend.

Then we saw Mr Cheng's face at the bottom of the stairs. He

looked as surprised as we were to see him. 'Who . . . is this? What's going on?' He sounded angry.

'This is my friend and patient, Lucy,' I said.

Connor emerged from behind me and said cheerfully, 'Hello, do you live here as well?'

'Oh, hello.' Lucy extended a hand. 'We've met before. You're Mr Cheng, aren't you?'

Mr Cheng steadied himself. 'I remember you. You're the asthma patient. How are you getting on?'

Lucy flashed me a smile. 'Thanks to Dr Lin, I'm improving more than I ever expected to.'

Mr Cheng smiled broadly. 'I'm so pleased that Chinese medicine works for you. I'm also pleased that you're here. You see, I'm trying to persuade Dr Lin to run a specialist asthma clinic for me, but she is too modest about her abilities.'

Once again Lucy was taken in. 'Well, I would be delighted if she did. I would certainly recommend it. If it had not been for Dr Lin. . .'

I didn't say anything. Mr Cheng delivered another lecture about the virtues of Chinese medicine, to which, again, Lucy listened carefully, nodding emphatically.

As he started to leave I walked him to the door. The smile disappeared from his face when he saw that Lucy was not with us. 'Have you considered my proposal?' he asked.

'Of course. And the answer is no.'

He stared at me for a good minute. 'You are the stubbornest woman I've ever known. Don't think the world will stop turning without you. Did you know you're running at a loss rather than making money for me? This is not a charity clinic. You are in my debt, Dr Lin, and I'll make sure you pay one day.'

With that he left me, slamming the door behind him. 'What was that about?' Lucy's concerned voice travelled down the stairs.

'Nothing,' I said, frowning. What would have happened if I had been alone in the house when he came in?

Lucy and Connor stayed for dinner, and we were in the

middle of eating it when the phone rang. I ran downstairs to answer it.

'Everything all right?' Lucy queried. Connor had tucked into the noodles.

'Wrong number,' I said, glad that they were there. Zhiying sometimes rang in the middle of the night, when he got the time difference wrong. Although I longed to hear news of Tiantian, I was always jumpy when the phone rang. Alone in the quiet room, I suspected it heralded bad news. Lucy and Connor's presence had reminded me of how it felt to have company.

16

Finally I was on the train bound for Tu Fei Wo. It was around the same time of year as I had last travelled there with Laoye. The trees were the same golden colour. Inside the carriage, a sea of green-uniformed Red Guards surrounded me, outnumbering the shabbily dressed peasants. I straightened my back, reminding myself that I wore the same red armband as the other young people around me.

The train jerked and suddenly a strange thing happened: the Red Guards, who had looked so confident and mature, burst into sobs. Out of the window, older people – their parents? – waved frantically, some covering their faces. The air quickened with the shuddering of shoulders – it was as if a huge wave had swept over us. Some tried to resist it and their mouths twisted into comical shapes as they sucked in their breath in an effort to swallow their tears.

I remained resolutely dry-eyed: I had no family on the platform to mourn my departure. They didn't even know I was here. I had left home because my stepfather, drunk, had asked why I did not address him as Father. When I had answered that he was not my father, he had beaten me. This time the shock was worse – since Laoye's visit I had thought him a changed man. When I had fallen to the floor he had kicked me in the stomach, and Mother had done no more than urge him to calm down. I had known then that this was no longer my home but I kept my mouth shut tight and didn't even whimper – I didn't want him to see me cry.

Ling might have had an inkling of my plan as I had stolen her best armband. As for my stepfather, my revenge had been to take money from his drawer. I felt the crisp notes in my pocket. There was no need to buy a ticket: I'd save the money to buy food.

I took a deep breath and looked into the sea of moist eyes around me. I felt superior. These Red Guards were bigger and older than I was. They spoke the language of adults and politics, and brandished their red books proudly, yet they were more emotional than I about leaving their families. If going to the countryside filled them with such dread, what grand revolutionary gestures were they capable of?

But suddenly I spotted a calm face. It stood out among its weeping, snivelling companions like a crane among chickens. When its owner's eyes met mine, he smiled, catching me unawares. I looked away quickly, but soon my eyes had drifted back to him. He was still smiling, so I smiled too.

The young man was sitting across the aisle on the opposite side of the train. He wore the green uniform of the Red Guards but, with his top button undone and his hat at an odd angle, he seemed to have dressed in a hurry. His smile broadened to reveal white teeth and there was a naughty glint in his eyes, suggesting childish mischief. He was certainly older than I – I thought he might be even older than Ling.

When he turned his head, I saw a tall, thin-lipped girl sitting next to him, whispering to him. Inside her green army jacket she wore a white shirt with a turned-up collar, which accentuated her long neck. I'd seen older girls with that sort of style and had always admired them, but Mother would never have allowed me to dress unconventionally.

I was afraid to stare so I pretended to look out of the window, but out of the corner of my eye I saw that the young man was a leader: once in a while, guards would come to consult him, then head purposefully away. He nodded intently as he gave instructions, and the faces of those he addressed were respectful and admiring.

For a while the seats between us were empty when the peasants sitting there went to the toilet. The young man leaned forward, as if we were old friends. 'Which school do you come from?' he said. His voice was like that of an actor, well modulated and smooth.

'Transistor-radio factory senior.' I thought I would pretend to be Ling.

'Where are you off to?'

'Tu Fei Wo.'

'So are we. Which brigade?'

I had no idea. Laoye had told me the name of his village, but I had forgotten it. I knew it only as Tao Yuan.

'We are going to number two. You don't know which you are going to?'

'Er. . .'

The girl, who had been listening to our conversation, nodded at the young man. 'I told you,' she said. Then, to me, 'You're a runaway, aren't you?'

'No, I'm not.'

'It's all right,' the young man said gently. 'We don't mind. We'd have done the same – anything to escape the old reactionaries. Well done for coming to join the Movement of Going Down to the Countryside. Chairman Mao teaches us that in the wide world of the countryside we can achieve a great deal.'

There were lots of so-called 'movements' then – movement of this, movement of that. I thought of the 'hygiene movement' when we had been ordered by the government to kill flies to stop them spreading disease. Now there was this Movement of Going Down to the Countryside. I met the smiling eyes of the young man and felt suddenly shy, even though his words, which I only half understood, had sounded kindly.

'In the wide world of the countryside, we can achieve a great deal.' The girl repeated what the young man had said in a high-pitched voice and pointed at the red banner spreading across the carriage. I nodded. I had heard this slogan often on the radio, though it had never seemed to have any relevance to me. Now I leaped on the words eagerly – they not only excused my escape, they gave it a reason. Of course that was why I had run away! I was not alone in feeling oppressed by the atmosphere at home. These Red Guards were my soulmates.

'You've done nothing wrong,' the young man said again, soothingly. 'You are answering Chairman Mao's call.'

'It's true. I ran away from my parents' oppression.' I felt more confident now.

His eyes gleamed as if this was what he had been waiting for. He smiled broadly. 'Welcome to the cause. I am Steel and this is Bell.' He stretched out a hand for me to shake. 'Come to number-two brigade with us. I'm sure they could do with another educated youth.'

'Educated youth'. I had never thought of myself in such dignified terms before, although I saw now that I was entitled to the description because I had been to school and came from a city. I was not a truant, much less a runaway, I was someone special, someone who could play a valuable role in the 'movement'.

'Yes?' His smile deepened.

I nodded noncommittally. Perhaps Laoye was in number-two brigade, but even if he wasn't, number two couldn't be very far away from him. I had learned during my last visit that number one and number two belonged to the same commune. Just for the moment, though, I didn't want to mention my grandfather – I was still nervous about how he would react to my turning up without warning.

Leaning forward, Steel handed me an open copy of Chairman Mao's *Red Book*. 'Read it,' he said. 'We have been studying this quotation for a while, and you will see how brilliant it is, so relevant.'

I took the book from him, filled with pride at his gesture. I pretended to read, even though I recognised only a few words. Would he expect me to comment on it? What if he wanted me to read it aloud? Suddenly I was sweating under my thick coat and took it off.

I spent several minutes staring at the page. When I deemed it safe to look up, I saw that he was still gazing at me expectantly.

118

I blushed. 'So wise,' I said, trying to sound grown-up.

'If you come to number-two brigade, we can study together. Wouldn't that be fun?' he said, in a tone that told me he was used to being obeyed. I felt as I had with Laoye, treasured and treated as an equal by someone I admired.

My admiration only increased when a ragged boy, one of the many orphaned children who slept rough at railway stations, came round the carriage begging. He had a bandage on one leg and a limp, and was in pain with each step. Many passengers either ignored him or shooed him away. By the time he got to us, the ticket collector was behind him.

As he stretched out his hand, the official caught his sleeve and twisted him round. 'How did you get on the train?' he said loudly. 'Have you got a ticket?'

The boy tried to wriggle away, but the man gripped him more tightly. 'I said, do you have a ticket? If you haven't, I'm going to throw you out of the carriage.' He towered above the boy.

The beggar boy cowered. 'Please, kind Uncle, I am starving. Please, let me go.'

I felt the money inside my pocket. I would have slipped it into the boy's, but I was too shy and too scared of the ticket collector. I, too, had no ticket.

Then I heard the voice I now knew well: 'Let him go.' It was Steel.

The ticket collector swayed. He saw Steel's armband and hesitated. 'I told you, let him go,' Steel said calmly.

The ticket collector loosened his grip, but didn't release the beggar. 'He has no ticket.' His voice was wavering – many of the Red Guards had no ticket, as he knew. I hated him for picking on someone who could not fight back.

Steel smiled sarcastically. 'Well, I have no ticket, neither does she, nor him.' He pointed to his comrades, who rallied round him. 'Go on, throw us all off!'

The ticket collector fell silent. He was no match for this. 'You . . .' He muttered something incomprehensible.

'We what? You dare not do it, do you? For we are on a

mission! We are answering the call of Chairman Mao and you are a reactionary obstructing us.'

'It wasn't like that – you all heard and saw.' The ticket collector looked around anxiously, but the carriage was packed with Red Guards, who stared at him accusingly. Quickly, to save face, he added, 'I welcome you all warmly to the countryside and am greatly honoured that you took our train, but this boy is breaking the rules.'

'He has no money because he is oppressed. It's not his fault, he's only a child. It is the parents who have deserted him whom you should ask for money, not him. Have you no heart? Look at what he is wearing – look at his toes. What if he was your child? Could you bear to see him starve?' Steel's expression was cold.

The ticket collector looked astonished, but the carriage filled with murmurs of indignation and sympathy, and he dared not object. His hand loosened and the beggar boy bowed to Steel. 'So kind, so kind, Big Brother,' he said, and edged away. But Steel put out a hand out to stop him. He turned to the people sitting around him: 'Who has some money for this poor boy?'

'Me,' I said, immediately taking out the notes I had been holding.

He took them from me, selected two five-yuan notes and pressed them into the boy's hand. 'Go and buy yourself some food at the next station,' he said, then, looking down at the boy's worn shoes, 'and get some new shoes too. You might have been abandoned by your heartless parents, but try to live with dignity. Prove to them that you are worth more than they thought.' Then he leaned towards the boy and whispered something to him. The boy nodded, bewildered, then Steel nudged him away and turned back to the ticket collector. The latter, whose face was now red like a ripe tomato, left without another word.

Steel gave me back the rest of my money. I felt like urging him to keep it, but realised that would be fawning. Something puzzled me and when the train stopped at the next station, I put my hand on the shoulder of the beggar boy before he had a chance to get off the train. 'What did he say to you?' I asked.

'What? Who?' He had the alert look of someone who was always on the run.

'The Red Guard who gave you the money just now.'

'Oh, him?' He smiled a smile too old for him. 'That silly big brother gave me so much that I won't have to beg for two weeks.'

'But what did he say to you?'

'Oh.' He gave me a funny look. 'What's it to you?'

I feigned indifference. 'I'm just curious, that's all.'

The whistle blew.

'Give me some money if you want to know,' he said quickly.

I gave him some notes. It had never occurred to me that money was precious and I enjoyed being free with it.

He stuffed it away quickly.

'So, what did he say?'

'He said, "Find them, make them pay".'

'What?'

'"Find him, make him pay."'

'"Him" or "them"?'

'I can't remember. I didn't understand what he was on about. If you ask me, there's something strange about that Red Guard.'

That was all I could get out of him. The train moved and I returned to the carriage. Whom had he meant? I didn't think it was the ticket collector. From the window I glimpsed the beggar boy running towards a middle-aged couple. The woman was holding a baby. The look on their faces said it all: they were his parents.

The ticket collector was walking past. 'That boy . . . he's not lame, and he isn't an orphan,' I stuttered, ashamed because I had witnessed the ticket collector's fall from grace. He craned his neck, but the train had long sped past the family.

'They are all the same, those tricksters.' He sighed.

I returned to my seat opposite Steel. I decided not to disillusion him by telling him what I had discovered. Besides, the words of the beggar boy had come back to me and for a while I sat there thinking about them. 'Find them, make him pay.' Who was he referring to? What could Steel's words mean?

I puzzled to myself and peered at Steel. There was a cold look in his eye that unsettled me and made me look away. After a while I turned back and saw that he was talking to Bell and his expression had softened. I decided not to think too much of the beggar boy's words. If he could lie about his identity, he could lie about other things. I shouldn't believe anything a trickster said.

The rest of my stepfather's money almost burnt a hole in my pocket – I was so keen to spend it that I bought buns and a whole cooked chicken at the next station, even though I was not hungry, and offered to share them with Steel and the guards. I ate a few mouthfuls and watched him gnaw the chicken to the bones.

From then on I felt I was part of his entourage, although Bell remained haughty and aloof with me. Steel became the young boy in the story Laoye had taught me, who treated the humble and abused with respect. Though the beggar boy had turned out to be not what he had claimed, the contrast made Steel appear nobler.

Having a new friend transformed the journey for me. The train was cramped and smelly, hot during the day and cold at night. Going to the lavatory was awful: I tried not to drink anything, but I still had to go. But my discomfort paled in comparison with the joy I felt at being accepted into this enlightened group. We sang songs and read aloud Chairman Mao's words, led by Steel. When I did the devotion dance, I performed with grace and a true feeling of dedication. It was more than just a stretch of the limbs, it was my initiation: I had now become a true member of this elite group. To have fled the pain and humiliation of home and find such good fortune seemed hard to believe. Now I knew there was nothing odd about me. It was just that until now I hadn't found friends of my own kind.

At night the carriage fell quiet, but every so often I opened my eyes to look at Steel, still not believing my luck in encountering such an exemplary young man. He slept leaning on his hands as if he was merely looking out of the window. The other passengers were exhausted and dishevelled, but he had taken to travelling as though he'd been doing it all his life. He reminded me of Laoye, I thought, as I drifted off to sleep – he had the same air of calm and elegance.

In the morning the Red Guards congregated around Steel, crowding our section of the carriage. They talked excitedly about plans for their arrival and complained about the discomfort of the night. The day passed more quickly than the previous one, with more devotion dances and readings from Chairman Mao's book. Soon the peasants sitting next to me tired of me squeezing past them so often and offered to change places so I sat next to Steel and Bell. Through the window the trees and houses passed as swiftly as they had when I had been on the train with Laoye, but this time, I had no time to watch them. I told Steel about my cruel stepfather and complacent mother, whose crime, as I recounted it, seemed even worse. His nods and sympathetic exclamations were reassuring, and I felt as if I'd found the big brother I'd always wanted.

At the sight of the mountains the Red Guards exclaimed loudly and leaned on the window to stare at them, much as I had when I had come this way with Laoye. I felt superior as I heard them debating the names of the trees and fruits. I had been there before with a man who knew the mountains better than almost anyone else alive. I was more at home in the hills than they were.

Steel was pensive. He watched the landscape, not exclaiming, rather as if he was searching for something. A question formed in my mind. Why had he chosen to bring his guards to this bit of the countryside? With his educated accent and obvious intelligence, he could have gone anywhere so why had he come to this particular place? Then many more questions bubbled inside me, but I was too shy to ask them. He looked forbidding, quite different from when he had been listening to me. It was as if he had retreated to a world of his own – a world that suddenly didn't seem quite so cheerful.

The Red Guards were swapping notes about what they knew.

'They said this area was famous for producing sweet chestnuts.'

'And women who smoke! It is said they can smoke more than a man!' They laughed.

'And bandits,' I said, showing off my knowledge. 'This mountain area used to be famous for producing the most fearsome bandits.'

'Oh, yes?' Steel turned to me with interest. 'How do you know that?'

'Oh . . . I don't remember – my mother?' I tried to make light of it.

He nodded slowly, as if this was not news to him, and I was disappointed that I had not impressed him as I had hoped to.

'And this is the area that produces the *lingzhi* herb,' I added shyly.

'*Lingzhi* the elixir?'

'Yes, the *lingzhi* elixir makes the person you most miss appear to you in your dream.'

Steel's mouth twisted and he murmured something. When I leaned forward to listen, he laughed and waved me away. Somehow, though, I couldn't let it go. Did he know something about the *lingzhi*? Why did I sense he was hiding something, even though he appeared open and friendly? I knew he was a good person – I had seen from the way he'd dealt with the beggar boy that he had a kind heart, but much about him puzzled me.

As we approached the station, I noticed that everyone apart from me had luggage. For a moment I wished I had a pack to sling over my shoulder. I wasn't a runaway, but I wasn't a proper Red Guard either, I thought sadly.

A number of tractors waited at the platform. I followed the crowds and wondered what to do. I hadn't planned anything beyond this stage, and I had lost sight of Steel in the rush to get off the train. At the sight of the tractors, however, I realised I might be able to find the driver who came to town often from Laoye's village. I was lucky. I spotted him in a group of drivers. 'Uncle Leng!' I shouted, and ran to him.

The Touch

'Juju, I didn't know you were coming. Your *laoye* forgot to tell me.'

I was so pleased to see him and my uncertainty vanished. 'Laoye doesn't know,' I said breathlessly. 'It's a surprise.'

'Well, I'm sure he'll be pleased to see you. Do you want a lift?'

I nodded emphatically.

'Listen, I will give you one, but not until later today. Come back here this afternoon when I have loaded the coal for the brigade.'

As I walked past another tractor I heard someone call my name. I recognised Steel in the sea of Red Guards. 'Make sure you come and see us in number-two brigade,' he said, tossed his hair and waved: 'Remember, in the wide world of the countryside, you will do great things! Remember Chairman Mao's teaching! Oh, I love this place already. I can feel the revolutionary atmosphere.' I waved back and walked away, pleased that he had sought me out.

I wandered aimlessly in the town, surprised that I remembered it so well and that it was not as big as I had thought. It was nearly midday, but hardly anyone was in the streets. As I passed a few restaurants the smell of food made me hungry, and it occurred to me that I could go to Auntie Hu.

I asked people for 'Hu's restaurant?' but they looked at me as if I was begging and hurried past without answering.

I tried to remember the way to her house, but ended up in front of a huge wooden door that seemed oddly familiar. It was Uncle Ma's chemist's. But why was the door shut in the middle of the day? Two big strips of paper were criss-crossed over it, like hands, barring the way. I couldn't read the words, but it dawned on me that lately I had often seen things like this. I knew enough to understand that it could only mean something bad. I looked through the crack in the door, but couldn't see anyone. Where had Uncle Ma gone? What was wrong?

I walked away slowly, my heart heavy. There was a definite atmosphere of unease in this town, which I hadn't noticed the last time I was here. Was this the mood of revolution Steel had spoken of? Why, then, should it fill me with dread rather than

125

jubilation? Did I see things he didn't or was his sense of revolution sharper than mine? My instinct was at odds with my new-found revolutionary fervour.

I continued away from Uncle Ma's shop, and soon stood outside the house where I had eaten the most delicious egg fried rice I had ever tasted. I read the menu pasted inside the window, the four-character names of the dishes that Laoye had helped to create. But although I could read them now, I suspected that they were not served any more. The restaurant seemed deserted, and bore the same black sign that I'd seen at Uncle Ma's. The paper appeared older than those on the chemist's door and some pieces had come loose to sway in the wind. I lingered at the door. No one was around, and the house was quiet. Then I saw a face behind a curtain in the upstairs room. I remembered the bedridden man, Auntie Hu's husband – was it him? I heard my name whispered. It was Auntie Hu. 'Auntie Hu!' I shouted. 'It's Juju.'

She put a finger to her lips to silence me and disappeared from the window. Moments later I heard the door open and her face emerged from behind it. She was so pale that I didn't dare come close to her until she smiled. Then she looked around quickly and pulled me inside. 'Did he send you here?'

'Who?'

'Your grandfather.'

'No, I came on my own. I came from home to see him.'

She stared at me. I could tell that she was thinking hard. Then she pulled me to her chest. Her lips were cracked and dry and she had wrinkles at the corners of her eyes. What had happened? Why did she look so frail and frightened? This was not the Auntie Hu I remembered. 'It's good to see you,' she said. Although her voice was not loud, it echoed. All the restaurant chairs and tables had gone, I noticed, and the hall was empty and big. I shivered in a cold draught. There was a soft sound upstairs and I jumped. 'What was that?'

She shook her head, then the corner of her mouth twisted as if she was going to cry. I waited, but she didn't speak. After a minute she sighed. 'I closed the restaurant. Orders. Listen.' She grasped my hand. 'You can't stay here long. It's lucky no one knows who you are. Can you deliver something to your grandfather for me?'

I nodded.

She disappeared upstairs and returned with a blue parcel. 'Make sure you give it to him, no one else,' she said.

I nodded again.

She felt my hair with her hand. I licked my dry lips.

'Are you hungry?'

'Yes.'

She went back upstairs and returned with something wrapped in a handkerchief. 'I made these dumplings for Uncle Hu's lunch. I know they are cold but . . . you mustn't be seen here. Now hurry along.'

On the bumpy tractor I ate the cold dumplings. They were delicious, but they felt heavy inside my stomach, unlike her wonderful rice. I kept thinking of her unsmiling face and the wrinkles that had deepened since my last visit. I had met her only once before, and now I was helping her with a secret. I was still in the dark about what lay between her and Laoye, but I knew that something bad had happened, was happening, and I dreaded to think what it might mean for him. For the first time I feared he would be angry with me for running away like this.

The sun was setting, a golden spread of colour marred only by the black smoke of the tractor. The driver asked, 'Why are you visiting us again? Isn't the city good enough for you? I heard their roads are as clean as our beds.'

'Laoye lives here. I want to be with him.'

'Crazy girl.' He shook his head, and then: 'You and your grandfather, there's a word for it, you know, *ge beir qin*.'

'What's that?'

'It means the special bond between grandparents and grandchildren. They spoil you, grandparents, don't they?'

I nodded, then remembered something: 'I don't have a grandmother, though.' I'd never met Laoye's wife.

'She was from an island in the south, and your *laoye* came

back here from his travelling without her. She had died giving birth to your mother, he said.'

My cars pricked up. A southern island? Laoye never talked about his wife – it was as if she had never existed. But I didn't want to reveal any of this to the driver so I kept quiet.

We drove past my aunt's house and I stood up. The driver stopped me. 'You don't know yet, do you? Your grandfather has moved.'

'Where to?'

'He wanted to live alone, and the brigade built him a new house at the edge of the village where the ruins of the nunnery were. Nobody wanted to live there, mind. Folks said it was haunted.'

'Haunted? By whom?'

'A wailing woman. She killed her son, then committed suicide.'

'Why?'

'Why?' He opened his mouth but shut it without saying anything. Then, after a moment, he said, 'It's not really a story for children.'

When we came to a quiet part of the village the driver slowed the tractor to point. 'See? There it is.'

I saw a brick and mud house not unlike others we had passed, but it was big and sprawling, with broken low brick walls extending all the way to the boundary of the village. The front door was pasted with bits of red paper, marking it out as a new house. I thought I could still smell fireworks here.

The driver stopped the tractor, and shouted, 'Dr Lin!' No answer. The door was unlocked so we went inside.

I picked out signs of our old life together to anchor myself. The familiar scent of dried herbs enveloped me, the little statue of the herb-god he prayed to raised its hand in salute, and the bowl he used to wash himself was clean and placed against the wall. Suddenly I felt tired, as the realisation sank in that I'd finally arrived. I wanted to be left alone with Laoye. I turned to the driver. 'I will wait for him here. I will be all right,' I said. I thanked him and bade him goodbye.

Unpacking, I found Steel's red book. I had forgotten to give it back to him. I sat down and flipped through it, feeling as if I was reading someone's diary. The book was well thumbed and inscribed with exclamation marks, some in red or green ink. I struggled with most of the words, but I read on, feeling privileged to have such intimacy. Though I didn't know Steel well, I had glimpsed something personal and important to him.

When I felt hungry, I cooked, the first time I had ever done so without Mother or Ling's supervision. That evening I had grown up, and knew how to keep a secret when I wasn't even sure what the secret was. I waited for Laoye's return as if I was more than his granddaughter. I searched for his white medicine box, and when I couldn't find it, I knew he'd gone to a patient. He might be a long time.

Darkness fell and I sat in it partly because I didn't know where the oil lamp was, partly because I wanted to surprise Laoye when he came in. Dogs barked, but otherwise all was quiet: we were far away from the rest of the village . . . I remembered what the driver had told me about the nunnery, and the woman crying. No, that was just the wind blowing at the papers on the window. Suddenly I did not like the darkness any more.

Then, in the moonlight, I saw a shadow emerge, on the other side of the vast field, from the foot of the mountain, a familiar, upright figure. Had he been to another village? As far as I knew there was no other house beyond this. But as he approached, I forgot everything except that I wanted him to hold me.

'Laoye!' I shouted, and he rushed to me.

'Juju, have I dreamed you?' He scooped me into his arms and I felt as if I'd never left him.

While he was eating I told him everything, including how my stepfather had beaten me. He put down the bowl.

'Juju, my Juju. If only I had known. . .' He couldn't finish the sentence.

When I told him how I had managed to get on the train without paying he laughed and shook his head. I didn't tell him about Stccl, partly because I was puzzled about him and partly because I would not be able to disguise my excitement – I didn't want Laoye to know how much I admired someone else.

When I asked him about Auntie Hu and Uncle Ma his face darkened. 'Something's happened, Juju, but it's too hard to explain to a child like you.' He sighed.

'Why did Auntie Hu have to close her restaurant?'

'I wish I knew. It happened so suddenly. It was almost like a curse.'

'What's a curse?'

'A curse?' He looked at me strangely. 'It's better that you don't understand for now. I'll explain to you one day.'

'She looked so pale,' I said. 'She must feel so sad that she cannot open her restaurant.'

Laoye was silent. After a long time, he nodded. 'Yes, she misses giving people a good meal. I think she is also sad because Uncle Hu is not well.'

'I thought. . .' I remembered that last time we were there, Laoye had said he was recovering well.

Laoye looked troubled. 'He was much improved but suddenly . . .' He trailed off. Then he said it was late and hurried me to bed. Before I closed my eyes, I made him promise never to send me back as long as my stepfather was in our house. This time, I believed him. Then I waited for him to come to bed: there was so much more I wanted to discuss.

Hours later he was still not in bed. I rose quietly and tiptoed to the kitchen. The moonlight was bright so that, even without an oil lamp, I could see what he was doing. He was holding Auntie Hu's blue parcel, sniffing it, with his eyes closed. I came back quickly to bed, as quietly as I could.

Lying there, I tried to work out what that gesture had meant. I knew what was in the parcel – I had been unable to resist the temptation to steal a glance – and had been surprised and disappointed by what I'd found: a pair of brand new children's shoes. Who were they for? Why had she given them to Laoye, and why so secretively? Why was he staring at the parcel as if tears were going to flood from his eyes?

It was a long time before I drifted off to sleep, thinking of

Laoye, Auntie Hu, her husband and the curse. The night was unsettled, with a strange sound that was either the wind howling or a woman wailing, a familiar voice that came closer and closer in my dream, like the saddest song I had ever heard.

17

There were five of us for dinner. The other couple were Mark's colleague, Steve, and his girlfriend, Molly, a nurse. The kitchen window opened on to the downs and I imagined standing at the top and looking down, as we had only weeks ago. Mark had pointed out the house to me then, and I had nodded even though I couldn't see it. But now, with the light on, the house would be easier to spot. It would look so small, but cosy. The heady summer scent of the honeysuckle and grasses outside mingled with the aroma of food. I felt drunk even before we had started on the wine. It was the first time I'd dined out since I'd lived alone, and I had been excited and heartened by the invitation. These feelings distracted me, so it was some time before I realised that Lucy was addressing me.

'More?' She leaned across the table and pointed at the white porcelain bowl of red cabbage. She wore a pink floral shirt and, with her rosy cheeks, she herself looked like a flower. I nodded, even though I didn't much like it, to hide the awkwardness I had felt for the last half-hour. Despite my affection for Lucy and Mark, I could not feel the same for their friends. Molly, who sat next to me, had made little effort at conversation, although her partner had asked what I did. I knew I was partly to blame: half of the time I could not follow what they were talking about. The conversation changed inexplicably in mid-sentence and by the time I had grasped what they were discussing, they had moved on.

'So, do you miss having your feet warm, then?' Molly asked,

turning to Mark as she had all through the meal.

He peered at Lucy, who kept her eyes on the plate from which she was serving me. 'Anything to make Lucy feel better,' he said slowly.

I realised they were talking about the carpet they'd discarded – Mark's prized Persian rug to which Lucy was allergic. I had had a role in this: I had told her that the carpet might be contributing to her symptoms. She had agonised long and hard over it.

'Allergies are such funny things,' Molly continued, between forkfuls of food. 'My sister was allergic to her cat, and she was thinking of giving it away, but then she discovered she was OK after all. The sneezing stopped as suddenly as it had started.'

Lucy said, 'I've got asthma, not an allergy.'

'Asthma, allergy, whatever.' Molly waved a hand dismissively. 'You two have a lot to put up with.'

Lucy blushed and the corner of her mouth twisted. 'Mark has a lot to put up with,' she said, to no one in particular.

'Darling.' Mark reached out but stopped half-way and sat back in his chair.

The clatter of knives and forks was all too audible in the silence. After a long while, Molly mumbled, 'Lucy, you're such a good cook.' Lucy stayed silent.

Steve leaned over to me. 'Tell me what acupuncture's all about. What makes it so special?'

I smiled at him. I liked him better now and wanted to explain, but it was hard to describe the essence of acupuncture. I could explain their own cases to my patients, but at a table with four English people, I felt tongue-tied. I began slowly: 'Acupuncture is only one part of Chinese medicine. In China, one is not fully qualified unless one is familiar with herbs as well. Herbs and needles complement each other, and sometimes herbs are more potent than needles.' I looked pointedly at Mark. Lucy beamed encouragingly, and I was reminded of our first rift. What a long way we had come together from then. Now I thought of her more as a confidante than a patient.

Incredibly Mark didn't seem to grasp my point, or perhaps he hadn't realised that his son had blown his cover, for suddenly his eyes sparkled as if he found all this amusing.

'I've read a bit about it,' Steve said. 'I must say, I'm taken with the idea. I might turn up at your clinic one day.'

'Of course you should, mate. I've tried it,' Mark told him.

'You have?' Molly and Steve spoke together.

'Yes, needles, herbs, moxibustions, the lot,' Mark said. Lucy and I exchanged a glance, and I knew what he would say next. 'The *ah-shi* point,' he added.

There followed a physical demonstration, to exclamations from Steve and giggles from Molly. The noise woke Connor, who came downstairs rubbing his eyes. When he saw our plates of cheese and biscuits he declared that he was hungry, too. His mother cut up an apple for him, which he ate, then demanded to watch his favourite video. Molly yawned, and Mark said, 'No, not now, Connor. This is our time. Go back to bed.'

'No.' Connor stood resolutely at the bottom of the stairs.

'Connor.' Mark's voice rose and Connor started to sob.

'Oh, Connor.'

Lucy rose, but Mark stopped her with one hand. 'Darling, he has to learn. . .'

Lucy brushed off his hand and walked towards the child. She picked him up, then turned to us: 'You carry on, I won't be long.' She took him upstairs.

Molly began to tease Mark about the *ah-shi* point, and then the conversation drifted back to topics I only half comprehended. I knew that they were old friends and had a lot to catch up with, but I felt resentful of the way that Molly kept nudging Mark. His eyes lit up as he drank: he was never as animated with Lucy. Steve tried to engage me in conversation again but now his questions seemed dull and patronising.

We were having coffee when Lucy came down, looking tired. Mark stopped talking to Molly and made her some herbal tea. But she had hardly touched it when we heard the sound of small feet.

Connor came down again and snuggled up to his mother. He was still wide awake after Molly and Steve had left. I sat awkwardly in the silence that ensued in the wake of their departure, wishing I hadn't accepted their invitation to stay the night. When Lucy yawned for the fifth time I had an idea. 'Go to bed, you two,' I said. 'I'll read to him – I'm not sleepy yet.'

To my relief they agreed to my idea. I didn't have to read for long: Connor was tired, and his pale face seemed almost transparent as he stared at his Lego. I recognised that dazed, tired look. I knew from experience with Tiantian that I shouldn't suggest he might be sleepy. He'd drop off quicker without a reminder.

His head drooped low until finally he fell asleep on the carpet. I rose to remove a Lego brick from his hand and wondered where to put him. I doubted that I could carry him upstairs so I laid him on the sofa with a cushion beneath his head.

I stood up to switch off the lights, then went to stand on the porch, gazing at the brightness of the moon. Spring had been so gentle and I could not have imagined that summer would be gentler still. It was hard to believe that this place was only a ten-minute drive from my clinic. On the day we had picnicked on the downs, I had felt an intruder in the family's English Tao Yuan, but here, now, I could almost imagine myself part of it. Somewhere nearby, an owl hooted. I lingered, hoping to hear it again.

At a different sound I rushed back inside. Connor had turned over and now lay dangerously close to the edge of the sofa. I bent down to push him back, but he clasped me to him and I changed my mind and decided to take him upstairs to his room after all. His sleepy body felt heavy and trusting. I held him tightly, closed my eyes and pretended for a moment that he was Tiantian. I was not sure now that she would let me embrace her. How long was it since I had seen her? Two months? Three? It felt much longer.

At the landing I paused: I didn't know which room was Connor's. Then I saw a door left ajar and glimpsed the shape of a rocking-horse. I made for the bed in the middle of the room and was about to put Connor into it when I saw that Mark lay spreadeagled on it. He murmured and turned to the wall. I put

Connor into the gap he'd left. As I turned away, Mark stretched out a hand to me. In his sleep, he had mistaken me for Lucy. 'Mark, it's me,' I whispered. He groaned softly and his hand fell to his side. I smelt alcohol on his breath before I turned to leave the room. On my way out I stepped on a toy, which let out a sharp squeak.

In my room I hurried to wash and went to bed. For some reason I felt scared. What was I doing so far from my home in this family's house? Was it safe to be growing so close to them? My hand tingled as I recalled the feel of their pulses: hers a distant, erratic flow, like a stream, and his heavy and rhythmic, as if his heart was beating there, just below the surface of his skin.

I want to touch it again.

18

'That's right, relax, don't let your hand tremble. There.' For a moment Laoye's hand rested on mine as he lowered his head and murmured, 'There, what can you feel?'

I closed my eyes and thought for a minute. 'It's . . . thin and thready.' I smiled apologetically to Grandpa Ying, whose pulse I was feeling.

'Indicating?' Laoye was unsmiling.

'Both *chi* and blood are weak?'

He nodded. Then, still with his hand on mine, he asked, 'What else can you feel?'

'It's slow.' It reminded me of a very old horse pulling a cart, but I did not like to say that in front of Grandpa Ying. Laoye gazed at me expectantly and I continued my diagnosis cautiously: 'That means it's a cold symptom.' Grandpa Ying nodded emphatically and beamed at me.

But Laoye was not satisfied. His eyes were still on me so I closed mine and felt for a few more minutes. The room was quiet but not quiet enough as I tried to listen to the pulse that was talking to me. Perhaps I was too nervous: my brain was blank.

Laoye breathed heavily. 'Concentrate. What more can you tell me?'

I thought hard. In my mind I pictured the cart as the old horse strained to pull it forward. Suddenly I saw light: 'It's tight, like a stretched rope.'

'Now you were getting somewhere,' Laoye said. He turned to Grandpa Ying. 'And I think our patient here is being very brave. What you have said indicates to me that he is in pain.'

Grandpa Ying shook his head. 'I know I can't fool you. They do say the older the ginger, the spicier it is.' He rubbed his thigh. 'Yes, I do feel some discomfort, but. . .' He turned to me: 'Ha, the hind waves of the great Yangtze pushed the fore waves ahead. She is becoming sure-handed. She'll be better than you when she grows up.' He spoke loudly: he was deaf in one ear.

Grandpa Ying was one of Laoye's longest-standing patients and friends. Arthritis had dogged him almost all his life, ever since he had been caught by bandits as a young boy and imprisoned in a water jail for ransom. Laoye's needles relieved the pain but never cured it.

After the diagnosis Laoye let me put the needles in, at Grandpa Ying's insistence. He said I would never improve if Laoye didn't let me practise. Laoye gave in, but watched me closely. Finally, at his nod, I took out the needles. Grandpa Ying made an appreciative sound and I straightened to wipe away the sweat from my face. Suddenly I felt tired, and my thumb hurt from the intense pressure. I lay back on Grandpa Ying's bed.

After a while I got up and went to the window, pretending to ignore Grandpa Ying, who was still praising me to Laoye. Outside the dried golden corncobs, plaited in a row that hung under the roof, swayed in the wind. It was a common enough sight at this time of year but today it filled me with a special joy. I knew we'd be given some when we left, and this time, whatever Laoye said, I would accept them. I had earned them.

As we took our leave the dog in the yard barked, alerting us to strangers. Grandma Ying rushed out and I glimpsed through the door she'd left open two tall figures with paler faces than those around us. Then a voice spoke: the voice that had left such a deep impression on me when I was on the train. It was Steel and his girl companion, Bell. I hesitated to greet them. Although I had been hoping our paths might cross again, I was surprised to see them there.

They didn't see me at first. 'Hello, Grandma and Grandpa.'

They stood in the middle of the dark kitchen, and mistook Laoye for Grandpa Ying. 'We are here to let you know of the new clinics opening in number-two brigade. From now on, you won't need to travel to the commune if you are ill. We are the barefoot doctors, sent by Chairman Mao.'

Grandma Ying opened her mouth, but said nothing. I looked down at their feet, at the green rubber army shoes that were not different from the ones I often wore. I didn't like wearing mine because, although they were comfortable, they made my feet smell. Barefoot doctors? I didn't understand. Why hadn't they told me this on the train?

Laoye was standing up slowly from the low stool where he'd sat beside Grandma Ying, and as I went to help him Steel recognised me. 'It's you, Juju. I've been looking for you. Is this your house? And your grandfather?' I nodded, then shook my head, and saw that Laoye was confused. I still hadn't told him of my encounter with Steel.

'This is my grandfather, and he's a real doctor, an acupuncturist,' I replied simply.

The smile disappeared from Steel's face, to be replaced by an expression I didn't understand. His eyes narrowed, as if he was trying to remember something. But then he came up to Laoye and smiled broadly. 'Old Ancestor,' he shook Laoye's hand firmly, 'we've heard much about you. I hope you will help us with the clinic. We have so much to learn from you.'

People always respected Laoye for what he did, but Steel's words meant even more than that to me. I felt as if I'd just drunk honeyed water. On Laoye's face, though, I saw the familiar expression of irritation that came whenever he was praised. He did not like to be the centre of attention. Usually I'd explain to the speaker that he was a modest man, but today I felt annoyed.

Stubbornly Laoye kept quiet and the rest of us remained awkwardly silent. Grandpa Ying's head poked out of the bedroom and we heard him cough, then his shoes shuffling. His loud voice reached the kitchen before he did: 'Have they gone? I haven't even said goodbye. Tell Lao Lin that Juju can come and practise on me any time.'

I felt Steel's eyes on me. He said, 'So, you are starting to learn, Juju, how wonderful. You and your grandfather are both welcome to join us in the revolutionary struggle.'

I nodded but tried to conceal my enthusiasm. I was grateful that Steel had been generous enough to forgive me for hiding that I was the granddaughter of an acupuncturist. 'We will be glad to,' I said, hurrying to compensate for Laoye's rudeness.

The dog gave another bark, friendlier this time. 'Who do we have here? Oh, the revolutionary Red Guards.' The brigade leader came in with the smile he usually reserved for visiting cadres. It was plain that he had been informed about the Red Guards' visit despite his surprise. It was strange to see him treat someone so much younger with such deference. 'So you've met Lao Lin, our village herbalist,' he stuttered, 'who sometimes helps us with our ills and pains.' It was as though he was deliberately playing down Laoye's status.

Steel spoke slowly: 'We know all about Dr Lin.' He paused and looked pointedly at Laoye. 'We'll pay him a proper visit some day.' He nodded to Grandma Ying, motioned to Bell and they headed for the door. As they moved past me, I smelt shampoo on their hair, a luxury the local peasants could only dream of. The brigade leader rushed ahead of them, shooing away the dog.

'Those young folk and their big words.' Grandma Ying shook her head as she wrapped some eggs up in old newspapers. 'For you,' she whispered to me. 'Barefoot doctors, I ask you! What is that supposed to mean?'

Laoye gathered up his medicine box. 'It is not a crime to be young. Juju is even younger but, as your husband said, she'll soon be catching up. Perhaps Lao Ying should go and see them one day. They might be able to help him in ways that I can't.'

'Lao Lin, how can you say that? You are our doctor and we will always come to you.' Grandma Ying seemed hurt.

'I mean it,' Laoye said briefly. 'You must.' He beckoned me and we left. Grandma Ying ran after me to press a bag of sweet corns into my hand.

Instead of going straight home, Laoye led us the long way

round the village. The villagers, most of them one-time patients, called out greetings and made appointments for their next treatment. Laoye nodded and responded, and his face, so serious at the start of our journey, began to soften until he had relaxed into his familiar contented self. Usually I was proud to follow him on his rounds but that day I had mixed feelings. I felt as though he was using our walk to restore his confidence. Surely the new barefoot doctors would not affect his status. Steel had said that he wanted to learn from Laoye. It was Laoye who had been rude.

After we had said goodbye to the people at the last house and returned to our own at the edge of the village, Laoye fell silent. As the silence bloomed I grew nervous and kicked stones randomly. 'When did you meet them?' he asked abruptly.

'On the train coming here. They were in the same carriage, but . . . I didn't know they were barefoot doctors. What does that mean, Laoye?'

'Barefoot doctors,' Laoye murmured. 'I've only just heard of them myself. They are young people trained to treat illnesses.'

'Young people like me?'

'Well, yes, though I think they are usually a bit older than you, like those two. How old are they? Seventeen? Eighteen? What are their names?'

'Steel and Bell.'

'Steel? That's unusual. Do you know them well?'

'Not well, but I like him,' I said. 'Why are they called barefoot doctors?'

'Oh,' he smiled, 'they are called barefoot doctors because they are meant to treat ordinary people and shouldn't give themselves airs. You could say I am a barefoot doctor, someone who does not dress like a prince.'

I looked at his plain blue cloth shirt and patched trousers. I thought of the handsome green jacket Steel wore and Bell's pristine white shirt. They were ordinary enough clothes, but their wearers had a style of their own that made them seem special.

When we were almost at home, we glimpsed Steel and Bell

coming out of my aunt's house. 'The sun is going down,' Laoye said slowly. 'Perhaps you should tell them to make their way back quickly or they will have to walk in the dark.' But no sooner had he spoken than we heard the hearty roar of engines and saw a tractor driving towards them. It had the words: 'Number Two Brigade Medical Co-operative Property' written on it. 'So they have transport,' Laoye commented. 'Barefoot doctors indeed.'

'Wait!' I called. I had remembered the book of Chairman Mao's sayings that Steel had left in my luggage, but before I could attract their attention, the tractor roared and was gone. Laoye turned to me. I didn't want to tell him about the book so I avoided his eyes.

At home we found the brigade leader waiting for us. He smoothed the still new bricks and mud, as if admiring the quality of the work, and I was reminded that we were indebted to him for the construction of this house – our home.

He sat cross-legged on the *kang* with Laoye. I cooked the eggs Grandma Ying had given us with some tomatoes. After dinner I withdrew to the kitchen, wiped the wok and the chopping knife, then put them away. I sat down on a stool in the clean kitchen and watched the fire in case it went out. The flames smelt of the dried corncobs that were burning. I smiled as I remembered my first diagnosis. Laoye had always been a kind if strict teacher, but he had only just stopped short of praising me today. I replayed my moment of glory again and again, as if I were chewing a favourite sweet, until I got to the part when Steel and Bell had appeared. Somehow something had not been quite right, although I could not say what it was. It should have been a pleasure to see them after our meeting on the train, but Laoye's coldness to Steel had cast a shadow, although I knew that gruffness was his usual response to praise. I was anxious that Steel should not take it amiss. But there had been something more troubling than awkwardness: something in Steel's expression had unnerved me. I sensed he had some other purpose that he had concealed from us. I was reminded briefly of his severity with the ticket collector on the train. I lit a lamp and, to soothe my uneasiness, I took out the red-covered book.

It took me a while to understand the writing inside the cover: Steel, his name. I turned a few pages and, to my amazement, found that I could read most of the words. But the meaning was another matter, and I allowed myself to be distracted by Steel's notes. Many were short exclamations, but some comments seemed to have no obvious connection with the printed work. On one page, he had written several times, with a black pen, 'unforgivable', beside a sentence about showing no mercy to class enemies. At the top of the page where it said, 'If the duster does not reach, the dust will not disappear of its own accord', he had scribbled, 'Seek them.' It was an enjoyable puzzle that I hoped would bring me closer to Steel.

I put the book down. Next door the adults' voice rose so that I could hear them clearly. It was the brigade leader's voice: 'So we still don't know why such a bright young thing asked to be sent to a backward area like ours, but he certainly had firm support at the provincial level. They say he was the adopted son of Director Li. . .'

'Adopted?' Laoye asked abruptly.

'Well, that's the rumour. Don't go spreading it, though. You know how people feel about being adopted. I'm sure he knows nothing about it himself.'

Laoye was quiet and my heart beat fast. Could Steel have been adopted and not know it? I held my breath and listened for more, but they were quiet.

Then I heard the brigade leader yawn, and shoes shuffling. Quickly I put aside the book and picked up my own writing book. Laoye came in and took the lamp to show out the brigade leader, then returned to the kitchen. He stood over my shoulder to look at the words I had written. Then he sighed. 'Good work. Now go to bed.'

It had been a long day. My head had hardly touched the pillow before I drifted off to an uneasy sleep. But something woke me in the middle of the night, and I realised that Laoye wasn't beside me. I sat up and saw him in the moonlight, kneeling in front of his herb-god statue, motionless.

What was he praying for? Who was in trouble?

19

I'd managed to double-book myself with Mark again. He said he couldn't make it now until he returned from a business trip, in a month's time. On the phone he sounded hurried and I tried to think fast, puzzled by how I could have made the same mistake twice. 'Another month is too long,' I said. 'The first treatment should be followed up.' I decided I could treat two patients at the same time. There was, after all, another couch in the room, although usually it stood folded up against the wall.

Neither patient objected and the other, Mr Robinson, the old man who was fond of talking, seemed to like the idea of sharing a treatment session with someone else. He asked how Mark had hurt himself and began to tell us of his own brush with death in a traffic accident. When I went out to the small storeroom next door to fetch a different size of needle that I seldom used, I could hear his voice from there. I lingered longer in the storeroom, hoping to catch Mark's response, but I couldn't hear him. As I made my way back slowly, I saw how much I had been looking forward to this time alone with Mark, and resolved not to let two patients share a session again. When I had worked in China it had been common practice to treat a roomful of patients simultaneously, but here I had grown used to the luxury of one-to-one.

Mark was silent when I went back into the room. He kept his eyes shut and only answered Mr Robinson's friendly queries with monosyllables. After I had inserted the needles, I felt both men's pulses. Mr Robinson's was as I had expected: weak, fast and superficial. When I had moved over to take Mark's, I noticed that his shirt was crumpled and his face unshaven. Usually he was so neat and tidy. He had told me that Lucy had gone to see her mother in the north, but a grown man like him should know how to look after himself, I thought. His hand felt hot and sweaty, and I remembered the scene I'd witnessed in their house last time I was there. Why had he been on Connor's bed?

I glanced up to the meridian chart on the wall to steady my thoughts. Concentrate, I told myself. What were Mark and Lucy's sleeping arrangements to me? Mark had complained of an ever-present pain, but that was not what I read in his pulse. I spent longer on him, tracing the rhythmic beat, which originated from his heart. What was his pain? Where did it come from?

Mr Robinson told us a story of a man who had had surgery with acupuncture as the sole form of anaesthesia.

'Sounds a bit far-fetched, wouldn't you say?' Mark said suddenly, frowning.

Mr Robinson seemed taken aback. Then he said, 'I believe it.'

'Well, I don't. Acupuncture isn't magic,' Mark grunted.

This was too much for Mr Robinson: 'Acupuncture is one of the world's oldest medical systems, young man,' he said indignantly. 'If you can doubt its efficacy perhaps you're in the wrong place.'

Mark said nothing but I could see that he was fuming inside. When I had taken out the needle and put my hands on his shoulders to massage them, he edged away. 'Don't bother,' he said, stood up and left.

Mr Robinson was slow to leave and I almost lost patience with him. Eventually I helped him on with his coat and sent him on his way.

Later that day I made several errors. First, I insulted Mr Lincoln by pointing out, in Xiao Jin's presence, that if he did not take the right doses of the herbs, I could not be responsible for his sperm count. Then I told a patient enquiring about eczema treatment to consult his GP. When Xiao Jin cautiously pointed out that my manner would send patients away, I had told her to mind her own business.

Xiao Jin left early, and I spent a long time pacing the room, angry with myself. The treatment couch was untidy but I didn't want to touch it. Feeling trapped in the treatment room, I decided to go out.

As soon as I opened the door I saw Mark leaning on the wall opposite. He crossed the road quickly. The sight of him made me angrier. 'You seemed in a hurry to leave,' I said. It hadn't occurred to me to ask why he was standing outside the clinic. Without waiting for his reply I started to walk and heard Mark following. I didn't look back. Traffic flowed past, people returning to their cosy homes, their families . . . I marched down to the canal path, with Mark beside me now, like a shadow. As I walked past the fishermen he was still there, but I found myself slowing. Why was I treating him as if . . . I had walked away like this whenever I was cross with Zhiying. I had used silence as a weapon against him. Better-natured than I, he always gave in, eager for me to talk. But this was no way to treat a stranger and a patient. I turned to meet Mark's eyes, ashamed of my childishness.

We held each other's gaze and then I lowered my eyes, confused. Mark was no stranger, but I wouldn't have called him a friend either. I tried to think of something appropriate to say.

After a long time I heard his voice, slow and tired. 'I want to apologise for my rudeness earlier. I should have said something at the time but your other patient was there and I was. . .' He trailed off. I felt relieved, touched, and was about to express my own regret when he added, 'The fact is, I don't know how to put it and this might sound like an excuse, but . . . as you've probably guessed, things have not been good between me and Lucy.'

I stepped back in alarm and nearly tripped. He reached out and grasped my arm. I steadied myself and pushed away his hand. He walked over to the water's edge and stood there, looking into the distance. Again I noticed how bedraggled he was. Then another image crossed my mind: of his face when he was lying alone on Connor's bed, mistaking me for Lucy. He'd reached out for her . . . It had troubled me ever since. It was so at odds with my picture of their relationship. Even now that I had heard of their rift from Mark's lips, I did not know what to make of it. But I was sure of one thing: a growing sympathy for the man in front of me.

Still facing away from me, he spoke again, his voice soft, as if he was talking to himself: 'I don't know how it happened – we've been together so long. I had a few girlfriends before her but never loved anyone the way I love her. You hear about how couples drift apart as time passes, but I never thought it would happen to us.' He reached up to rub his shoulders, and I was reminded of how he had rejected a neck massage. And yet – I smiled to myself – he had been too stiff to perform even that simple movement earlier. His gesture meant my treatment had been effective. But my smile froze when I saw how sad he looked and I chided myself for being insensitive to his pain. Then he spoke again. 'We moved to the country to have children. When Connor arrived . . . first there was the joy and excitement of being new parents, then exhaustion – the night feeds, no sleep. . .' He looked up at me. 'You must know what I mean. Is this what happened to you and your husband?'

I stared at him. Not even Lucy had spoken to me like this. My first instinct was to back away, to leave him with these thoughts, which should remain private. I almost resented being told something so intimate. He moved closer to me, as if he'd read my thoughts. 'I'm sorry to have said all this,' he said, 'but it's not something I can share with our friends here. . .'

Suddenly I thought I understood what he meant: 'You mean because I'm a foreigner I don't count?' I blurted out, hurt.

'No, that's not what I meant at all. Please, Juju.' He looked at me as if he was seeing me for the first time. Something in his eyes made my heart leap. 'I though you would understand.'

I stared at the water, my mind blank. After what seemed like a long time I heard him again, his voice low: 'I don't know what's happening to us, to me. I don't see how Lucy and I can find the old closeness again.' He looked up. 'Juju, I'm sorry. You're treating us both, and I know how important you are to Lucy. I've no idea why I'm telling you all this.'

Apart from the fishermen we were the only people about. The sun was setting, the still water and the greenery were as soothing as I had always found them. But something was burning inside me that could not easily be cooled. Feeling drained, I searched for somewhere to sit down and saw, just a few steps away, the stone slab on which I had often sat to rest. The first time I had done so was when I had felt the photo of Lucy and Connor in my pocket.

He moved closer but I didn't dare look up. I wanted to run away from him, from all that he had told me, but I also wanted him near me.

'Excuse me,' I said, 'I must go.' I turned for home.

20

It took me no time to get out of the village now that we lived on its edge. I set off early, soon after Laoye had left at dawn to hitch a lift with the tractor on its usual trip to town. He didn't tell me what he had to do. He made these trips often now and always returned tired.

He didn't insist that I told him where I was going – he never did, which saddened me a little. His lack of interest in my movements was new and, whatever the cause, it seemed as if he was almost pleased when I was out of the way.

I left the main track and followed a narrow path to the cliff. I don't know why I thought to look for him in the hidden cave when he had told me he was going to town – perhaps it was the mud and moss I had noticed on his clothes recently, their dampness and the dank smell that hung about them. Perhaps he was storing something secret and precious up there – but if so, why didn't he tell me about it?

I found the cave, which dipped just below the cliff top. This was the *yin* side of the mountain, which sunlight hardly ever reached. The descent into the cave was so steep that I felt dizzy standing on the edge. Laoye had discovered it when he was looking for the elusive *lingzhi*, when he was trying to save someone's life – as the monkey king had discovered his paradise cave beneath a waterfall. Laoye had fallen from the cliff and was saved from death by the branch of a tree. As he hung there, he had spotted the cave mouth.

The cave couldn't be seen from above, which was why it was secret. The first time he had taken me there, Laoye had warned me to watch my step and climb down cautiously. A thick creeper grew out of the rocks and he had taught me to cling on to it and swing down. I took a deep breath and held on. It felt cold and damp in my hand. At first I was nervous, not only on account of the drop, but also because I was doing something he had forbidden. 'Never come here on your own,' he had said. 'Were anything to happen to you, no one would find you until it was too late.' Now I tried to block out his voice.

Eyes closed, I slid down carefully. When my feet felt an opening in front of me, I threw myself forward, trusting blindly that it was the cave mouth. I landed gently, and let my eyes get used to the darkness inside. Of course I didn't expect to see anyone. In the old days Laoye had come here with two other pickers. They had worked in a team to harvest the *lingzhi*, which liked to grow on steep cliffs. Now the other two had died, and Laoye had sworn me to secrecy.

For a moment I sat looking out. It was a cold, sunny day, so clear that I could see almost as far as our house on the far side of the valley. For a moment Laoye occupied my thoughts. I felt close to him here. It was as if this was where his heart was now, not in the house we shared. I could almost feel him breathing. In the house he was my grandfather. Here, he was himself. I thought of what he might be doing now, and of what he might be thinking. Perhaps he was at the town school, asking if I could start next year – it was something he'd often talked about. He could teach me all about medicine and writing, he said, but I should probably learn other subjects and mix with other children. But I felt his heart was not in it: he was doing it because my mother – who had been relieved to know I was safe – had insisted I have a formal education. I couldn't care less about school: I learned all I needed to know from Laoye. Nor did I lack friends: in the village there were several children of my age whose families were too poor to send them to school, and there was my cousin – he was a bit older but we still played together.

I imagined how often Laoye would have rested here, and how pretty the valley would look in the summer, full of colour and fragrant blossom. Then my mind turned again to the *lingzhi:* might this cave be the sort of remote place where it flourished? I started to search but I found nothing, apart from a few dried twigs that must have fallen off Laoye's basket when he had rested there. At the far end of the cave, where the light hardly reached, I found the curious little mound of earth that I had noticed the first time I had come here. I wouldn't have thought anything of it but for the way in which he had murmured to himself as we approached it, almost as if he was talking to someone. He had told me he stored some of his herbs there to keep them cool. I wasn't convinced.

I approached gingerly, and reached out to touch the earth. It was loose. For a fleeting moment I wanted to dig through it to find out what was buried inside. But a noise in the cave made me pause. And then I realised what the mound reminded me of. A grave. I had seen many earth mounds shaped like this in the *yin* side of the Black Hill, which Laoye had told me marked the places where people were buried. I stepped back and shivered. If it was a grave, why was it here?

Suddenly I wanted to get out of the cave. I reached for the creepers and clambered up – easier than going down because I could see where I was going.

I hurried back up to the main path. I thought again of the curious little mound but now I laughed at myself. How could it be a grave? It was not big enough to bury a cat in. Then I heard footsteps coming towards me. Was it Laoye? Or someone else who had discovered our secret cave? The person came into view and I saw that it was Jinni, another local herb-gatherer, whom we sometimes met on the mountains with his basket on his back. He grinned when he saw me. 'What are you doing here?'

'Nothing. . .' I said, then asked, 'What are you doing? Where are you going?'

'Oh, I'm going that way,' he said, pointing to where the path forked out away from the cliff. 'Did you come up from the cliff?

You be careful – it's a sheer drop. It's not called Devil Never Dare for nothing.'

So he hadn't discovered the cave after all.

'Where's your grandfather?' He supported himself on his stick.

'He's gone to town.' I pointed down to the valley.

'Today? Did he forget the market was cancelled? I nearly did.' He breathed heavily.

'I'm not sure.' Laoye hadn't packed any herbs.

'Can't stay at home and do nothing, though,' Jinni continued, as if he hadn't heard me. His basket was nearly half full already, and I asked what he was going to do with the herbs now that the market was cancelled. He shrugged. 'Somebody always needs them. They never go to waste.' He looked at me. 'So, what are you doing? Where are you off to?'

'Number-two brigade.'

He peered at me curiously. 'You know those student doctors from the city?'

'What students?'

'Oh, Red Guards calling themselves barefoot doctors. The boys had hardly developed moustaches, but the girls were pretty enough. I wouldn't trust them with my health in a million years – "Three generations of doctors, then you can trust them," as the saying goes. We all know your *laoye* and he's the one for us. Those young ones? Well, mark my words, they won't last.'

A show of solidarity with Laoye was what I had expected from the villagers, but I was taken aback by the almost universal condemnation of Steel and his friends. No one had given them a chance. Laoye was the only person who hadn't dismissed them out of hand. I refrained from showing my contempt. 'I'm going to see Cousin Guo Li in number-two brigade. He's expecting me,' I said.

Near lunchtime I walked slowly down the hill towards number-two brigade, unsure how I would be received. Would Steel remember me? Would he even want to see me? He had treated me warmly on the train, but last time we'd met, with Laoye, he had been cooler. It was not his importance to others

– the Red Guards who deferred to him on the train and the brigade leaders who treated him as if he were an adult cadre – that made me shy of him, but because I held him in the esteem I had reserved so far for Laoye alone.

There was nothing to distinguish the so-called clinic but the red characters 'Number Two Production Brigade Co-operative Medical Society' painted on the outside wall. A heavy woollen curtain hung outside the door with the words 'Consultation Room' written above it. A huge water jar stood in the dark corridor. Disappointment rose in me: this was like an ordinary peasant house, bleaker than most. I listened, but there was no sound. I flipped up the curtain and knocked on the door frame. Then, when there was no response, I pushed open the door.

I blinked at the brightness of the room and looked around. In contrast to the hallway, the room was spacious, the wall covered with white paint, rather than the usual old newspapers. The smell of antiseptic prevailed. A huge portrait of Chairman Mao sitting in a field surrounded by healthy-looking peasants and golden crops hung on the wall opposite. His face glowed, as did those of all around him. The words at the bottom said: 'Put the emphasis of medical hygiene to the countryside.' A bed with a white sheet stood in a corner, a treatment couch or Steel's bed? Opposite, a wooden shelf was crammed with boxes and bottles with neat labels. It was the cleanest room I'd ever been in, and I felt ashamed now of Laoye's dark, shabby herb store in the kitchen. He was tidy and the herbs were sorted neatly, but it lacked the glamour and professional efficiency of this room.

I hesitated. What to do next? Steel was not there, but evidently he was not far away – I had glimpsed a basin of steaming water in the corner of a little side room, whose door had been left ajar. That must be his bedroom. But what was that little mirror doing by the basin? Only girls used that sort. Then I remembered Bell, whom I had managed to banish from my mind. Was that her room? I thought doubtfully, and turned to face Bell herself, holding a gloved hand to her mouth to suppress a laugh.

My face felt hot as I struggled for words: 'I. . .' I had never dreamt that she, rather than he, would be here. That was stupid of me because of course they worked together.

'What are you doing here?' She arched her eyebrow in that haughty way and I remembered my excuse for coming here. I held out a newspaper-wrapped parcel. She reached to take it but I drew back. 'Actually,' I said collecting myself, 'it's not for you, it belongs to Steel. I need to return it to him personally.'

'Well, well, if you must. But he's not expected back until this evening. He's gone to see a family on the other side of the valley.'

Suddenly I felt so tired. I turned to leave, dreading the climb back up the hill. Besides, I was starving. I paused. 'I'll wait,' I said.

'Till evening?'

I nodded.

'Whatever.' She waved her hands impatiently and it was then that I noticed she wore a pair of blood-stained gloves and the front of her shirt was spattered with red spots. She saw that I was staring, looked down at herself and shuddered. 'Wait here. I need to get changed.' She went inside the little room and slammed the door.

I heard water splashing. then drawers being opened and closed, the rustle of clothes, and imagined her putting on a top, another impossibly white shirt. She didn't seem to wear any other colour.

She came out in a clean white shirt, as I had imagined. I laughed despite myself. 'What's funny?' She frowned.

'Oh, nothing,' I said, feeling foolish.

She sank onto the bed and squinted at me. I shifted uncomfortably from one foot to the other and wished she'd ask me to sit down.

She didn't. She examined her hands, then put them over her face. When she looked at me again, her face was almost humble, an expression I had not seen on her before. 'I'm so tired,' she murmured.

'Why?'

She said slowly: 'I've just delivered a baby.'

'Really?'

'Yes. It was . . . quite an experience – though I'd learned all about it at the training school, of course.' I knew she was really talking to herself, but I listened avidly.

'Nothing, absolutely nothing, prepares you for it,' she continued. 'It's amazing to see a new life in front of you, just like that . . .' Her hands were trembling and I was alarmed by her emotion when usually she was so cool.

'My *laoye* has delivered many babies,' I said, after a few minutes.

'Your . . . *laoye*?' she repeated, with a raised eyebrow. 'Ha, yes – the old man.'

We were interrupted by voices outside and four Red Guards strode in, carrying a big pot that smelt delicious. 'Get your bowls, Bell,' they shouted.

Bell went to help them, ignoring me. They pulled out the table and chairs and fetched the bowls and chopsticks from a shelf. A short man with a black mole on his chin put most of the pot's contents into a bowl for Bell. As she sniffed it he leaned forward to whisper something to her and they giggled. When he looked up he noticed me. 'Who's this? Your little sister?'

Bell turned. 'I'd nearly forgotten that she was there.' She waved a hand at me. 'Come and have some food. You must be hungry.'

I wanted to refuse, but the smell of the steamed rice and soup was too much for me. I went and sat down. Someone passed me a bowl and I started to eat without a word.

A few minutes later, we heard footsteps outside. 'Bell! Bell!' Steel's voice shouted. I put down my bowl as I had suddenly lost interest in the food. Would he be as pleased to see me?

Bell jumped up to greet him, and at first he didn't notice me. 'I'm back early. The patient recovered quickly.' He stood at the door smiling at her and I saw that he was thinner and darker, almost peasant-like, with his shirt sleeves and trousers rolled up.

Bell rolled them down: 'How many times do I have to tell you that just because you're in the countryside, you don't have to behave like a peasant?'

He frowned and made no comment. Then he saw me. 'Hello, Juju, you came at last.'

I struggled not to blush. So he had expected me – he had wanted me to come all along! Trying my best to look serious and businesslike, I handed him the book wrapped in newspaper. 'I've come to return this.'

He took it from me, almost absentmindedly. 'What's that delicious smell? Juju, have you brought us something to eat?' His tone was warm and I almost wished I had been the bearer of the food.

I shook my head. He turned to Bell, and I noticed that the short man and his friends were looking nervously at their feet. 'What is it? Bell?' Steel insisted.

'Chicken, I think,' Bell said, glancing at the short man.

'Chicken? Where from?'

'They caught it stealing our food,' Bell said, gesturing to the others.

Steel glared at the short man. 'Zheng Yi, have you been stealing the villagers' chickens again?'

'It's not stealing. They should make sure the birds don't get out of their yards . . .' the man argued.

'But you've jeopardised all the work we've put into building a good relationship with the people here. Your greed will spoil our reputation,' Steel growled.

Zheng Yi lowered his head.

Steel felt in his pocket, brought out some money and threw it onto the floor. 'Apologise to them and give them that.' His voice was harsh. When Zheng Yi did not move, he stepped closer to him and raised his voice: 'What are you waiting for?'

Zheng Yi murmured something and Steel moved closer to him. 'Speak up.'

'I said it's not fair,' Zheng Yi repeated, defiant. 'It's all right for those who have pretty girls to cook for and wait on them.' He said it in a low voice, but we all heard.

Steel stared at him, then laughed. 'Are you jealous?'

Zheng Yi glared from Steel to Bell, then shouted, 'Jealous? I'm not jealous of a deserted mongrel. . .'

Steel was so quick that I hardly saw how Zheng Yi ended up on the floor with a bleeding nose. The other men rushed to him as he lay there moaning. Bell went to fetch some cotton wool, then bent down to attend to him. When she stood up she said, 'You didn't have to hit him so hard.'

'He asked for it,' Steel said quietly, not even looking at Zheng Yi. 'You're not so innocent yourself, are you? That's why you're defending him, isn't it? Did he sweeten you up with it?' His voice was soft now, but I felt the ice in his words.

Bell's eyes filled with tears. 'We all ate it, including your little running dog there.' She threw me a contemptuous glance.

'Juju?' Steel kept his eyes on her. 'She's just a child. You should know better.'

'Do you think I'm made of steel, like you? Why do you think I'm putting up with all this, starving myself and sleeping in a flea-infested bed?'

'Why?'

'Why?' she shrieked, then dropped the roll of cotton wool and covered her face. 'If you don't know the answer, you're more heartless than I thought.' She ran from the room.

For a moment Steel stood silent. Then he spoke, calmly but with authority: 'Get out of here, all of you.' We started for the door, but Steel stopped me. He motioned me to the couch Bell had been sitting on, then went into the side room and shut the door behind him.

I picked up the roll of cotton wool that Bell had abandoned and put it back on the shelf. My eyes met the portrait of Chairman Mao on the wall opposite. When I had seen it earlier the picture was just a decoration, but now I realised that Steel reminded me of these young men surrounding Mao. He belonged to that ideal world, which I had never experienced. What was more, he had behaved like the heroes of the old days that I had only heard of in stories: the Red Army martyrs who would starve themselves rather than pilfer from poor peasants, like the Nationalists did. His violence towards Zheng Yi didn't bother me – he was simply setting an example to others. Anyway, I didn't like Zheng Yi. The more noise he had made, the more I had taken Steel's side.

The fact that Steel and Bell were in disagreement also secretly pleased me.

Zheng Yi had called Steel a deserted mongrel. It was such a strong insult that anyone would have lashed out. Suddenly I remembered the words of the brigade leader that night when we had come back from Grandpa Ying. Steel's reaction to what Zheng Yi had said suggested that he knew he was an orphan. I was intrigued, but it was not something I could ask him about, and I suspected that Steel would never allude to it.

Quietly Steel walked out of the side room. He'd changed and looked calmer. He held the book I'd returned to him. 'Would you like to keep it?' he said. 'I thought I'd lost it, so I got a new one. Thank you, though, for looking after it for me.'

'I can't keep it,' I said. Should I remind him of the notes he had made inside? But to do so would be to admit that I'd read them. I couldn't risk that.

'No, I want you to have it.' You of all the people I know, he seemed to imply. Overwhelmed, I took it back from him.

'How are you doing in number-one brigade? Do you still like it there?' he asked, and I was flattered. When they saw me most people asked about Laoye first. They never seemed to think I had any life of my own. But Steel was different. I told him everything, chattering away about my daily routines, most of which involved Laoye anyway. I boasted proudly about how I had begun to practise on Laoye's patients and how, as a result, we had started to receive gifts. Steel seemed fascinated so I told him of how Laoye would accept no payment and how his scruples heightened his reputation. That was why, I hastened to add, Laoye had acted so coolly when Steel had met him – he hated to be praised.

Steel laughed with a twinkle in his eye. 'That makes me want to praise him more. What a remarkable man.' I was delighted, and told him about Laoye's other habits, including his bathing and praying. It was all I could do not to mention the secret cave.

When I had stopped for breath he was rubbing his face.

'Are you all right?' I asked, I wanted to smooth the deep wrinkle between his eyebrows – it made him look so much older.

He nodded. After a while he sighed. 'It's so hard, Juju. The countryside is beautiful, but the villagers resent us and I know why. You saw what happened. The others don't understand what I tell them. They are so arrogant. They talk about the peasants as if they are stupid because they don't read and write. I keep telling them to learn from the peasants and treat them with respect, but they don't seem able to.'

Touched by his trust and by his words, I was filled with the desire to help him. 'Laoye can talk to the villagers,' I said boldly. Where my grandfather was concerned, I paid no heed to modesty.

'Why didn't I think of that? He is the one who can bridge the gap, help me to win over the peasants. Do you think he will? Juju, you are closest to him, will you help us?'

I nodded.

Then Steel explained the new initiative he was planning for the co-operatives. The idea was to encourage the peasants to gather herbs, and donate them to the barefoot doctors, who would then use them to treat local people. This would save everyone a lot of money and, with the barefoot doctors' help, we would eventually be able to produce more sophisticated medicines. Did I think it was good idea? Did I think I could persuade Laoye to support it? Of course, I said.

He smiled and squeezed my elbow, a comradely gesture that made me feel grown-up and important. As he rose to fetch some water I realised something else: the admiration I felt for him was now mixed with a new closeness. He seemed to feel it too: when he returned with the water he clicked his mug to mine as if to seal our friendship and I met his smile with a laugh.

I left number-two brigade with a feeling of elation. I hadn't wanted to go but Steel said he did not like to think of me travelling in the mountains in the dark. 'Your grandfather will say I didn't look after you properly if I keep you any longer,' he said, as if he was my elder brother.

I sang all the way home. It had not been just a day in another village: it had been a step into another world, an exciting, modern world that included me. I ran through every moment I'd spent there, anxious to remember all the things I had learned. I gripped the red book Steel had given me: a gift from him, a token of his trust and faith in me.

As I began the downhill trudge to my village it was getting dark. Loud noises and lights came from the central stockyard, where the sweetcorn and potatoes were kept. As I went closer I heard music and laughter, and under a gas light I saw a group of musicians – a travelling opera band. I remembered their visit last autumn, at the end of harvest when the villagers had time to listen and money to pay them. The children were not allowed to join in the fun as the songs were bawdy. I hid behind a low brick wall and watched the adults, my uncle and auntie among them, screaming and laughing and nodding to the insinuating tunes, different from the songs that peasants and other workers sang during the day. This music was full of words that puzzled me about Big Brother and Little Sister, who missed each other all the time. My cousin and I had tried many times to get into the circle, and when we had failed, we clambered on to roofs and other high places to watch. When the adults discovered us we were scolded.

I crouched low and edged closer. I heard a raucous peal of laughter and saw my auntie's sharp profile as she raised her hand to slap at a man's leering face. The music took on a new intensity when he gripped her hand, forcing her close to him. She struggled and slapped him again. Nobody stopped them – not even my uncle, who sat back laughing. I thought of the remark I'd heard on the train on my first trip down about the people in Tu Fei Wo: 'They are descendants of bandits, the men are drunkards and the women, well, they might be good-looking, but their virtue. . .' The man hadn't finished his sentence but, watching my auntie today, I understood what he had meant.

I was pleased Laoye wasn't there, but I wouldn't have expected to find him at such a scene. I rose to go. This grown-up world had lost its appeal. I'd found my own world, full of action and drama. Steel's romantic view of the villagers made him seem even nobler to me.

I got home, cooked and waited for Laoye. As I ate my lonely meal it occurred to me that I knew what Laoye was doing: he'd gone into town to get moon cakes. That was what the music and dance were about. It was Mid-autumn Festival today when we were supposed to eat moon cakes and admire the moon at its fullest.

I waited in the dark, murmuring a poem Laoye had taught me. Then, to pass the time, I opened my writing book. I drew the character for the moon, then the characters for the organs that had moon in them: lungs, liver, kidneys, face . . . and heart. I remembered what Laoye had taught me about their corresponding elements: heart is related to fire, kidneys to water, liver to wood . . . In our world everything is related to everything else and medicine is all about these connections.

I looked down at the paper, full of the words I'd written. There were many moons. I paused over 'yue jing, the moon repetition'. This was something that happened to girls when they reached a certain age: their bodies responded to the movement of the moon. *Yue jing* would be a sign that I was a proper grown-up woman and that one day I would have a child of my own. Laoye had explained it to me and I had accepted it, but later, when I had told other girls in the village what he had said, they giggled. Afterwards, an older girl took me aside and advised me not to use the words *yue jing*. People would laugh at me, she cautioned, and told me that they referred to it as 'the curse'.

I thought of Bell. I was sure she had had the 'curse'. She thought of herself as a real woman, and dismissed me as a child. And I remembered how Steel had described me in front of her – something that I had managed to forget: 'She's only a kid.'

I knew he had meant well, that he had said it to exonerate me for having eaten that stolen chicken. Still, I hated the implication that because I was a child I could never be their equal. The more I thought about it, the more it clouded the day. Perhaps we were not as close as I had thought. Perhaps he had indulged me, as one would a child.

I went over his words again, trying to tease out his real meaning: 'We trust that you will persuade him to join us in this great proletariat struggle of serving the people and purging the superstitious beliefs of the past.' Those had been his exact words to me when we said goodbye on the edge of the village.

I had nodded eagerly, although I only half understood what he meant. No, I decided, these were not words with which one would address a mere child. This was a declaration one would make to one's comrade, one's equal. Anyway, I had proof of his trust in me. I had his book. One would not readily give away something so special, and he had given it to me, not Bell. I comforted myself with the thought.

Late that night I heard Laoye's footsteps, irregular, heavy. I hurried to put the book down. 'Laoye, you must be starving,' I called as I started to heat the food I had cooked and saved for his return.

'Oh, no, I've eaten,' he said apologetically. My heart sank – and further when I saw that he was empty-handed.

He stepped closer and I smelt the aroma of cooking on him. For some reason Auntie Hu came into my mind. Perhaps he had been away so much lately because he had been with her.

21

The phone rang again, with shrill aggression. Could it be the same person who had rung just now and hung up when I answered?

'Dr Lin?' said a man.

'Who are you?'

'A voice from the past.' It laughed, then: 'Don't you know the voice of your own employer?'

'Mr Cheng?' What did he want now?

'Good. I see that you have a better memory than I after all. If I'm right, you're only a few years younger than me.'

'What do you mean?'

'I mean it was stupid of me not to recognise you. That story you told the *Gazette*, it was a pack of lies, wasn't it?'

I gripped the phone and the room closed in on me.

'Dr Lin, are you there? Dr Lin? Don't worry, I won't tell anyone. Rest assured, your secret is safe with me. I can quite understand why you'd want to hide the facts. Please relax.' He giggled. 'Stupid of me not to realise it sooner. Now I think about it, your accent should have given you away. You must have tried so hard to change it.'

Accent?

'And yet,' he sounded puzzled now, 'you've done a strange thing for someone who wants to keep her past hidden. You've adopted his surname. Dr Lin, you could have called yourself anything else, and it would have taken me longer to work it out.

If I remember rightly, he was your maternal grandfather, your *laoye*, is that right?'

So he knew. I remembered when I had made the decision to change my name. It had seemed the most natural thing in the world. How could I practise medicine in any other name than Laoye's? Everything I knew, I had learned from him. I wore his surname like a lucky charm, safe in the knowledge that nobody else could know what it meant to me. But how had Mr Cheng known my secret, and who was he?

'You're confused, aren't you? Let me enlighten you. I was one of the educated youths sent to your part of the world. I wasn't there very long, of course. It's not called Tu Fei Wo, the nest of the bandits, for nothing.' He giggled again.

As he said 'Tu Fei Wo', the air seemed to be sucked out of the room.

'If the newspaper editor hadn't called me to check some facts about you, I would never have realised. But then I started to think. Of course, you didn't know me then – in fact, I don't remember seeing you. I was too busy chasing bigger girls. . .' He belched. 'Oh, it was such a long time ago. But I do remember your grandfather, a most impressive figure.'

Something cold and heavy was creeping up my back. His words came from the phone as if from another world, unreal and frightening. What to do? I couldn't run – not any more: I had been running all my life.

'I went back to the article and put two and two together. I should have remembered much sooner, but . . . well, it's quite an honour to have the granddaughter of such a celebrated asthma expert working in my clinic. I will pay you a proper visit soon. I'm sorry to have neglected you and treated you as an ordinary member of staff.' His tone was sarcastic.

I let the phone slip as he jabbered away. Finally the past had caught up with me in the unlikely person of Mr Cheng. How much did he know? I felt a sharp squeeze of pain. I stood for a moment in the middle of the room, steadying myself. I should switch off the light and go back upstairs, but I was reluctant to do either. I stared out at the darkness beyond the circle of light from the table lamp, at the mass of silence crouching there, waiting to pounce when the light was extinguished. Suddenly I yearned to touch someone.

22

The crowds on their way to the fair in number-two brigade reminded me of the villagers on their way to the market. They had dressed in their best. The baskets, donkeys, horses and wheelbarrows of produce were draped with red flags. Ours were the plainest-looking: neither Laoye's basket nor my schoolbag of herbs was adorned in any way.

When he had asked me where I had been all day that mid-autumn night, I told him about my trip to see Steel and Bell. I hadn't intended to, but I was still angry with him for going to Auntie Hu's and not telling me. I hadn't expected him to respond immediately to Steel's idea of herb donations, but nothing prepared me for his rage when I mentioned Steel's name. Where previously Laoye had been the one to say, 'Give the barefoot doctors a chance', that night he had used rude words. I didn't know what I was doing, going off to see that man like that, without telling him, Laoye said. Did I know what a nasty piece of work Steel was?

His outburst knocked me sideways and I cried. My tears seemed to calm him and he tried to hug me. He explained that he had discovered how dangerous Steel was: he was calculating and cruel; he had done terrible things to some of Laoye's dearest friends, who'd never done anything to invite such misfortune. I asked him who these friends were and what Steel had done to them, but Laoye wouldn't tell me. That night, I sobbed myself to sleep. I had seen how nobly Steel behaved, and now the man I trusted and loved most in the whole world had told me that it was all a veneer. And who were the friends whom Steel had wronged? I recalled Auntie Hu's terrified eyes. Could Steel have been the cause? But then he had only just arrived. Besides, Steel would never do such a thing – I remembered how he had championed the poor homeless boy. Laoye was wrong, so wrong. If only I could convince him.

I saw then that it would be impossible to persuade Laoye to help Steel – he had practically forbidden me to mention his name. But we soon heard from the brigade that all farming families were to donate herbs to the new medical co-operatives, and the leader came specially to Laoye to warn him of the danger in not obeying orders. People would be watching him, he advised. So, we prepared the herbs as we were told. I felt ashamed that I could not fulfil Steel's request: instead of leading the herb donation, we had become its least active participants. The thought of Steel's disappointment was unbearable, but I dared not show it in front of my grandfather.

From the animated conversations of those around us, I gathered that today had been a traditional day of harvest thanksgiving. They talked about dances, markets and visiting musicians who had told traditional stories. But the brigade leader, who was among us, had warned that no such things would be allowed, and reminded us that, despite the coincidence in date, this was to be called Herb Donation Day. He briefed us on the forthcoming meeting at number-two brigade to study a quotation from the works of Chairman Mao and to celebrate the official opening of the new clinic. But for all this, I saw people surreptitiously carrying goods they must have hoped to sell: eggs, dried meat and seeds. Even the brigade leader's wife had a bag that I recognised as one in which she put dumplings to sell at the market. Perhaps, despite what the leader said, some transactions would be carried out and there might be some fun and colour, apart from the monotonous red flags.

Near the foot of the hill we heard the beating of drums. An even bigger crowd from number-two brigade greeted us, headed by a giant placard of Chairman Mao carried by a dozen young men. We followed it and the procession made its way slowly but steadily to the centre of the village. I stole a glance at Laoye: the atmosphere had had no effect on him – he seemed to be in a world of his own. Occasionally he shut his eyes when the shouting of slogans and beating of the drums became too loud.

Soon the stream of people came to a halt and we children ran ahead to investigate. We saw another crowd heading our way, holding a figure almost as large as our placard, made of grass, flowers, twigs and fruit. The bearers were the village elders, some so old that I had thought them dead. Their appearance cast an air of ceremony, even gravity, over the proceedings. There was a sudden hush.

Slowly we heard the chanting: 'Yao Ren, Yao Ren, the medicine man, the medicine man.' Soon more voices joined in, chanting in unison. Children scuffled for a better view and before long even the bearers of the Chairman Mao placard had come to admire it. Someone tapped my shoulder and I turned to see Laoye, smiling broadly. 'Come on.' He nudged me. 'Let's go and meet the Yao Ren.' He pulled me after him.

A familiar voice called Laoye's name. It was Uncle Ma, the chemist from town, one of the bearers of the Yao Ren. Laoye raised a thumb at him: 'Lao Ma! I thought I would never see anything like this again.'

Uncle Ma beamed. 'It was the elders' work, mainly. Their talk of the old days gave me the idea, and when I suggested it, everyone fell for it.'

People were relaxing after their initial surprise at the arrival of the Yao Ren. They chatted loudly, forgetting their slogans and revolutionary songs. They called out to acquaintances and relatives, slapping each other's shoulders and joking about each other's secret baskets and bags. 'Of course it's Yao Ren, you remember Yao Ren,' one villager said, and another answered, 'The last time the Yao Ren was made, Jinni had his wedding. . .' I watched Laoye whispering animatedly with Uncle Ma. What was the Yao Ren and why was everyone so excited?

Jinni, the herb-picker, appeared out of nowhere and grabbed my hand. When I struggled he whispered, 'Ssh. Go and touch the Yao Ren – everyone else is. You touch it for luck. Then you won't be ill for the whole year. Go on.'

I reached out a hand tentatively to feel the cool prickly leaves, then turned back to Laoye. Would he mind? I couldn't see him anywhere and Jinni was gone too, swallowed up in the crowd. The old days. I mulled over Uncle Ma's words and tried to imagine what they might have been like.

'Move along! Move along!' someone shouted, and soon the Yao Ren joined Chairman Mao at the head of the procession towards the central stockyard where the commune leaders sat on a red cloth-covered platform. Steel and a man in green army uniform with only one arm were among them. At our approach, the dignitaries stood up to greet us. But as we came closer I saw the look of horror on Steel's face. He said something to the man beside him, but I couldn't hear what it was. A few Red Guards congregated around him and came our way, gesticulating wildly.

I glanced around wondering what had caused the commotion. My eyes came to rest on Chairman Mao's portrait and I wondered if it had been damaged.

But the Red Guards went past the placard and headed for us. They stopped in front of Uncle Ma. 'Stop this immediately,' a guard ordered, hands on his hips.

'Why? I thought we were celebrating the donation of the herbs to the commune,' Uncle Ma stated.

'But what is that?' The guard pointed contemptuously at the Yao Ren towering above him.

'It's Yao Ren, the medicine man, a village tradition – we made it to mark the herb festival,' Uncle Ma answered.

'How dare you raise a feudal relic to the same level as our beloved chairman.'

'Feudal relic?' Uncle Ma repeated. He lowered his head as if he was thinking, then raised a hand and said, 'Chairman Mao teaches us, "Traditional Chinese medicine is a treasure. We must utilise it to help the people." Haven't you studied his latest teaching, young man?'

There was a sudden burst of laughter. The Red Guards

retreated to the centre of the stockyard and Steel. The crowds cheered Uncle Ma and I saw Laoye smiling.

I stood apart. Fond as I was of Uncle Ma, I felt uneasy about the tone in which he had spoken. People began to pile the red-covered table in the centre of the stockyard with herbs. They walked with their heads high, their baskets and bags aloft as if they were being photographed. Drums sounded as each placed his or her offering on the table.

I watched the performance half-heartedly, catching frag-ments of Laoye and Uncle Ma's conversation: '. . . self-criticism . . . confession . . . asking questions about . . .' Laoye looked worried. Once in a while they both stopped talking and glanced silently at the platform where the leaders were sitting. I tried to work out what they were talking about. Who had been made to confess? Who wanted to know what?

Now the commune secretary stood up on the platform and read a long speech about Chairman Mao. I caught the eye of a schoolgirl in a bright yellow costume, one of the dancers who would perform later. Children were chatting to each other all around her, but she had no one to talk to. Why? I felt sorry for her – there was nothing worse than being alone in a crowd.

I didn't recognise the next person on the platform. He talked in a ragged local dialect, stealing furtive glances to left and right as if seeking approval. It took me a while to understand the gist of his speech: in the old society he had suffered from arthritis while working for the exploitative rich landlords, and had found it hard to get help. Now, the young doctors whom Chairman Mao had sent had cured him with just 'a needle and a bunch of herbs'.

'It's Grandpa Ying,' I whispered to Laoye, as the man started rolling up his trousers to show where the needles had gone in. 'Laoye, he was cured!'

'Cured?' Laoye sneered. 'Watch him walk.'

He walked straight and easy through the applauding crowds. But when the clapping finished and the next speaker stood up, I saw him try and fail to sit down. He winced and stood leaning on his walking-stick instead. He was far from cured, so why had he lied?

Laoye whispered, 'You see that? This is what your hero has done, he has turned my old friends and patients into liars. He is a bully, that young man, and he's done worse than this.'

'How do you know it was Steel who made him lie? And why are you being so mysterious, Laoye? What else has he done?' I asked anxiously. Laoye said nothing, so I persisted: 'Laoye, tell me, what has he done that's so terrible?'

Laoye hissed: 'Forcing people to lie – is that not bad enough? And I don't care what he does to me – he can spread all sorts of rumours, discredit me and my reputation – but he's hurt someone I care about very much and I won't forgive him for that.'

'Who? Tell me,' I asked, although I knew he must mean Auntie Hu. Laoye stared at me in silence. 'It's not true, is it?' My voice trembled. 'You're just jealous of him, because he's younger and more successful than you.'

Laoye's back stiffened and he glared at me. Uncle Ma, who had been listening intently, bent down to me and whispered, 'Juju, you don't know what you're talking about.'

'I do!' I said, almost hysterically. Now that I was beginning to speak my mind I no longer cared that I was upsetting Laoye. 'I've seen Steel defending the peasants and trying to discipline the Red Guards. He's a good man!'

People were peering at us curiously as my voice rose. Laoye shook his head, and Uncle Ma stared at me with disbelief.

I felt so alone. Part of me wanted to beg Laoye's forgiveness, but I was angry too. I'll show you I'm not a child any more, I thought, and stormed off.

After I had gone a safe distance I looked back. I could still hear the speeches on the stage as they were relayed by the loudspeaker, although the people on the platform were just dots. Now I could make out figures in bright yellow and red and realised that the girls must be doing their sunflower dance. 'Chairman Mao is the sun,' they sang, 'and we are the sunflowers. We thank you, our dear beloved leader. . .'

176

An old man standing all alone beside me murmured, 'It used to be the gods we thanked. Now it's Chairman Mao. . .' His voice was drowned by the song. Suddenly finding it all too much, I covered my ears and walked off.

It was getting dark and all around me people were drinking and chatting, enjoying the opportunity to get together with family and friends. Word spread that the village canteen was open for dinner, so I followed the crowds into the simple wooden barn and joined the queue. Beer was being served and soon men and women were red-faced and laughing. In one corner, a woman was sobbing, with a group of others. As I went closer she began to shriek, 'Give me back my baby!' Those around her echoed, 'Yes, you want your baby back.' Noisily they made their way towards where the Red Guards were sitting. When Bell stood up they surrounded her and the sobbing woman clutched at a corner of her jacket. Bell struggled free and looked haughtily at her, eyebrow raised. The woman caught her arm: 'Killer! Killer!'

'What do you mean? Get off me!' Bell said.

'You killed my baby!' the woman shouted, and spat on Bell.

Bell leaned backwards, looking frightened now. 'Let me go – it wasn't my fault he died.'

'You were the doctor, weren't you? You were responsible.'

'Babies die sometimes – everyone knows that. . .' Bell protested weakly, but her voice was drowned by the shouts of angry women. 'Killer! Killer!' Then, 'We want revenge, we want revenge,' they bellowed, pointing at Bell.

Bell retreated to a corner and the crowd closed in on her. She raised a hand and her eyes darted around wildly. I ran for help. I searched for the Red Guards, but an even bigger crowd of drunken men had formed around them chanting, 'Thieves! Thieves!' I had no idea what an angry crowd might be capable of, but I had seen how my auntie behaved when she was drunk. I headed for the exit and ran to the platform. All of the commune and brigade leaders were there – there would be more Red Guards, and perhaps Steel . . . As I ran, an image crossed my mind: Bell's blood-stained gloves when I had chanced upon her at the clinic. The blood grew redder in my memory and made me run even faster.

I bumped into Steel. The look in his eyes told me that he knew what was happening. 'Steel, quick, Bell – the villagers—' I caught my breath and coughed.

He nodded, and touched my shoulder. 'Don't worry, Juju. Calm down.' With that he turned and walked steadily towards where Bell and the crowds were, accompanied by two Red Guards.

I stood where I was, reassured by his calm. I watched as he reached the grieving woman, and whispered to her. Suddenly there was a hush: it seemed everyone knew how important Steel was.

'I understand your feelings,' Steel said loudly to the grieving, drunken woman. His voice was slow and solemn. 'I know that nothing I say can bring back your baby. I'm so sorry.' He glanced at the crowd. It seemed to me that in that swift movement he captured everyone's attention. Suddenly, he dropped on to his knees in front of the mother and hung his head: 'It was my decision that Bell should deliver the baby. If you want revenge, punish me. I am responsible.'

She waved away Steel's words and knelt beside him. 'No, no, no,' she kept saying tearfully, and suddenly tears came into my eyes, too.

Steel's voice rose again: 'I know we are not the most accomplished doctors yet, but both Bell and I have always tried our best for all our patients. We practised the needles on each other and would never use any herbs without tasting them ourselves.' He paused and caught my eye. I smiled at him through my tears, willing him to win over the villagers. He continued: 'I do not want to sound as if I am trying to find an excuse, but it is our duty to perfect our skills as barefoot doctors. Chairman Mao has sent us to serve you, the people.' He stood up and motioned to Chairman Mao's portrait. Then he turned to the bereaved mother: 'What we lack in experience we make up for with dedication. What we ask from you,' he lowered his head again, 'is a little patience.'

I sighed with relief as I watched the woman nod. It seemed that the crisis was over. Steel took her hand. 'Auntie, may I be permitted to pay my respects to the little brother?' he asked.

The woman burst into fresh tears. She lifted the corner of her jacket to dab at her eyes. 'There is no need,' she sobbed. 'He's dead, and there's nothing anybody can do about it.'

Steel led her to a chair, where she sat down, still snuffling. The tension dissipated as conversation resumed in a low murmur. Feeling the warm glow at Steel's goodness, I hurried through the crowds to the front, eager to be with him. But before I reached him, I heard new voices coming from the entrance. I craned my neck and saw Laoye approaching with Uncle Ma and some others. At the sight of him a woman shrieked, 'But we wanted to fetch Dr Lin to help! He knows about childbirth. Why didn't she let us?'

'Yes, why didn't she let us?' another voice shouted from somewhere in the barn, and the village women raised their fists and protested. I tiptoed away to search for Steel and saw that he was now with Bell, whispering to her. At the sound of more angry voices he raised a hand and I saw his lips move in an attempt to calm the women. But this time they ignored him and carried on shouting, pointing at Bell. I had never liked Bell, but the look in her eyes made me want to beg Laoye for help. I knew that he was the only person who could calm the villagers now.

Then my heart sank. Laoye would not be on Steel's side. I searched anxiously for him and saw that he and Steel were staring at each other across the barn. I was struck by how similar their expressions were: the knotted eyebrows and the intensity in their eyes. Then Laoye went to the mother. The hall quietened once more. 'Dr Lin, Dr Lin,' I heard them whisper, and felt the authority his name carried.

Like Steel, Laoye spoke quietly: 'Sister Yan,' he said to the woman, who was looking up at him like a helpless child. 'They did send for me.' He paused and hung his head. The crowds murmured in surprise. 'I should have come sooner. I stayed away because I was told that, despite her age, the girl was an experienced midwife.' He glared at Bell. The chill in his eyes made me shiver.

Bell had paled, and now I remembered she had told me that she had never delivered a baby before. Was I the only person who knew this?

Steel squeezed Bell's shoulders, a protective gesture that I found both touching and uncomfortable to witness. 'Bell has all the qualifications a barefoot doctor needs,' he said, in a hoarse, sharp voice. 'How experienced would you expect a sixteen year old to be? I know plenty of twenty year olds who would faint at the sight of a needle. Bell has had to learn the hard way.'

Bell burst into tears and my heart went out to her. I remembered how Ling and I used to talk about having babies and how frightened we were by the idea of birth. But Bell, who was the same age as Ling, had delivered a baby. She must have been terrified.

But Laoye's voice was unrelenting: 'These are matters of life and death. Experience is paramount.'

There was a long silence as Steel stared at him. Then he sauntered towards the grieving mother and stood near Laoye on the other side of her. He addressed her as if Laoye wasn't there. 'Dr Lin is indeed experienced,' he said coolly. 'So experienced that he has never made a mistake and lost a baby in his care.' He looked Laoye in the eye. 'Have you, Dr Lin?'

I understood Steel's words, but there was something in them that eluded me. But I had no time to think about it: Laoye's face turned ashen and he gripped the woman's chair. Uncle Ma stepped up to steady him, and there was chaos as people flocked around him. I pushed my way through the crowds and when I reached him his eyes were closed. I didn't know what to do. Steel was hovering close by, evidently bewildered, with Bell beside him. For once, he had lost his cool.

Uncle Ma took charge. 'Lay him down,' he ordered and they laid Laoye flat on the ground. Uncle Ma tried to revive him, pressing the *ren zhong*, the point between Laoye's nose and upper lip. I searched his medicine box, brought out the needles and stuck them into him. I called his name desperately and

Uncle Ma told me not to panic. He said Laoye had fainted because he had been tired and weak after the long climb on an empty stomach. The emotional scene had been too much for him.

Laoye stirred. When he opened his eyes I held his hand tight and pressed my face to it. 'Laoye,' I whispered. I was sure my storming off earlier had contributed to this. I had never treated him like that before. For a moment his eyes held mine and I saw that he was looking for something. But when I bent down to ask him what it was, he said nothing. Uncle Ma told someone to fetch some soup for him from the canteen. After he had drunk it, he lay in Uncle Ma's arms with his eyes closed.

A little later, we moved him to a warm shelter by the Yao Ren, and I snuggled next to him. A fire was lit, and soon friends and patients congregated around us. A Red Guard even came to ask how Laoye was, claiming Steel had sent him. I dared not tell Laoye as I feared the mention of Steel's name would make him angry again, so I said to the guard that he had recovered. He nodded and walked slowly away.

As the night drew on the crowds dispersed. The wind died down as the moon rose higher. 'Harvest moon,' Laoye murmured. He seemed to have forgotten our earlier arguments, and pointed to the Yao Ren, telling me the names of the herbs woven into the giant form. Once in a while I would pluck out a leaf or a twig at Laoye's bidding. I felt almost as if the giant figure was alive and breathing, and hastened back each time to the safety of Laoye's arms. There I lay, hypnotised by the rich fragrances mingled with the smoke from the fire, and the music of the travelling band who came to play for Laoye. The lead singer, who was blind, performed unaccompanied, stopping occasionally to cough. Another man clanged the gongs from time to time, almost absent-mindedly. Despite the lateness of the hour, a small group of villagers remained, huddling round the fire. Nobody sang or giggled: they were all intent on listening to the words. I couldn't hear them clearly, but the tune spoke to me, a sad melody that was as insistent as a beggar, who wouldn't leave me alone until I had given him something.

I watched the faces of the people around me. They included the grieving mother and a few of her friends, their bags empty now that the herbs had been handed in. The seeds and fruit were gone, too, I noticed, and wondered how the transactions had been made without my noticing them. Was a secret market going on despite the orders of the brigade and commune leaders? How had they managed it? I sensed that I was glimpsing another world here – a secret world, like Laoye's cave – full of mysteries I could not understand. It was a world from which the adults excluded me, for my own protection.

Against the fire the villagers' eyes were dazed and their faces softened. It was hard to believe that they were the same crowd that a short time ago had demanded revenge. The proof of their respect for Laoye comforted me, but I felt guilty that I had sided with Steel and his Red Guards.

The music continued. But while the blind man's chanting seemed to touch a sad place deep inside me, I knew that I could never truly comprehend his story: it belonged to a world I could not enter.

23

'How is she coping?' Xiao Jin asked.
    'Fine,' I said, peering at Lucy.
    'I don't envy her,' Xiao Jin said, fanning herself. The small window opposite the couch was open and the door to the treatment room stood ajar. But still it felt hot. Lucy's half-naked body was covered with the warm ginger paste I had made especially for her. On the hottest day of the year she was stuck in a tiny room with a hot compress covering her body. Whatever made her trust me enough to suffer this? I had explained the principle of the treatment – that her type of cold asthma responded best to hot treatment on the hottest day of the year – but, I had expected her to protest. However, as she had on her first visit, she seemed to accept what I said.
    When I removed the paste she sighed, as if only now feeling discomfort. The smell was more pungent because the paste had baked itself to her skin. I, too, sweated as I wiped away the residue with cotton wool. Her skin looked red and sore.
    After she had dressed, I walked her to Xiao Jin in the reception area. I wondered how long I could continue to see her yet think of Mark. I wanted to cut short her treatment, but she was already booking her next appointment with Xiao Jin. She turned, radiating health, to thank me. 'Well, that was . . . hot,' she said, smoothing her hair. A sense of normality returned. She asked, as she had before, how my daughter was. She talked about Tiantian as if she were with me, rather than in China,

thousands of miles and many hours away. Usually I found her concern soothing, but today I found it intrusive and painful.

'Is Tiantian on holiday now?'

'Yes,' I said.

'And she starts school in September?' she asked, unaware of the change in my mood.

'Yes.' I nodded. 'How's Connor? How's his eczema?'

That took her attention away from me and my family. There followed a long list of Connor's symptoms and remedies recommended by friends or family. Lucy was not just into acupuncture but other 'alternative medicines'. The latest was homeopathy, which was 'not dissimilar to acupuncture' in principle.

I listened, but I wasn't taking in all that she was saying. My sympathy with Connor's condition was bound up in its similarity to my daughter's. Yet, it wasn't Connor I felt close to but Lucy. My affection for her had brought me closer to her family. But now a member of that family had taken a step away from them and come closer to me, and I did not know how to handle it. Instead of pushing away Mark, I wanted to run from them all.

Later that day the weather changed. The sky was dark and pressed down low, as if in anger. I felt restless but decided not to risk a walk: it was plain that a thunderstorm was imminent. I walked instead from room to room, but could not settle. I longed for company, and thought of ringing Xiao Jin, who'd left for the day, then laughed at myself because we had already exhausted any small-talk.

I lifted the curtain upstairs. Lucy had made me look at the street outside while before I had been content to read the few Chinese books I had brought with me, safe and happy in my own world. I had eaten most of my meals in their company. But since I'd met Lucy, even though I wouldn't talk to other people, I had started to wonder about them: the postman was a cheerful young man who wore an earring, which puzzled me; he sang to himself and was growing a beard that I thought too old for him. Occasionally he'd smile at me, which was when I dropped the curtain and hid behind it.

I had so few friends.

Mercifully the suffocating closeness did not last: rain splashed down and gave me an excuse to dash round the house, shutting windows. In the steamed-up treatment room I was enveloped in the smell of the ginger paste I'd used on Lucy. The close air had a sourness that was almost tangible. I could feel her presence there. I bent down to where her head had left a dent on the pillow and put my hand on it.

She shouldn't place so much trust in me. I was not to blame for her unworldliness.

24

I was worried about Laoye. Since the herb-donation fair, he had been a changed man. It seemed that collapse at the barn had not only harmed him physically but had affected his personality. Before that day he had been self-effacing but quietly proud; now he was suspicious and jumpy, and fell into a rage at the slightest provocation. I kept replaying that night in the barn, going over everything that had happened, but I could not understand why Steel's question had had such a profound effect on him. I watched him closely and nursed him with herbs that he'd taught me to use, and was pleased when he improved.

But just as things were looking up, an order came from above, forbidding those without formal medical qualifications to treat people. The brigade leader came to warn us that, as a traditional doctor, Laoye should be extra cautious: he was exactly the sort of person at whom the order was aimed. Overnight he seemed to lose his soul. He wandered the village like a ghost. Normally he would have been called here and there for a consultation or a chat, but now all doors were shut to him. Even Grandpa Ying didn't see him any more. Laoye spent a long time standing in front of the herb-god statue. I tiptoed round him. I wanted to see Steel and ask him all sorts of questions but thought it wise not to antagonise Laoye by mentioning it. It would not be so easy to visit him without Laoye's knowledge because now he stayed at home all day.

As he recovered, Laoye started going frequently to town,

which seemed to agitate him: he'd come back coughing and heaving like an old man. Uncle Hu had been unwell again, he said, when I asked where he'd been, and as an old friend he was doing his best to help. I asked him how Auntie Hu was, and he told me that she herself was unwell too. When I suggested that I should go with him to see them, he said he would take me.

Even though this was only the third time I'd met Auntie Hu, she made me feel as if I'd known her for years. Laoye must have talked to her about me, even before he decided to take me to the countryside. But beneath the smell of the lunch she was cooking, I picked up the stale, thick odour of sickness – the herbal brew Uncle Hu must be drinking. What was his mysterious illness, and what had caused it? I sat in a corner, wondering, while Laoye and Auntie Hu chatted.

A knock at the door interrupted my thoughts. It was Uncle Ma. He looked even thinner than he had the last time I had seen him. Neither Auntie Hu nor Laoye seemed surprised by his arrival. It was obvious that they often met like this.

We sat round a big table. A poached egg floated on top of each bowl of noodle soup, and we began to eat. 'I need some *gan cao* for Brother Ying,' Laoye said to Uncle Ma, when he put down his bowl.

'I'll bring some tomorrow. What else?'

'Some *ren dong teng* would be helpful, but I don't want to make trouble for you.'

'Trouble?' Uncle Ma laughed. 'What more trouble can I get into? They couldn't take much more away from me now. I must say, I rather enjoy not running the place any more. It was nice treating people at the front desk, I miss that, but I hated all those political meetings and now I can escape them. It's you who should be careful. Are you sure it's wise to carry on practising?'

What did this mean? What had Uncle Ma done wrong? Had he given someone the wrong herbs? That was the only reason I could think of for his dismissal. And what was this about Laoye practising? Did 'Brother Ying' mean Grandpa Ying? If Laoye was treating him again, he must be doing so secretly as I'd not seen them together. Suddenly I remembered those quiet knocks after dark and the whispering in the kitchen. People had come for treatment when they thought they weren't being watched.

'Lao Ma, Lao Lin.' Auntie Hu put down her chopsticks.

I noted how tired they all seemed. This meeting was such a contrast from the last one, when Laoye and Uncle Ma had bantered, joked and behaved like naughty children. Now they looked their age. Perhaps, as Laoye had often said lately, I was growing up.

Laoye murmured something through his teeth and I thought I heard Steel's name. Auntie Hu frowned at him warningly but Laoye protested, 'It's time she knows what that boy is up to. This silly girl still thinks he's a saint.'

My face burned. I did not like to be reprimanded in front of Uncle Ma, but I did not want to protest and upset Laoye – his collapse at the barn had frightened me so much. Besides, we were in Auntie Hu's house and I should refrain from showing anger. I pretended I hadn't heard him. But he continued, 'She needs to know.'

'Lao Lin, calm down,' Uncle Ma said. 'You don't want to frighten her.'

'Frighten her? If I don't watch her every day she'd run to him at the first opportunity. I want her to see sense.'

Laoye coughed again. He gulped down the glass of wine Auntie Hu passed him. 'I've been practising all my life, and now I have to apply for permission to treat my patients. You yourself, in giving up all your property to the country, to the poor, have been humiliated. Why does he hate us all so much?'

'Well, we can't be sure it was him,' Uncle Ma murmured.

'Can't we? I'd bet you anything he was behind your dismissal and my disqualification. As for Sister Hu, I'm even more sure. Isn't he the leader of all the Red Guards in this area? How could they do what they did to her without his knowledge?'

'Lao Lin, calm yourself. You are confusing Juju,' Auntie Hu chided and took away Laoye's wine glass.

Laoye looked at me, breathing heavily. 'I'm not that old yet. I can still pick out a fish eye from among pearls.'

I sat in silence but the questions kept forming in my mind. I had known about the order that forbade Laoye to practise, but that had applied to all doctors who were not formally educated, so Laoye could not take it personally. But was Steel really responsible for Uncle Ma's downfall? Surely there had been a misunderstanding. How could a young man have such power? He was barely older than Ling. I bit my lip and said nothing. I knew that when Laoye was angry he would not listen to me.

'Neither of you deserves this,' Auntie Hu said softly, looking from Laoye to Uncle Ma.

Uncle Ma shook his head. 'It's not just us – you know what things are like nowadays. No one is safe. Quite a few old friends of mine . . . Anyway, let's not talk about these unpleasant things. Life must go on. I'm fine, I assure you.' He turned to her. 'You must look after yourself. You must be strong for Brother Hu.'

'I know.' Auntie Hu nodded. 'I must go and give him his medicine.' She left the table and went upstairs.

Laoye followed her swiftly, without a word to me. I was left with Uncle Ma, who was tapping his chopsticks impatiently. I had a sense of *déjà vu*. But I was not that naïve little girl any more. I rose to follow Laoye. As last time, Uncle Ma tried to stop me, but I stood my ground. 'I want to be with my *laoye*, Uncle Ma. Please let me through.'

'He is working. He is not to be disturbed.'

'He likes to have me with him when he works. It is how I learn. Besides, don't you think it's time I met Uncle Hu?'

He sighed deeply and stepped aside.

My heart beating fast, I tiptoed upstairs. The mosquito net had been flipped open and Auntie Hu was leaning over a man lying prostrate. I edged closer. He had the palest face I'd ever seen, like rice paper. His large, vacant eyes, though wide open, did not seem to see. At the sound of my footsteps Auntie Hu glanced over her shoulder and beckoned me to her. She took my hand. 'This is Juju, Brother Lin's granddaughter,' she whispered, and the corner of the man's mouth stretched as he tried to speak. She leaned close to him, nodded, then straightened. I smelt something familiar and realised that Laoye was standing beside me, but the hushed atmosphere held me still.

He, too, bent over the sick man, and listened to the laboured breathing, nodding, frowning, as if he understood. Then he reached for Uncle Hu's hand, his expression familiar now – that of an attentive doctor.

I was puzzled. How could Laoye understand him? All I could make out was a soft grunt. It was as if Uncle Hu was talking through a thick mask.

When Uncle Hu was quiet, Laoye went to a little side table, next to a bed with a floral cover, where Auntie Hu stood gazing out of the window. I followed him, not daring to stand alone near the sick man. 'He's not at all well,' Laoye said, in a low voice. 'Does he eat much?'

'Hardly anything,' Auntie Hu said. 'I think he could, but he won't.'

Then Laoye said softly, 'And you?'

Auntie Hu did not reply. Just carried on gazing out of the window as if the answer lay somewhere outside. They were separated by the side table, but somehow, I felt, their bodies touched. It was as if a magnet drew them close, that despite themselves they had to be together. Suddenly the jealousy I had felt when I first met Auntie Hu returned. I went to them, wanting to come between them.

Startled, Auntie Hu turned and knocked a saucer off the side table. As she reached down to pick it up, her sleeve fell back and I saw a red mark on her arm. 'Auntie Hu!' I exclaimed. She hastened to cover herself, but Laoye stepped up and held out her arm for me to see. 'What is it, Auntie Hu?' I asked. 'Were you bitten by a wolf?' I knew what wolf bites looked like as I had been with Laoye when he had treated one.

Her eyes searched Laoye's, as if for an answer.

'Oh, this is worse than the work of a mere wolf,' Laoye said, between his teeth. 'It was your friends the Red Guards who did this. Your Steel.'

'Are you sure?' I sucked in my breath and turned to Auntie Hu.

She shook her head. 'It was a bunch of Red Guards I'd never met before.'

'But why?' I watched her closely.

Laoye said indignantly: 'She'd done nothing to deserve it, nothing.'

'Surely you are mistaken about who did it.'

'If only she was.' Laoye snorted.

'But. . .'

Auntie Hu peered at both of us, then seemed to make up her mind. 'I was up here giving my husband his medicine when some Red Guards stormed in and started to smash things, upsetting him. When I asked what they wanted, they said . . . they said they wanted to find out about my past.'

'Your past?'

'Yes, and when I said I had nothing to say they said I was lying and hit me.'

Laoye clenched a fist. 'Juju, now you know what he's done.'

'But, Laoye,' I whispered, 'did they say on whose order they came?'

'You silly girl! If she'd asked, they would only have said "Chairman Mao sent us".'

'So, how can you be sure that Steel was behind it?'

Finally Laoye's anger and frustration burst through and he roared like thunder, 'We are not sure, but we know someone is after us, Uncle Ma, Auntie Hu and I. Someone wants us dead, but we don't know who or why. We don't know what they want from us. Are you satisfied now?'

'But why do you keep accusing Steel?'

'Because everything began with his arrival in the area and I see his mark in this persecution. I don't trust him.' Laoye sank down on to the bed, his chest heaving.

Uncle Hu whimpered, and Auntie Hu rushed to his side. I sighed with relief. Laoye had no proof that any of this was Steel's doing. He was stubborn, and once he had set his mind on something, nothing could change it.

Laoye and Uncle Ma whispered to each other for a long time before Uncle Ma bade us goodbye. Auntie Hu stayed at the top of the stairs as Uncle Ma waved and disappeared. I was puzzling over his brief goodbye when I remembered the last time I'd been there: she had not wanted others to know she had had visitors. I glanced up at Laoye and saw that he was looking intently out of the small window facing the street, checking that no one was around. They truly believed they were being persecuted, I thought, and felt uneasy.

On the tractor we huddled together to fend off the chill. The wind was cold and merciless. There had been no snow so far. Looking out at the bleak grey mountains and empty roads, I remembered the scar on Auntie Hu's arm. Although I had been certain Steel was not responsible for her suffering, I was appalled by the way she had been treated. Surely Steel should know that some renegade Red Guards were abusing their authority. Then a question formed in my mind and I turned to Laoye. 'Auntie Hu hasn't always run the restaurant, has she? What did she do before that?'

'She used to be the wife of a bandit,' Laoye said slowly.

'Uncle Hu, a bandit?' I exclaimed. The exotic word summoned an image of a knife-wielding villain, but the bedridden man under the mosquito net was more like a hermit.

'Uncle Hu was not a bandit. He was one of her admirers and was badly punished by the bandit leaders who heard of his love for her,' Laoye said.

I thought of Uncle Hu's face and felt a wave of fear. Although Laoye didn't expand, I understood this was why he was bedridden.

'What about Auntie Hu? Did the bandit leader do anything to her?' If he was as cruel and jealous as this, why would he have let her go? He might easily have killed her.

Laoye paused for a minute. Then he said: 'He tried to hurt her very much.'

I clung to Laoye. I was desperate to know Auntie Hu's story, but somehow I knew Laoye considered the subject closed. And however the bandit had tortured her, Auntie Hu had survived. But suddenly I understood her silence. 'She must have been very beautiful woman to inspire such jealousy,' I said, after a minute or two.

'She is,' Laoye said.

I tried to imagine what Auntie Hu's life had been like as a bandit's wife. Questions began to pour out of my mouth: 'Laoye, how did she become a bandit?'

'She didn't become a bandit.'

'But you just said—'

'She became a bandit's wife because the bandit leader heard how beautiful she was and snatched her from her family. She was the daughter of the local herbalist, and practised herself, although, of course, she was not as good as her father. They were a family of doctors. If she had been a boy, she would have been taught more but, alas, her father only taught her a little . . .'

He sounded bitter and I remembered how he had defended me when my auntie had spoken dismissively of me because I was a girl. I had heard about Auntie Hu's family from Uncle Ma but the story sounded so much more real when Laoye told it.

'How did you know all of this?' I watched Laoye curiously.

He gazed into the hills as if searching for an answer. Then, he pointed to them: 'That was where the bandits used to live, high up these. Nobody could reach them, not even the new Communist government in the beginning.'

'But eventually they captured them?'

'Yes, and the bandit leader was punished.'

'Punished?'

'Put to death, for he was a wicked man.'

'What happened to Auntie Hu?'

'She married Uncle Hu, who had always loved her,' Laoye said briefly.

I thought of Uncle Hu's vacant eyes and shuddered. He was like a dead man – how could she bear to live with him? Yet she did. I'd seen her making brews to treat and nourish him, and she must have been doing so for years.

The ride got bumpier as the road narrowed. I peered at Laoye's frowning face and realised in a flash that he would have shared Auntie Hu's secrets. There were things about her he would never tell, not to me, not to anyone, and I felt another pang of jealousy. He might be my grandfather, but he seemed much closer to her.

That night I reread Steel's red book, trying to find clues as to why he might be responsible for the misfortunes of Laoye and his friends. But the more I read, the more I was convinced of his innocence and nobility. My sense of the injustice Laoye had done to him was so strong that I spent the whole night arguing with him in my head on Steel's behalf. The image of Steel defending the poor beggar boy, scolding Zheng Yi for stealing the chicken and speaking at the herb-donation fair in defence of Bell was in the front of my mind and, try as I might, I could not reconcile it with the cruel, calculated man that Laoye had made him out to be. My conviction of Steel's innocence made me doubt everything about Laoye. Might he bear a grudge because of something Steel knew about his past? What had Steel said at the fair? Something about Laoye being such a good doctor that he never made mistakes. I thought over the scene and remembered how serious Laoye and Steel had looked. Suddenly I understood what Steel had been trying to suggest: that Laoye had been negligent – he, too, had delivered a baby that had died.

I sat up suddenly, wide awake now in the dark.

25

Half an hour after Mark's appointment was to have started, I sat alone staring at my notes. He was often late, but this time he was very late. His was my last appointment of the day. Idly I inked over his name in the diary.

Xiao Jin popped her head into the room: 'The patient rang to cancel his appointment.'

'Mark?' I looked up.

'He said he was tied up in a meeting. Shall we charge him? It's less than twenty-four hours' notice.'

I watched her too-eager face. No doubt Mr Cheng would be delighted by her officiousness. 'Are you sure he said he couldn't come? He might just be late.'

'I'm sure,' she said smugly. 'I suggested another date but he said he'd ring back later. He was very offhand.'

I nodded slowly, expecting her to leave, but she lingered – I could see that she was curious. I looked down at Mark's name in the diary, now etched thickly in dark ink, and covered it. 'You can go now,' I said coolly.

She nodded. Soon I heard her high heels tapping on the floor of the corridor. 'Shall I lock the door?' she called.

'Don't bother, I'll do it.' I was desperate to be alone.

Silence. I was used to it. I should have known he would not come, after last time.

I rose, kicked off my shoes and sat on the bed. I tried to imagine how my patients felt in my consulting room. Lucy and

I always chatted, and I knew she trusted me. But Mark was usually silent and when he spoke, as he had last time, it had only made things more awkward. Still, it didn't matter any more: he was not coming. I lay back, exhausted after a busy day, and allowed myself to close my eyes. 'Mark,' I said to myself. It was safe enough to say it now: no one was around.

When I opened them, someone was standing next to me. 'Did you call me?' He bent down. 'I thought I heard you. Sorry to just walk in like this – I did knock but there was no answer.'

I didn't stir. 'Mark,' I murmured.

'I had to come,' he said.

Slowly, my hands went up to my face, as if the sight of him was too much for me. There was a moment's silence, then, very gently, he moved away my hands and stroked my cheeks. A sigh came from deep inside me. I felt at peace. When his hands slid off my cheeks, I took them in mine and squeezed them. They were cool and comforting, and I longed to hold them.

Then a strange electronic sound intruded: his mobile phone. He cursed. The look on his face told me who it was. For a moment we stared at each other, then he slipped out of the treatment room. I heard a few murmurs, then silence.

I sat up and blinked as if I had woken from a dream. Mark stood exactly where he had when he had dropped me off after the picnic. Then he had leaned forward and kissed my cheek. Watching him now, I realised that that peck on my cheek, innocent in his culture, had sparked in me this flicker of desire that now threatened to engulf us. I had massaged his shoulders and back, I had felt his pulse, but that kiss had let something loose in me and I had craved his touch ever since. I lifted a hand to my cheek. It was not too late to stop. I could prevent this act of betrayal unlike the other one.

I rose from the treatment couch.

26

'I'd rather die!' I shouted, and rushed out of the house into the wind. Without thinking, I raced towards the mountain path. Behind me, I heard Laoye and Mother calling to me to stop, but I ran on.

The wind was howling by the time I was half-way up the hill but I couldn't stop. A fire was burning inside me and the person I was most angry with was Laoye. When Mother and Ling had told me the reason for their visit, I stared at Laoye and saw guilt written on his face. 'But you promised,' I hissed at him, not quite believing that he could do such a thing. He had remained silent.

Mother, looking older and fatter, in spite of her expensive new clothes, had sat down next to me and said that this time there was no negotiation. Laoye had been labelled a 'bad element' and condemned by the 'movement', which meant it was no longer safe for me to live with him. There was no future for a person connected with a bad element, and my life had only just begun.

'Bad element?' I repeated.

Laoye nodded. 'I'll protect you from anything I can, Juju, but I cannot protect you from myself. Your mother is right, you should not stay with me. Go home with her.'

Go home? To the man who beat me? Mother seemed to read my mind. 'Your father has promised to be gentler. He always meant well – he just wanted you to grow up knowing right from wrong.'

Ling, also in brand-new clothes and polished shoes – bought, no doubt, with our stepfather's money – nodded. So, they were in this together. I remembered how she had called him 'Father', making me cringe. For a moment they all stood there watching me, as if we were on opposite banks of a river, and tears filled my eyes. That was when I had turned and fled.

Now that I was at a safe distance from them, I realised where I was going: to Steel. Only he could release me from this trap. Breathless, I rested where the path forked towards the cliff, and looked down to the valley below: Laoye and I often rested there. But today the memories of our happier times together made his betrayal all the more unbearable. How could he send me back to the man who'd beaten me? I didn't care if he was a bad element, he was still my *laoye*. I was sure he wanted to be rid of me for other reasons, which he was too cowardly to tell me. Mother's arrival had given him the perfect opportunity.

I thought once more of the conversation I'd overheard the first night Mother and Ling had been there.

'How did it come to this? They say you refused to co-operate with the authorities. Is that right?' Mother had chided.

Laoye didn't respond.

'What do they want you to do?'

Again Laoye didn't speak. Mother sighed. 'You're mingling with undesirables,' she said. 'Think of yourself and Juju. What will people say? With that as well as what you are, Father, you must be careful.'

'What do you mean?' Laoye spoke for the first time.

'You know very well what I mean. I've heard a lot from Juju's auntie.'

'That woman!' Laoye snorted. 'Don't tell me who to mix with. I will stand by my old friends.'

'Friends? Bandits, black elements! That woman who, everyone tells me, was a bandit's wife! You are in enough trouble of your own without her as well.'

'Don't talk about her like that.' Laoye sounded so angry. 'You don't know what you're saying. You ought to be ashamed of yourself, woman. Even Juju has more sympathy than you.'

'Oh, yes, sympathy with bandits and whores! You really are bringing her up properly! I should have known better than to trust her to you.'

'All right. Take Juju away – she's your child, after all. You do whatever you want.'

'Father,' Mother pleaded, but I could still hear the anger.

There had been no more from either of them and I dared to take a deep breath. But even after that, I had thought Laoye's words were no more than an angry retort to Mother. I had not thought he'd meant it.

Now I was cold and decided to walk on, but as I was moving away I saw a tiny figure coming up the path. At first I thought it might be Jinni, the herb-picker, and wondered why he'd come out in such dreadful weather. But as the figure came nearer, I saw that it wasn't carrying a basket. It was Ling, struggling against the wind in her city shoes and a big scarf. She saw me and called. Still angry, I turned away, but as the wind hit me, I relented. I paused to wait for her.

Panting and wheezing, she collapsed next to me. 'You shouldn't have stormed off like that. Our stepfather has changed. He's a different man now. He has stopped drinking.'

I was still angry with her for betraying me to the adult world, but touched that she'd made the trek to find me. 'Come home,' she begged.

I kept silent.

'You're so stubborn. You should have stayed calm and shown Mother that there might be other possibilities. What about boarding at the school in town?'

I turned back. Ling was good at compromise, and anything would be better than returning to the city. I nodded slowly. But would Mother accept it?

I voiced my doubt and Ling said, 'Let me talk to her. She's just worried for you and wants you out of Laoye's house. Why don't we say to her that for the moment you'd better stay at the town school to finish the term – you wouldn't be able to catch up if you came to the city school now. After you've caught up, you could come back to the city. That way, you won't have to leave with us now, and things being as they are with Mother, it might be a long time before she thinks again of coming to fetch you.'

It sounded like a good idea. But whether the adults would agree to it was a different matter. Still, I was grateful to Ling. I sat closer and touched her hand. She put an arm round me protectively, like the big sister she was. Suddenly I had found someone who could help me to make sense of my confusion, and I told her everything that had happened since I'd last seen her, starting from when I had found Auntie Hu looking frightened, the closure of Uncle Ma's chemist's and the desolation in the town. I told her of Laoye's initial acceptance and eventual denunciation of Steel.

'He sounds almost too good to be true,' Ling said.

'But he's like that – you'd see it, too, if you met him. He's a selfless, brave man, always thinking of the beggars and peasants.'

'So why did he do these horrible things to Laoye and his friends?'

'That's just it. I don't think he did. Someone else did it and people blamed him.' There was my suspicion about Laoye too, but I didn't think it would go down well with Ling so I kept it to myself.

'Who is responsible for forbidding Laoye to practise, then? That must be Steel's order – he's the only person who would benefit from it,' Ling said, sounding like a detective.

'The brigade leader said that it was an order to protect people from rogue doctors.'

'Laoye? A rogue doctor?' Ling glared at me.

'I know, I know, but rules are rules. Laoye is applying for permission to practise, and the brigade leader is behind him. He just has to wait for the permission to come through.'

'Think of it from Laoye's point of view, how important his work is to him – it's practically his life. Remember how he did it all for no payment. Now imagine how hard for him it is to be forbidden to do something he thought was his birthright,' Ling said.

I hadn't thought of it like that. All of a sudden Laoye's anger and frustration made sense to me.

'Why didn't you talk to Steel about it?'

'I wanted to, but he wasn't there when I arrived to see him. They said he'd gone to the capital for an important meeting of the Red Guards and the central leaders.' Shortly after our visit to Auntie Hu's house I had gone to see Steel behind Laoye's back. I had so wanted to clear the air with him.

Ling was silent for a while. Then she said, 'But, Juju, Laoye is no fool. There must be something he knows that you don't.'

'Why doesn't he tell me, then?'

'Perhaps. . .' Ling kicked a stone and looked up at me with a sly smile. 'Perhaps he's protecting you, or perhaps he thinks you like Steel so much that you might tell him what he said.'

I stopped in the middle of the track, speechless.

'Well, do you love him?'

Love? She had said the word so casually, but I was shocked. I stared at her and she laughed. 'You do. I can see it in your eyes. Well, he must be very special, this Steel.'

I thought of his face. I could not tell if he was good looking or not. But the memory of his eyes had filled me with the desire to see him. Love? Of course not. I just needed him to explain things. And now the urge was stronger. I felt almost suffocated by the pain of not having seen him for so long. He had to be back now – he had been gone for days.

I stamped my foot. 'Don't be silly,' I said. 'I have more important things to do than talk about love.'

'Where are you off to now?' Ling asked.

'To see Steel,' I said simply.

'You are mad. Listen to the wind! Come back, please,' she begged.

'Tell them I'll be home this evening. Don't worry,' I added, when I saw her face, 'I know the way.'

She looked back down the path she'd taken. Coming all the way up here had frightened her, I could see that, and I urged her again to go back. She hesitated. Impatient to leave her, I turned.

'Juju,' Ling shrieked, 'look where you're going!'

I stopped. I had left the track to approach the cave. 'Go,' I said, retracing my steps. 'I promise I'll be all right.' I waited until she had started reluctantly down the path. Then I turned back to the cliff. Before I bent down I looked round to make sure she'd gone and that no one else had appeared. I needn't have bothered. The weather was so appalling that no one would have wanted to come up here. I felt for the creepers and slipped down.

The cave felt damp and forbidding, but I ignored that and went straight for the far corner and the strange mound. But before I reached it I stumbled on something. I picked it up and saw, in the faint light, that it was the herb-god statue. Recently it had been missing from our house. I remembered when I had noticed its absence and asked Laoye about it. He had smiled, but said nothing. I told him about my cousin leading the village children on an expedition to destroy the local deities. Although they had mainly been looking for kitchen-god posters, Laoye's herb god would have been at risk. But Laoye had told me it was safe. And every night he stood where the statue had been and murmured his prayers as though it was still there. I had thought then that he didn't miss it, but he had sighed and said it was not a good omen: gods did not like being moved and he feared bad things might happen because of it.

And now this. I put the statue down hastily, sad that it had ended up in such a place. Then I turned to the mound. I took a deep breath, bent down and began to dig with my hand. The earth was soft, as it had been before, and, overcoming my feeling of apprehension, I continued. Cold sweat accumulated on my forehead, but I dared not stop because I knew I might not be so brave if I paused to think about what I was doing. Not only was I defying Laoye's strict order not to come near the cave, worse, I was trying to find out what secrets he was hiding from me. Somehow I knew I would find an answer here to all my doubts and questions. Finally my cold, sore fingers felt something and I stopped.

I had expected to find bones: I was still convinced, from the shape of the mound, that it was a grave, and perhaps that of a baby who had died after Laoye had delivered it. As to why he would bury it here, I had no idea. But my trembling hands dragged out nothing more than a pair of old shoes, tied together with the laces. At first I sat back and laughed, as my fear evaporated, but as I looked at them, I realised I'd seen them before. They were the shoes Auntie Hu had given to Laoye: I had been the messenger, had admired their embroidery and had witnessed Laoye's strange, sad reaction to them. What were they doing here? Why would Auntie Hu give Laoye shoes that he had to hide? And what a strange place to hide them! As I wondered, my hands felt about in the loose earth. They encountered a lump and I let out a cry. It was another shoe, with the same embroidery but slightly smaller. I shook the loose earth off my hands and stood up.

Suddenly I felt sick. The relief I had felt not to discover tiny bones had disappeared. There was no dead body, but I could smell something decaying, something ominous. I rushed to the entrance of the cave and vomited. What did the shoes mean? From the shape of the mound I was convinced there was more, but I had lost the urge to find out. I was no closer to discovering Laoye's secret. On the contrary I was more mystified than ever.

I waited for the sickness to pass, and held on to the familiar view of the village in the valley for comfort. I tried as usual to find our house, a tiny dot on the edge. When Mother and Ling had first seen it, they had fallen silent. I realised how bleak it must look to them. They did not know that Laoye's heart had left it, or that he and I were estranged. I noticed he had looked at me anxiously lately, as if at a tree he had replanted at a crucial stage of its growth. He'd explained to me how you used different parts of plants, that you harvested spring leaves, summer blossom, autumn berries and winter roots. Miss the right season, and the whole year's growth was wasted.

There was a new restlessness in me that drove me to run, to shout at the top of my voice. Laoye complained that I kicked him at night when I was asleep, and that I would wake him, talking or crying in my sleep. I knew I had nightmares because

I would wake in a sweat feeling as I had when I had first realised that one day Laoye, like my father, would die.

The thought of death made me peer again at the mound. The longer I gazed at it, the more afraid I felt, just like the first time I'd seen it. I decided to head back.

The creeper felt slippery as I grasped it but I thought nothing of it and started to climb. Just before I reached the top, my hand slipped. I screamed and clawed at the wet grass, until a pair of hands clutched me and hauled me up the cliff. It was Ling.

We lay in a heap, panting. I was sobbing, but she didn't say anything, just put her scarf over me. After a while I stopped crying. She stood up and glared down at me. 'What on earth were you doing?' she shouted. 'If I hadn't waited, you'd be dead. Now, come home with me.'

I said nothing. Something was wrong. My face itched and I tried to raise a hand to scratch it, but I couldn't move it.

Suddenly Ling screamed: 'Blood!' She pointed to me and I felt something trickle down my face. I tried to move my arms again and felt a sharp twinge in my shoulder. 'Ouch,' I said.

'Oh, my goodness.' Ling tried to dry the blood with her scarf. 'Let's go home now,' she pleaded. 'Laoye can treat you.'

'No.' I shook my head slowly. 'I'll go to Steel. He'll have medicine at the clinic.' Before she could object I added, 'We're nearer to the clinic here anyway.'

'If you go, I'll come too,' Ling said. 'I can't leave you alone.'

It would be good to have company, I decided.

'What were you looking for down there?' she asked, as we started up the path.

I didn't see any harm in telling her. 'It's a secret cave,' I said. 'You can see our house from there, the whole village, even. No one can see Laoye hiding in it but he can keep an eye on everything.'

'But what were you doing there?' Ling asked, her leather shoe scuffing the hard surface of the mountain path.

'I. . .' Although I longed to I decided not to unburden myself of this secret to Ling. Beside, I was still trying to work it out. But Ling was watching me curiously and I hastened to answer: 'It's a special place – where the *lingzhi* grows. I didn't want to tell you that because Laoye swore me to secrecy.'

She seemed to believe me and I relaxed. But the pain in my shoulder worsened. I must have dislocated it when I strained to hold on to the creepers. I clamped my jaw and groaned quietly. The bleeding had stopped, but my face hurt in the cold air. The path felt longer than before and I was filled with dread that Steel might not be there. Perhaps I should have gone home with Ling to Laoye.

Two figures were standing outside the clinic. I recognised Bell's white shirt, but at first I wasn't sure who the other was, a tall figure talking animatedly to her. Then at our approach they turned to look and my heart leaped at the sight of his face. Bell was flushed, and it seemed they had been arguing. When she saw us she went inside the clinic without a word.

I introduced Ling to Steel, forgetting about my shoulder in my excitement. Ling said, 'She's bleeding. She needs treatment.' Steel steered me gently by my other shoulder towards the treatment room.

He searched through the cabinet for what he needed, and then he sat me down, and gently examined my injured shoulder. I winced. 'I'm sorry to do this to you, but it'll be over very quickly—' Even before he finished his sentence, I felt the firm force of his hands on me. I screamed.

Ling and Bell rushed in. 'It's all right,' Steel said. 'I've just put her shoulder back into its socket.' He turned to smile at me and I nodded through my cold sweat – now I remembered Laoye treating someone with a dislocated shoulder, and his description of the pain. 'Now for your face,' Steel said, and examined my scratches. Our eyes met briefly but he dropped his. He called for Bell and she swiftly located the balm, without speaking. It was plain that she was still angry with him. Steel didn't seem to notice. He swabbed off the blood then applied antiseptic while he talked to Ling. She blushed at his questions and flicked her hair every so often – I'd seen her do this with boys she wanted to impress. All of a sudden I felt sick. I wished she knew that Steel wasn't impressed by coquettes.

But Bell smiled when Ling started to talk, and before long they had retreated to the small side room. Steel and I were alone in the main treatment room where a fire was burning.

'Now tell me,' he smiled, as we sat on two low stools beside it warming our hands, 'what were you doing up on the hill?'

'We were on our way to see you, of course,' I said, 'and here you are.'

He laughed. 'Of course I'm here. Where else would I be?'

'You were not here last time I came.'

He frowned. 'Last time?'

'I came a week ago. Didn't they tell you?'

He shook his head and his eyes rested on me thoughtfully. I felt shy suddenly, and bent down to the fire. 'Ouch,' I exclaimed, as the pain in my shoulder flared up again. He had bandaged it deftly, reminding me of Laoye's careful hands. 'How did this happen?' He pointed at my shoulder.

I told him I had slipped as I was climbing out of the cave.

'What cave?'

'The cave where—' I stopped, suddenly remembering my vow to Laoye.

'Well, I can't tell you because I'm sworn to secrecy.'

His smile broadened into a grin. How I wished I could tell him. I would have done anything to please him. 'What an honourable person you are,' he said. 'If a friend of mine told me a secret, I would keep it, too. I understand.' He rose to fetch more wood, but looked serious now. I feared that, despite what he had said, I had offended him. After all this I could not afford to lose him.

'Wait,' I said, before he left the room.

He was walking away slowly but he turned round. 'Yes?'

'It's just below the cliff near Devil Never Dare. You have to swing down the creepers to get there. You can't see it from this side. My *laoye* discovered it.'

'Your *laoye?* I see.' For a moment he waited as if he expected to hear more. I struggled not to tell him what I had discovered in the cave – Steel was the ideal person to help me unravel the mystery. But that would be a betrayal Laoye would not forgive.

Steel must have guessed what was going through my mind, for he laughed bitterly. 'Is he still angry with me, your grandfather?'

'No, of course not,' I said, but saw from his face that I had not fooled him. I dropped my eyes; somehow, I thought it was all my fault that they did not like each other. In the long silence that followed, Laoye's unhappy eyes were in my mind, reminding me of the purpose of my visit. But I was lost for words. I had so much to say to Steel that I didn't know where to begin.

'They want to take me away from here,' I said.

'Who?'

'My family – my mother and her new husband. They want me to go home with them.' I didn't mention Laoye's betrayal. It hurt too much.

'Oh.' He nodded. 'I remember. If it hadn't been for your stepfather, we would not have met. How extraordinary fate is. What will you do?'

How could he be so philosophical about it all? This was not the reaction I'd had in mind. I had expected him to be angry on my behalf and his detached tone was wounding. I pretended not to have noticed it. Perhaps Steel was showing me a mature way of dealing with my crisis. Perhaps he was even thinking of ways to get me out of it. I watched him closely.

After a long time he still hadn't said any more, so I volunteered, 'I'd rather die than go back with Mother. I will look for somewhere else to go. I wondered if the clinic . . .?'

'I'm afraid that's out of the question. We cannot take you here. People would think it odd.'

'I don't care what they think.'

He smiled strangely. 'But they would gossip about me, don't you see? They'd say I was behind all this, stirring up trouble between you and your grandfather.' The smile told me he was aware of all the rumours about him.

I leaped to his defence: 'Don't listen to what people say. They're just jealous.'

Steel nodded. 'Bell keeps telling me to move on,'

'Move on?' I repeated, incredulous.

'There is a position in another county, thirty miles from here. I have had an interview, and they want Bell and me to go there.'

So that was why he'd been away. He was thinking of leaving without me. For a moment I was speechless. Suddenly my nose prickled, and tears formed. What was the point of staying here without Steel?

'Why don't you go, then?' I blurted out. 'Nobody is stopping you.' I stared at the fire, Although it was crackling fiercely, I felt cold inside.

For a long time he made no sound. Eventually, I turned, and he was gazing into the fire. He reminded me of Laoye: lately he had often looked like that. I dared not disturb him, as I dared not disturb Steel now.

Then suddenly he smiled, eyes fixed on the fire. 'I am not leaving here. I have unfinished business to see to.'

'What kind of business?' Now I was intrigued, and the tears had dried.

He looked up at me. 'Let me tell you about a little boy,' he said, 'who grew up in a poor family in a village in the south. He had thought he was his mother and father's boy, like everybody else, until all the other children started calling him names. "Deserted mongrel! Deserted mongrel!" they shouted at him. At first he didn't believe them, but the taunting grew more intense so he confronted his parents and was told that they had indeed adopted him. They had no idea who his real parents were. Can you imagine what that meant to him? His whole world collapsed. He left the village, got on to a train and drifted. He got into street fights, was put into prison, where he learned to steal and fell in with bad company. But he survived. He was worth more than a mere foundling, he decided, and began to rebuild his life.'

He stopped and glanced down at the fire. I waited, hardly daring to breathe, but he made no sound. I stuttered: 'Is that boy. . .?' I dropped my eyes, couldn't quite bring myself to say 'you'.

'Yes. Now you know my secret. I am, to borrow Zheng Yi's words, a deserted mongrel.'

Although his voice was calm, the muscles of his jaw were tense. I remained silent. I could not quite believe he was telling me all this.

'So, you see,' he said slowly, 'I cannot encourage you to run away from home when I am running back to mine.'

'Running back?' I was puzzled.

'Yes, I intend to find my birth parents. I know they are around here somewhere. The peasants who adopted me told me that much. I've also done some detective work and I'm getting close.' At this he clenched a fist.

'And what are you going to do when you find them?' I asked.

He stared at me, then leaned forward, his eyes shining with a strange light. 'What would you do?'

'Me?' I thought for a minute, but I simply could not imagine.

Steel was watching me, waiting. Then, suddenly, I remembered the words of the beggar boy on the train: 'Find them, make them pay.'

'Make them pay,' I murmured, and saw Steel's smile deepen. So he had said those words to the boy. For a moment I felt as if I did not know him – not when he smiled like that. The feeling I had experienced in Laoye's secret cave returned to me. Once more I was unsettled by my ability to notice things that others seemed to overlook. The fact that both secrets concerned the two people who mattered most in my life made it even more frightening.

As if he'd read my mind, Steel stretched out a hand and pulled me up – carefully, on the uninjured side, supporting my back with his other hand. 'Little Sister,' he said gently, 'keep my secret.' His arms slipped round my waist. 'I have never told this to anybody else,' he said, looking me in the eyes. 'I don't know why, but there is something about you. . .' He trailed off and I saw a flicker of confusion in his eyes, so unlike the confidence I was used to seeing there. I held his gaze as if my life depended upon it. 'You are a curious girl,' he continued, in that mesmerising big-brother voice. 'There are so many things you should not know. . .'

I felt strong and weak at the same time. Poor Steel, he had no one to confide in but me. The pain in my shoulder disappeared: his arms radiated a warmth that made me feel heavy-headed. What was the matter with me?

Bell and Ling's giggles in the other room made us step apart, but even when they came in and Ling spoke to me, I still felt absent. It was as if I'd entered another world and left her behind. I'd grown up in that half-hour with Steel and felt close to him in a way I'd never felt with anyone else. Part of me, I decided, would always remain with him, wherever I was. And it was this that enabled me to leave him that day.

When Steel summoned a tractor to take us home I didn't remember to thank him: somehow our new closeness had entitled me to the favour.

When we were nearing the village, Ling, who had been quiet most of the way, raised her head. 'Juju, can I ask you something?'

'What is it?'

'Whatever you feel for Steel, forget it now, before it's too late.'

'What do you mean?' I raised my voice, although I knew exactly what she meant.

'You are too young for these things and . . . he has a girlfriend.'

'So what? Bell doesn't understand him.'

'You have no idea, do you? A girlfriend is more than a friend. She is the woman he's going to marry and have children with.'

A wife, then, like Mother. It didn't mean much to me. I was Steel's special friend and it meant something quite different, but I knew Ling would not understand.

'Besides, you told him too much.'

'What?'

'I heard you telling him about the cave. I thought you'd promised Laoye to keep it a secret.'

'But, Ling, I trust him.'

'Well, you'll see.'

After this there was a long silence between us. But as I watched Ling's serious face, I grew worried. It wasn't what she'd said that bothered me: it was what she might say to Laoye.

When our village was in sight I said, 'I promise I'll be more careful with Steel.' I tried to look as if I meant it. She stared at me doubtfully and didn't say anything. I added, 'But, please, don't tell Laoye we met Steel at the clinic.' Still silent, she kept her eyes on me. 'What I mean is,' I tried to phrase my sentence better, 'Laoye is so old fashioned he might believe I cared for Steel too much.'

'Don't you?'

'Not after what you've just said about him and Bell. I know how to protect myself.' I kept my eyes on her.

'Well, I hope so, Juju.'

That night, I stared at the ceiling and replayed in my mind the time I had spent at the clinic. As we had done at our house, we all slept in one big bed. But the breathing around me did not make me feel part of the family. I resolved to tell them in the morning that I would be happy to leave and go to the town school. My innocent days with Laoye were over. Once I had thought family ties were strong but now I knew that families could betray you. Steel's had abandoned him at birth and mine wanted to send me back to the man who had struck me. Why should I trust them now?

I hugged Steel's red book. Steel, we will look after each other, I said silently in the dark, and thought briefly of his birth parents. Whoever they were, I wished them ill for causing him such pain.

27

'Dr Lin,' Xiao Jin had rushed in, 'Lucy wants to see you.'
'I'm busy – can't you take a message?' I knew Lucy was due for one last session, but was surprised to be interrupted mid-treatment.

'She said she needs to see you now.' Xiao Jin hovered around me. 'She seems upset about something. I've never seen her like this before.'

I hastened to put the last needle into Mr Robinson and assured him I would be back soon.

Lucy stood in the reception area, gripping the chair in front of her as if she might fall. She wasn't wheezing. As I came in she turned, caught my eye, then averted hers. Something stirred in me. Finally, I thought, she had come. I told Xiao Jin to take the needles out of Mr Robinson in twenty minutes' time if I was not back. She looked surprised. 'Where will you be?' she asked.

'Upstairs,' I said, and motioned to Lucy. She followed without a word. The silent climb up the stairs seemed longer than usual.

I went straight to the window and pushed it open, as I always did when Lucy visited. For a moment I lingered there and listened to the traffic outside, then moved towards her. She drew closer to me, her chest heaving so much that I feared she might have an attack.

I reached for her hand. She didn't resist, but turned to stare at the photograph of Tiantian. She didn't give me long with her pulse, but I detected its unmistakable slipperiness, like a well-oiled marble rolling across the balls of my fingers. I glanced up at her pale, drawn face and made up my mind. I let go of her hand just as she withdrew it.

'How could you do this to me?' Her voice shook.

'Do what to you?'

'You know very well what I mean. Do you really need me to spell it out? I thought of you as a friend.'

'I don't know what you mean.'

'He came home in the middle of the night stinking of your herbs, and when I looked at his mobile I found he'd been calling the clinic. He wasn't ill at all – he didn't need treatment. It's not whiplash you're seeing him about, is it?'

I sank down on to the bed. I had known what was coming, and I had been prepared, but I was still shocked. On the table stood the vase she had given me full of chrysanthemums. I had bought the flowers a few days before Mark's last visit. When I had come back upstairs, their cheerful blooms had eased my heavy heart. I had stared at them as I congratulated myself on pulling away from him just in time.

'Lucy,' I said. My lips were dry and I didn't know what to say.

'What's going on? Tell me!' She spoke louder, more sure of herself now.

'You're right. It was not whiplash I was seeing him about,' I said slowly, and registered her surprise. No doubt she had not expected me to be so calm. Encouraged, I went on: 'He came to the clinic after his treatment was finished.' She straightened her back and watched me. 'You know how lonely and homesick I sometimes feel.' I took a deep breath and continued, almost believing myself: 'I rang your number. You were away and Mark answered the phone. He came over.'

She was silent.

'We chatted. I told him about me and Zhiying, what I've told you, and about Tiantian. He comforted me. The next time, we talked about you.' I glanced briefly at her and saw her eyes widen. 'He told me how much he missed you and Connor. He also seemed excited about something, a new adventure, he said. I wondered what it might be, but he wouldn't say. He wasn't sure, he said, and he thought it would be better for you to tell me.' I turned to face her.

Her mouth opened, then shut, and I saw a flicker of a smile that she tried to hide. For a moment we stared at each other across the bed. I knew words were useless in situations like this – she would see my innocence better without them. I stroked the medicine box on the table. How were sins measured? Was a gesture needed? Was a touch required? Then I remembered that in my other life, so many years ago, when I was a mere child I had done no more than say a word.

'So, yes, we did meet, but Mark was being kind, listening to a lonely woman. Nothing happened between us, Lucy. Nothing of the sort you imagine, I promise you,' I said finally. It was the only answer I could give her.

She sighed, yet her face glowed. As she stood up she put a hand to her belly. I waited for her to speak, but smiled to myself, for I knew what it was she was going to tell me. As I had just read from her pulse, she was pregnant again.

28

It was with a sense of foreboding that I left the house Laoye and I had shared. The ever helpful Uncle Leng came with his tractor; Laoye and Mother sat at the front, while Ling and I huddled at the back. The village disappeared far too quickly with the roar of the tractor, and I pictured our home, grass growing out of its roof; I saw the kitchen, with the now vacant niche where the herb-god statue had been kept. I saw Laoye standing in front of it, praying earnestly to nothing.

Then I remembered all the people in the village: my cousin who had taught me how to crack open a hard nut with my teeth, Jinni the herb-picker, who had dressed my cuts and scratches numerous times when Laoye wasn't round; Grandpa Ying, who had let me practise on him without complaint.

I thought of all these people, of their goodness and weakness, of the height of the men, and the chiselled good looks of the women, their uncompromisingly loud voices. I had found them intimidating at first, but now, as I was leaving, I felt attached to the land of bandits.

I closed my eyes to see it all more clearly. Somehow I felt I might never return. This farewell was different: instead of a ride to town with a cloth bag, the tractor carried my luggage and my schoolbag, just about all I possessed in this world. The luggage was extra heavy as I'd stolen Laoye's medicine box. And I knew Laoye's house would be that much emptier. In the rush to pack he had forgotten it: he had only asked about it when we were on our way and it was too late to turn back. I suggested that perhaps he had left it with one of his elderly clients, whom he was still seeing secretly. This was the main reason why I had stolen it: I had wanted him out of trouble, but I had also wanted to take something that would remind me of him. I knew this alone would not stop him, but at least he would be less visible without it. People might think he was simply visiting friends. His sadness had almost made me relent and give it back to him, but then I realised that that might have something to do with my departure rather than the disappearance of the box. But I couldn't be sure. Which one of us would he miss most? I wondered, as I stared at his hunched back in front of me.

As the distance increased between me and the village, the Black Hill appeared. Soon the shape of Devil Never Dare emerged, and I thought of my trips there, the cave, my discovery and the now familiar journey to number-two brigade. What would Steel be doing? I tried to imagine. I would not be going there to him any more, but I might see him in town, where I understood he went often for meetings. And away from Laoye, everything would be easier.

Something had happened between Laoye and Steel. During the last week Laoye had stopped ranting about him. When I thought back, the change had coincided with a mysterious late-night visit from Uncle Ma. They thought I didn't know about it and Laoye hadn't said anything the next day, but I had kept my ears open and had heard Steel's name mentioned many times. Since that day Laoye had stopped cursing him, and kept quiet when anyone else said anything about him. It was not as if he wasn't interested in Steel, though: suddenly he couldn't hear enough about him. A couple of times he tried awkwardly to find out Steel's whereabouts from me. I was mystified. What had Uncle Ma told him?

I faked indifference to Laoye's interest. I could afford to do so because my feelings for Steel were more complex now: I felt secure in our friendship. He'd told me his secret and it was as if he'd given me his heart. I knew now that there would always be things that I did not understand about him, but that was because of the difference in our age and experience. There was a special place in my heart for him. Ling called it love, but I preferred to think of it as intimacy.

I barely recognised the town. For a moment I felt as if I'd returned to the city I'd left behind. Red posters were everywhere, with black crosses on some shops and houses. The earth-god temple where Laoye had come to pray had been demolished; only two pillars remained like sad guards. I peered at Laoye and was surprised that he seemed so impassive. Then it occurred to me that he travelled to town regularly, and had probably witnessed this sort of transformation in progress, had perhaps been there when the destruction had taken place. He had suffered so much, I told myself. The world must have seemed to change before his eyes. I stared at his back again and read in it his sadness.

The tractor drove past a large, empty but familiar space. After we'd left it behind I realised it had been the market place. Some workers were busy erecting a platform at the far end of it to the edge of the town. I closed my eyes to fill the silent ride and the empty space with fruit, vegetables, people and smells, but what I couldn't replace was the feeling of joy I had experienced there, with the cherries in my hand, in my mouth and close to my nose. Years later I knew that that was called growing up, but then I was simply filled with regret.

The station was thronging with young people. On the platform Ling waited demurely. With her upturned collar and white shirt, she cut a smart figure.

I watched her from a slight distance. Some of the young men, homesickness on their faces, looked at her as men do at pretty women. She knew it, but was not interested in them and it showed on her face. She couldn't wait to leave the dirty countryside, she'd told me last night. But I didn't mind. Despite our differences, she was my sister, a cherished elder sister who had looked after me when I had needed her most.

A few days after we had come back from Steel's clinic, I had woken to discover I was bleeding. It was just my period, Ling had reminded me. It was a bit inconvenient and uncomfortable

221

but you got used to it. Hadn't I heard about it from the other girls?

Was it the curse? I said hesitantly, remembering the village girls' giggles. Ling nodded. She gave me her special knickers to wear and some soft papers. Remember, you are a city girl, she said. We keep ourselves clean and use this instead of the straw that country girls use. Later that night my belly had hurt, and my groans had woken Laoye and Mother. Laoye got up to brew something for me, which had dulled the pain. In the morning, it had gone, and I'd remembered that this was what Laoye had told me about: the moon repetitions, which marked me as a woman. It occurred to me then how lucky I had been that Ling has there – Laoye would have explained everything in his elegant, concise way, as he had always done, but this was not an abstract concept: it was bloody and real and I preferred to have Ling holding my hand and saying, 'It happens to all of us and it'll get better.'

Now I stepped closer and huddled up to her. As I lifted my head I caught Mother looking at her with pride. She frowned when she glanced at me. At the sound of the train's hooter she sighed and stroked my head. I brushed away her hand. 'Shall I tell your father that this is from you?' She pointed at the honey she had bought at the town shop.

'No,' I said. As the image of him entered my mind I felt sorry suddenly for Ling. She took the honey from Mother. 'Let's go, or we'll miss the train.' She hooked her arm round me. 'We'll say it's from all of us.'

'Don't wait, Father,' Mother called from the train window, which she had opened. 'Get Juju to school.' Beside me Laoye cursed, very softly but I heard.

The driver had unloaded the luggage from the tractor and Laoye slung it over his shoulders. I carried my schoolbag and followed him out of the station.

He walked slowly and I had to wait for him several times. In the end, impatient, I strode back and took my case off his shoulders. I had wanted to carry it anyway, as I had feared he might discover the medicine box wrapped inside an old jacket.

I was now nearly as tall as him and enjoyed my new strength. I could carry him on my shoulders and spin him round, I joked, trying to cheer him. He laughed briefly, then said it wouldn't be good for his bones.

At the empty space that had been the market place, we walked right through the middle. Laoye fixed his eyes straight ahead and walked fast now, as if he was in a hurry but I let my gaze wander. The sadness I had felt on the tractor had disappeared: I was excited about my new life in the town. A platform had been erected and some workers were slowly putting up some large paper characters across the front. I read 'Down With. . .' but before I could finish we had arrived at the school gate and Laoye hurried me inside.

It was lunchtime, and I had been hungry but when we stopped at the school canteen I was put off by the smell. Laoye frowned, as I did, but as the canteen was closing and we had no other choice we went in.

He bought me a dish of stir-fry noodles and egg. I ate because I was hungry and needed something to fill my stomach, but the noodles were dry and salty and the egg burnt with crisp black bits that stuck to my teeth. We sat at a dirty, greasy table as workers swept the floor beside us. Laoye watched me eat, but swallowed little himself. I couldn't help comparing what was in front of us with Auntie Hu's food. At the thought of her I pushed aside my bowl.

'Eat a little more,' Laoye begged.

'I've had enough,' I said.

'You will have to get used to the food here,' he said, but didn't force me to eat more.

I walked with him back through the playground. At the gate he waved me away. 'Go back,' he said, slung his small parcel on to his shoulder and turned, but I held the corner of his jacket and pulled him back.

'Say hello to her for me.'

'To whom?'

'Auntie Hu, of course.'

'Who told you I was going to her?'

'Tell her I'll come to see her once I'm settled here.'

He stared at me, then smiled. 'I think I might have left my medicine box there,' he said.

'Laoye.'

He sighed. 'Besides, she needs me now.'

'Why?'

'Uncle Hu died and she's all alone.'

Uncle Hu dead? I remembered the vacant eyes: he hadn't seemed alive when I'd seen him. Perhaps his death had not grieved her too much. But Laoye looked sad, and I knew, by now, that there were things between them that went back a long time, secret things he'd never tell me. She was part of his life that was outside the family but somehow mattered more. It was special to him, like Steel was to me.

Now he was off to Auntie Hu's, where he would meet Uncle Ma. Perhaps he was already there, waiting for Laoye. 'Be careful, though, if you go.' I was worried, I didn't know why.

Laoye put his hand on my shoulder and patted it. 'I should be here to fetch you for the new year, but if I'm not, go to Auntie Hu. She will know where I am.' Before I could reply, he turned and strode off.

I stayed to watch him walk away, head held high, back straight. But there was something odd about his step and it took me a while to realise it was because he wasn't carrying the medicine box, which was usually strapped on his left shoulder. His left hand hovered over his left hip, securing the missing box. Suddenly I felt sad. He was still within sight yet I had started to miss him. His parting words had had an ominous ring.

I stayed at the gate until he had disappeared. For a moment there was nothing to see apart from the empty square with a few pasted-up characters, which still read 'Down With'. The workers must have stopped for lunch. No tractors or bikes passed. Just as I was about to turn, I saw a procession coming from the centre of the town. It seemed they were heading for the track leading out of town. Another school outing or a factory honouring its retired workers with a picnic, I thought, but I was intrigued at the lack of fanfare. There was no drum or red flags and it was eerily quiet. The school caretaker, an old man who had been watching me and Laoye from his little hut, had come out and we stood in silence as the procession neared us.

They wore black and their heads were wrapped in white scarves. The men carried a strange black box on their shoulders. A woman headed the procession clutching something. Her head bobbed up and down as if she was swimming. Then I realised she was wailing and there was something familiar about her red, swollen face. Something stirred in my memory as the old man next to me said, 'It's a child, poor woman.'

I turned to him. 'What do you mean?'

He peered at me. 'The shoes, of course, my child.'

'What shoes?' I whispered. I had recognised the woman now: it was she who had lost her baby to Bell.

'We have a custom here that when a baby dies, he or she must be buried with a new pair of shoes the mother makes for them. It is so that the child will grow up and find their way home. Some mothers make a new pair every year.'

I didn't want to look, but as my eyes settled on the woman I saw what she was clutching. She was beating her chest with a little pair of shoes.

Not as pretty as, but almost identical to, the shoes I'd discovered in Laoye's secret cave.

29

Lucy's visit helped me to make up my mind about something. When Mr Cheng visited again, I was ready for him. I was in the reception area chatting to Xiao Jin when we saw the familiar figure. He nodded at Xiao Jin, then turned to me. 'I have come for your decision. I want to know whether you will join us at the special asthma clinic. If not, a new doctor will come next month and this clinic will be closed.'

Greed makes people ugly. I stared at him for a minute. 'You know my answer. Must I repeat myself?'

Mr Cheng's face became purple. 'Dr Lin, if you think you can leave here and find another job, think again. I'm in possession of certain information that will interest any potential employer of yours in this country.'

'Really?' I said slowly, and closed the appointments book. Outside, the traffic flowed. I would join it myself, soon, when I got on to a plane. I felt light already. I thought of the suitcase I had taken out by my bedside, the one I had used to leave my marriage. Things would be all right, I told myself. Sunshine streamed in on to Xiao Jin's tender skin and Mr Cheng's ravaged features. I thought briefly of how he might have looked back then, when we were so much younger.

I pushed the appointments book to the dumbfounded Xiao Jin, and turned to Mr Cheng. 'I wouldn't bother if I were you,' I said. 'I'm sure it wouldn't do any of us any good. It's so dull to other people anyway. Just another tale of the Cultural Revolution, they'll say.'

'Dr Lin, don't try to be funny. I mean it.'

'I'm sure you do, but I don't care any more.'

For a moment we stared at each other and I was filled with sadness. I had wanted to forget and had managed so well. Why had he felt the need to bring it all back? It was not as if he would gain anything from it.

But I must have touched on something that Mr Cheng could not forgive. Perhaps fearing that he might lose face in front of Xiao Jin, he pointed a finger at me: 'What she did was unforgivable,' he said to the girl. 'She has blood on her hands.'

'Dr Lin!' Xiao Jin stared at me in horror.

'Come here, Xiao Jin.' I beckoned her and she followed me into the treatment room. I reached for the medicine box on the table. When I had made up my mind to leave, I had brought it downstairs. I had wanted it to witness my last few treatments. I wanted it to be part of my present. And what better time than now to open it and face the past I had spent all my life running away from?

The latch was a little rusty and hard to undo, even though I had oiled it from time to time. But eventually it gave and the lid opened. I caught a whiff of a stale scent. I closed my eyes for a second. Perhaps there wasn't any smell. Perhaps it was just in my imagination. I opened my eyes and saw that Mr Cheng had slipped in quietly behind Xiao Jin. I sat down and put the box on my thigh.

Slowly I took out the contents one by one: a plastic-covered red book, a notebook full of childish handwriting, with dried flowers between the pages, a single child's shoe . . . Each time I took something out, I felt the box lighten on my thigh.

I looked at Xiao Jin: 'This box belonged to my *laoye*, who was a traditional doctor. And I was thirteen when it happened.'

30

How can I be sure of what had happened on the last day of that year? How can I be sure of anything that had happened in those years? So much was guesswork or deduction. I had spent the next twenty-eight years reliving every moment of those days.

I remembered the weather. It was an extremely cold day, with dark grey cloud in the sky. The air was filled with the scent of the fireworks and I stood in the doorway just outside the dormitory, sniffing uneasily. I hadn't smelt fireworks since I'd left the city I was born in – nobody could afford fireworks in the village. For that reason I had been indoors for the last week or so – my asthma, which Laoye had cured, or thought he'd cured, had returned after I had spent just three weeks at my new school. I stayed in the town hospital for a few days before they sent me back.

Even before that I had been an odd sight – I could see that from the strange looks with which the teachers and my fellow students greeted me. I was several years older, taller but shyer than the eldest and tallest of them. I arrived when the term had nearly finished, so there was no time to make friends and I had sat silently at the back of the classroom staring out of the window. The teacher frowned at me. After the asthma attack, on days when I didn't feel like going to my lessons, I told the other girls to say I was feeling ill again and lay in bed, daydreaming.

Every day since I'd been ill I had expected Laoye to appear as he had before, but he didn't. Now it was holiday time, when we were expected to go home to our families. When the last boarder had left, the teacher in charge was ready to lock up and asked me if I knew where to go. I lied and told her I had a relative in town through whom I could get in touch with my *laoye*. She hesitated and then, perhaps impatient to join her own family, agreed to let me go.

Stepping gingerly, I made my way through the middle of the former marketplace. In the days that I'd lain in bed, I had heard from my classmates that there had been a mass rally to criticise the 'Yao Ren gang', headed by the town chemist, Ma Deyou. They mentioned casually the slogans they had shouted, 'Down with the reactionaries' and 'Defend the honour of Chairman Mao to the death.' They described how the chemist's head had been pressed down when he refused to bow. For self-preservation I had kept my mouth shut at the mention of Uncle Ma and during my illness these things had seemed unreal. But now, walking past the square, I could sense the atmosphere. The platform had gone, but strips of posters remained. I hurried past them, not daring to look closely. But surreptitious glances were enough, and for a while the big black crosses hovered before my eyes, shocking. I remembered how Laoye had avoided looking around on the day he'd left me at school – he had seen it coming. I knew what happened to people who were publicly criticised – we all did: it meant the end of their public life, it meant anyone could spit at them. I shut my eyes at the thought of the ever-smiling Uncle Ma being humiliated. Although I was no longer a wide-eyed child, and knew enough not to be surprised that another formerly respected official had fallen from grace, I was saddened that Uncle Ma should have been treated like this. He had seemed so kind to everyone.

But my sadness for Uncle Ma had soon turned to concern for Laoye. I remembered him saying he feared there was a conspiracy against himself, Auntie Hu and Uncle Ma. Now that Uncle Ma had been criticised, what would become of Laoye? Had anything happened to him? Was that why he hadn't come to the school to fetch me? I was still convinced that Steel hadn't been behind Uncle Ma's downfall – the public meeting of criticism had been organised and conducted by the municipal government, not the Red Guards. But what had been the significance of Uncle Ma's late-night visit when he and Laoye had whispered so earnestly about Steel? Could Laoye have found out that he'd been wrong about Steel? Was that what Uncle Ma had told him that night? That Steel was, as I had always thought, a noble and honest man?

It was a reassuring idea, but it did not explain why Laoye had not come to see me, as he'd promised he would. He had said someone was trying to hurt him. A former patient bearing a grudge? But Laoye had never had enemies, and he had never accepted payment for his treatment. I quickened my steps towards Auntie Hu as if the answers to my questions lay with her. Laoye had been going there on the day he had left me at school and had told me to look for him there if he didn't come for me. He must be there now – it was New Year's Eve. Now that her husband had died, it made even more sense for Laoye to be with her.

I came into the main street, which would normally have been thronged with people. But it was deserted and eerie, like walking through a stage set in an empty hall. I looked at the clock at the top of the town-hall building and saw that it was nearly midnight, about the time when everyone would sit down and feast on dumplings. I turned off the main street. The thought of seeing Auntie Hu and perhaps Laoye after so long made me feel both excited and apprehensive. Besides my concern for him, I had another tricky question to put to him. It wouldn't be easy, but at least the thick air of suspicion between us would be dispelled. During my long days of illness I had had time to think things through and I had dwelt mainly on our earlier happy days together. I was homesick and missed him. I wanted to confront him, but knew that when he confessed to me, I would forgive and comfort him: I knew how hard it must be for him to have caused the death of the child of one of his dearest friends, Auntie Hu. I wanted to tell him that I

231

understood why he had refused payment for all the treatment he gave people: he had been atoning for the one death he'd caused.

Near her house I began to tremble. Something dark lurked at the back of my mind and wouldn't go away. For some reason I was transported back to the darkest corner of the cave, breathing the damp smell. I was digging, even though I had discovered the shoes. There was something else in the mound, a voice hissed in my mind.

Now I was standing outside her door, panting, my chest tight and painful, short of breath.

The door was ajar, releasing the smell of food. I pushed it open, followed the hot steam and found my way to the kitchen. An old woman emerged, walking unsteadily, holding a plate of steaming dumplings. I knew it must be Auntie Hu, but I couldn't be sure until she looked at me. She was wearing a white jacket, which was unusual – in the time I'd known her, she'd always worn different shades of red. But as she came closer, I realised she'd aged since I had last seen her. The hairs at her temple had turned from grey to white.

'Juju.' Her smile widened. 'You are just in time for dinner.' She beckoned me to follow her and I felt a huge weight lift off my shoulders. The smell of the dumplings made my mouth water. The school food was so bad that for these last few weeks I had eaten little and I was ravenous. Now I expected to see Laoye, jumping out of his seat, delighted to see me. I could almost picture his smile.

But the dinner table, although it was laid with four sets of chopsticks and plates, was empty. Who else was she expecting? I peered around but saw no one. She put down the big plate of dumplings and went to fetch another chair. 'Sit here,' she said, and came back from the kitchen with another plate and a pair of chopsticks. 'You can have your special pretty bowl,' she murmured, pointing at the little bird pattern, which I recognised. 'They will have to do without. The men can have plain ones.'

'Men?' Why did she say 'men' not 'man'? 'Where is Laoye? Is Uncle Ma coming as well?'

'I meant the rest of my family, of course.'

'The rest of your family?' I looked round the empty room, and noticed for the first time the smoke spiralling from an incense stick in front of one place. As she spoke, Auntie Hu leaned forward to pick up a dumpling and placed it on the plate in front of the incense. I sucked my teeth. Of course, that was for her late husband. That was why she was wearing white. She was in mourning. But it was strange to see the plate with dumplings and the way she raised a hand at it as if to invite someone to eat, as if Uncle Hu were sitting there. I tried to imagine Uncle Hu staggering down the stairs and frightened myself so much that I sat back a little. Surreptitiously I peeped at the other sets of plates and was relieved to see that there were no incense sticks in front of them. But why had she spoken of 'men'? Which others was she expecting for dinner?

She sat down next to me and looked me in the eye. In all the time I'd known her, she had never looked at me like that. It was as if I were her equal and she my friend, rather than an auntie who smiled down at me. I met her gaze and caught sight of the red paper flower she wore tucked behind her ear. I dropped my eyes and noticed her trousers. 'You are wearing red,' I said foolishly.

'Yes, mourning and celebrating at the same time,' she said, with a strange twinkle in her eyes.

My ears pricked up.

She licked her lips. 'You must be wondering why I am wearing red when my husband is dead.'

I didn't say anything, but that was the question I had asked myself. I was also thinking of the dead baby. The grief-stricken face of the village woman floated into my mind. I hoped I would never know what it felt like, but I would never forget how she had looked. If Auntie remembered her dead husband, why wasn't she thinking of the baby too?

She sighed. 'You saw Uncle Hu, you know the condition he was in before he died. It was a relief for him, and for me. He had been like that for nearly twenty years, almost as long as I knew your *laoye*.'

Laoye? 'Auntie Hu, where is Laoye? I haven't seen him for—'

She put a finger to her lips and continued, ignoring my question: 'Juju, I never dreamed that I would tell another soul, but now . . . Uncle Hu's dead and I am nearly as old as your grandmother. Anyway, it's a small town, rumours run round it, and I'd rather you heard this from me.'

'Auntie Hu. . .'

She put the finger to her lips again. 'Don't interrupt. I want you to judge me only after I've told you the whole story. Your *laoye* said I was never to tell you but I think differently. You are a special girl.'

'Auntie Hu,' I said quickly, 'I know about the baby you lost.' I averted my eyes to the incense smoke that had now encircled us. 'I was sorry to hear of it. You must be so upset.'

She sat back. 'The baby?'

'I guessed. I saw the secret grave Laoye made in the cave.'

'So you know. My goodness, Juju, and you came here to. . .'

'I came here to find Laoye, and to see you.'

'Juju, so . . . you forgive us?' Her large eyes opened wide, and I thought I could see tears in them.

Forgive? Had grief made her mad? She had done no wrong – it was Laoye who needed her forgiveness. For a moment I didn't know what to say. 'Auntie Hu,' I started, glancing quickly upstairs in case Laoye was hiding up there, 'I'm just sorry your baby died.'

At this point a strange thing happened. Auntie Hu closed her eyes, took a deep breath and smiled. Briefly it was as if she had become once more the Auntie Hu she had been when I'd first met her, coming out of the kitchen in that alluring red coat, and holding all of us under her spell. She sat closer. 'You'll never believe this, Juju.'

'What?'

'The baby boy I'd thought dead has come back. He's alive. Ming Ming's alive.'

'Alive? Where?' I looked about me again, half expecting a toddler to charge from the kitchen. Then I laughed at myself: of course he wouldn't be a baby now, he would be . . . a young man.

It was as if she'd read my mind. She raised her voice and spoke fast, eyes darting about the room. 'Well, you'll never believe what a fine young man he is, tall, handsome and such a beautiful voice. And . . . Didn't Lao Lin say something about you knowing him well?'

'Lao Lin said that?' I repeated, not understanding.

'Yes, your grandfather, your *laoye*. Ming Ming's father,' she said quickly, with a smile.

'Laoye, Ming Ming's father,' I murmured. Suddenly the room became smaller and my mouth dried. Ming Ming's father, Laoye, my grandfather. Something was not right. But . . . my mother was Laoye's child. Where had Ming Ming come from? Who was he? Auntie Hu's voice was somewhere near me, but it sounded faint.

'We met after your grandmother died, of course. Your *laoye* came to help with treating my husband. Hu Yue was the kindest man I'd ever met and he was devoted to me, but he was already so disabled. What can I say? I was a woman, after all. You will be a woman one day and you will understand. It was hard . . . hiding my pregnancy . . . and when the baby was born Lao Lin delivered him.'

I was only half listening. I wanted to cover my ears. What did it all mean? Laoye delivering her baby, no, their baby. How confusing it was. In my mind I was back in the cave digging again, deeper into the loose earth.

She moved closer, her breath on me, hot and uncomfortable. I leaned back in the chair, the heavy column of incense smoke following me. I waved a hand to dispel it. 'And he told me the baby was dead. I mourned him for seventeen years, my baby, seventeen years.' My baby, my baby, wailed the village woman, beating her chest with the shoes she had made. I shut my eyes, wanting to escape the image, but was taken back into the cave again. Dig! Quick! Dig the other way. So many children's shoes emerging from the earth.

'He had lied. He told me the truth only recently and I should have been so angry, but . . . Hu Yue died and I had no family left but now I have a son. My own son, alive and healthy, big and strong, my flesh and blood. I should have been angry, but. . .'

Anger. Someone's angry – the little boy who was taunted by his fellows, the little boy who fought for himself and grew up. I had heard a story of a little boy like that somewhere before. Where? So many shoes – dig, dig, dig.

'Like father, like son. So they say. You only had to look at them and, what's even more extraordinary, an acupuncturist too. You know him, don't you? It's as if you and Lao Lin had a misunderstanding about the boy.' She cocked her head to one side.

Suddenly I felt the blood rushing out of me. 'Ming Ming, does he have another name?'

'Ming Ming is the pet name I gave him. His proper name is . . . Can't you guess yet? I gathered from Lao Lin you thought well of him.'

I heard my voice say it: 'Steel.' But I wasn't sure whether it *was* my voice. It had been a long time since I had said his name, although he had been on my mind every day.

'Yes, Steel. He was here just now. He has gone to look for his father. Your *laoye* could not be found anywhere and Ming Ming said only Uncle Ma knew where he was, so he's gone to him. He said he'd bring his father here for dinner, and we could have a family gathering. It's New Year's Eve after all, and I've made so many dumplings. . .'

It was 'family gathering' that got to me. A strange sound came from me, like a whistle or a cough, and it startled her. She stopped and stared at me. 'What's the matter, Juju? Don't you . . . like him after all?'

Like him? A flame ignited inside me and I jumped up. My eyes darted about the room and I caught sight of the dumplings. I reached out for them, now cold and sticky, huddled together like a family of fat-bellied siblings. I flung them at her, and watched them hit her face and fall down to stain her red trousers. As she flinched I laughed, a strange sound that scared me.

I fled the house. At first I simply ran, I didn't know where to.

236

The Touch

At the centre of the town I dodged fireworks, set off from buildings opposite each other like an exchange of fire between troops. It gave me an excuse to scream and run hysterically. In my mind my hands had exposed the secret I had been digging for. Now it had staggered up from the earth, a resurrected ghost. It grew taller, and taller, and came for me. For a long time I didn't know where I was until a group of Red Guards patrolling the town found me and took me, panting and wheezing, to the chemist.

The door was wide open. There were Red Guards everywhere, standing at the entrance. 'I want Steel,' I hissed at the two boys on the door, and when they tried to stop me, I lashed out at them like a wild cat. 'Let me in!' I shouted, and then, when they had tried to hold me back, I screamed, 'I'm his family! Let me in!'

This worked and they took me into the dark hall where Laoye had shown me the herbs. Steel stood there alone with his back to me.

'Steel!' I shouted his name, then paused to catch my breath. Something was pulling the muscle inside my throat, trying to strangle me from inside, and I remembered the panic I had felt when I was a young child. Then I had had someone to lean on, but now I had no one.

'Steel,' I said again, panting. Ever since I'd left Laoye's house, I'd expected to see him again and had imagined all sorts of encounters, but now, when I finally saw him again, it felt unreal. Perhaps it was all a bad dream. For a moment I wished he wouldn't answer me.

Slowly he turned and we stared at each other like two strangers. Perhaps we were. As my eyes locked with his I saw no sign of recognition. The sleeve of his shirt was rolled up, reminding me of our last meeting when Bell had rolled it down – such an intimate gesture. Something tugged inside me.

Suddenly he grinned, and it was once again the face I had missed these last few weeks. 'You came just in time,' he said, as if we'd been parted only for a day or two. 'Finally I made Ma Deyou talk, and now I know the truth.'

237

'The truth? What truth?'

'That Lin Ji had wanted me dead. He told Hu Lingzhi that I was dead, then arranged for Ma Deyou to pack me off to some distant peasant family. When his conscience tortured him too much, he'd send Ma Deyou to drop in with some money so that they'd keep me fed and dressed. The peasants were grateful, and he seems to have expected me to feel the same.'

His voice was calm and quiet and I heard each word clearly. I stepped closer, cautiously, as Laoye had told me to do near wild animals. Despite myself, I was drawn to him. Even now, all I wanted was to be near him.

I saw blood on his hand, and he grinned. 'Well, Ma Deyou needed persuasion. But I believed him when he said he didn't know where Lin Ji is. So.' He fixed his stare on me. 'Where is he? Where is the holy sage of the mountains? He must feel quite pleased with himself, don't you think, because the world thinks him such a noble man, treating people without charge? Now we know why.'

I leaned against the compartments of the wooden medicine cabinet. They had been emptied and the contents lay spilled on the floor. I was back in the cave again, and now, running from the spectre of the past, I had crawled my way to the mouth, gasping for fresh air. The view outside was alluring. It was where I wanted to be.

'Juju, where is he? Do you know?'

His voice tugged at me, but I was back in the cave. As he persisted, I covered my face. I hated the way the voice was interrupting my dream. I was nearly out of the cave, into fresh air, safety.

A cold hand touched my shoulder and I shuddered. 'Don't.'

He pressed his face to mine. 'Why not, little niece?'

Finally, the spectre caught up with me. Sneering, it pushed and I fell helplessly into the void below.

'The cave,' I screamed, and heard him repeat the word. There was a sudden commotion as the Red Guards outside ran at his command.

I was left alone.

It was quiet but I seemed to hear sounds, and it was not just the wind coming in through the window that had been left open when they rushed out. Was that Uncle Ma's moaning? What had they done to him? Where was he? But the sound was near and I looked up at the wall of gaping holes – the drawers of herbs, each one a little mouth, now crying like an angry baby. I covered my ears, but I could still hear the sound, which maddened me. Clutching at my tight chest, I stepped up to the wall and started to close them, one after another. 'Clang, clang,' the drawers went. 'Blossoms at the top, stones at the bottom. Honeysuckle for internal heat and wild chrysanthemum for bright eyes,' I whispered, breathing fast, coughing and wheezing, and heard an echo from a long time ago.

Outside, snow was falling. I should have known. It was always especially cold just before it snowed.

31

I had packed my luggage and drifted now to the park. I stood in front of the brass band again to listen to their sentimental songs. This time I realised that half of the audience were family or friends of the musicians. A woman was holding a baby and it occurred to me that she had been one of the trumpeters. She had a broad face and an easy smile that had stayed with me. The performance was over quickly this time and I stayed to watch them disperse, unscrewing Thermoses of tea, yawning and chatting.

I followed the path to the pond, where I had seen Lucy with Connor and the paper boat. The fountain had dried up, leaving a small puddle of dirty water clogged with dead leaves. I sat on one of the wooden benches that faced it. A few steps away from me, an old couple strolled by, warmly dressed in thick jumpers. As the sun dimmed a chilly wind blew. 'Chunwu qiudong,' I murmured, and was transported, back to my first outing with Lucy and Mark. It seemed like only yesterday.

I had said goodbye last week, when Lucy had come to the clinic. Xiao Jin must have rung to tell her I was leaving. When Lucy had asked why, I had answered, 'For Tiantian.' What had happened with Mr Cheng and Mark had brought forward the date of my departure but I had always known that I would not let Tiantian grow up without me. I thought of Laoye coming to collect me from the countryside, and the feeling I had had of coming home. I had wanted to do something similar for my daughter – reclaim her as my own. I knew Zhiying might have other ideas, but I missed her too much to care. I didn't explain any of this to Lucy, but she had looked at me in a way that told me she understood, and I thought she did. I was glad we had parted like that, sitting on my bed with the window open, Connor hanging on to her like a monkey. It was how I would remember them.

I pictured them now and rose to go, willing that rare feeling of light-heartedness to stay a while longer. When I reached the oak tree by the gate I saw her, them, coming towards the centre of the park. Before they spotted me, I switched to another path.

I could just make out the bump of the baby beneath her jacket. In the shade of the oak tree she paused to point something out to Connor – a squirrel? Mark's hand went to her waist and they embraced, a lingering kiss. A shaft of sunlight caught her face: she was radiant. My throat tightened. A leaf fell and I caught it, then hurried home.

32

The path feels less steep, but it's winter again, and snow is falling, just as it was last time. . .

'Mummy, why are we here?' Tiantian holds my hand tight and I smile at her. It is only in the last few days that she has begun to call me 'Mummy' again.

'I want to show you something.' I kneel down, and reach out to grab the creepers. It is not where I expected it to be. I lean and look down but can't see the cave.

'What are you doing?' a voice calls behind me. I turn and see a man with a basket on his back.

'I seem to remember there was a cave here.'

He looks me up and down as if he's debating whether to tell me the truth. 'There was one a long time ago. My grandfather told me about it,' he said. 'Somebody died trying to reach it, so the commune decided it was dangerous and sealed it off.'

'Who died?' Tiantian asks.

'A young man. Very sad. He was looking for someone.'

'Who was it?' Tiantian asks.

The man peers at me again. 'It was his father. The son was trying to find him, but he slipped and fell.'

'Oh, he should have been more careful,' Tiantian says, stepping back from the cliff and I hold her hand tightly.

'The father must have been very upset,' she says, 'mustn't he, Mummy?'

243

Before I can say anything the young man answers, 'Well, the father was injured in trying to—'

I raise a finger to my lips.

'Who are you?' the man asks.

I smile. 'You are Jinni the herb-picker's grandson, aren't you?'

'Yes,' he says. 'And you. . .'

'I'm Dr Lin's granddaughter, Juju.'

'Juju! I thought you'd gone to England for good.'

'I was away too long and I'm back now. This is my daughter, Tiantian.'

He looks at Tiantian and shakes his head. 'My grandfather said Dr Lin always thought you'd come back, and often kept the light on in his room night.'

'My grandfather and uncle – do you know where they're buried?'

He points. 'Down there.'

'Down there' is a wilderness with twenty or so graves dotted around, gentle mounds in the earth. Snow has given them white caps, pretty but eerie. I remember picking herbs there with Laoye, the *ma huang*, which had to be picked between descent of Frost and Arrival of Winter. I remember the faces I saw on the train coming here, how people's features had seemed to soften as I grew to know them better . . . or had that been wishful thinking? But the ground is as hard as ever.

I stand in front of the largish mound that is theirs. Tiantian's hand wiggles in mine restlessly. 'Go and pick some flowers,' I whisper and send her away.

I kneel down and close my eyes. Snowflakes buffet randomly on my face. Here I am, Laoye, with Tiantian. At the thought of her I pause and look behind me, Tiantian waves, then bends down to pick something up. I turn back to the grave.

'Laoye,' I whisper. 'They said that in trying to stop Steel falling, you slipped and broke your leg. You were lucky to have Auntie Hu to look after you – it seemed she was destined to look after sick men – but you never fully regained your strength. I could barely imagine how the two of you lived together, defying the frowns and scorn of the villagers. Did you ever wonder about me? Steel had died, and I had put your life in danger. I was the one to blame.

'Take comfort, Laoye, because in the last moment of his life, Steel knew you cared. And I knew you did too, from the very beginning. I was there all those nights you sat awake, regretting that you had given him away. I was there when you prayed to your god for his safety; I was there when you refused payment from grateful patients, atoning for your crime. I was there at the shrine you'd built for him in that dark cave, where you were alone with your memories and your remorse. I was there all those times, but I was blind. I was a child.

'Tell me you've forgiven my betrayal. The one word that revealed where you had gone is the word I have spent my life until now trying to forget. Twenty-eight years is a long time and no time at all. Laoye, Steel, I am here. Can you hear? Let me know that you both now rest in peace.'

But I hear nothing, just the wind howling. They will give me no answer. Instead, I feel they want something from me.

I stand up. I had been away from Tiantian for so long that since our reunion I have hardly let her out of my sight. I call her. Then I see her coming towards me with something in her hand.

'Mummy, there are no flowers left. It's winter and they're all frozen. But I found this.' She holds something in her palm and gazes up at me.

I take it from her, a purplish-brown plant shaped like a mushroom. For a while I stare at it, speechless. Then I hold her tight. 'Where did you get it? Did you go near the cliff?'

She nods slowly. Then, seeing my displeasure, she smiles to charm me: 'But, Mummy, I was very careful. Mummy, it's pretty, isn't it? Can we pretend it's a flower and give it to your grandpa and uncle?'

'Yes, honey, it's exactly what they would have liked.'

'What is it, Mummy? Is it a mushroom?'

'No, Tiantian. It's a herb called *lingzhi*. It makes you dream of the people you miss.'